THE RELUCTANT EMPRESS

TERESA HOWARD

This is a work of fiction. Names, characters, places, and incidents are products of the author's imagination or are used fictitiously and are not to be construed as real. Any resemblance to actual events, locations, organizations, or persons, living or dead, is entirely coincidental.

World Castle Publishing, LLC
Pensacola, Florida

Hardback ISBN: 9798250390385
Paperback ISBN: 9798891265387
eBook ISBN: 9798891265394
First Edition World Castle Publishing, LLC, May 11, 2026
http://www.worldcastlepublishing.com

Cover: Cover Designs by Karen

Contents

Prologue

Retiring Ambassador Gibbons looked out over the graduating class of 3043 at the League of Seeded World's Space Academy. He ran a hand through his thin, gray hair.

In his monotonous, slightly nasal voice, he began, "If you are planning a trip to Bengar, don't. If you are *fortunate enough* to be assigned to Bengar, there are a few things that will help you. They produce great wine." He paused. Laughter rippled throughout the room.

"It's a third-tier planet in a distant quadrant of League space, far from Earth and League headquarters. Its only importance is that it is near the fringe of League territory and would provide an excellent base to monitor far space. So every year, Bengar is invited to join the League, and the answer is always the same: no. That won't change.

"To understand the people, you must understand their World War that happened two hundred years ago. To say it was bad is an understatement. The Empire and a couple of the southern kingdoms fought against the rest of the planet. Bombs, invading armies, and chemical warfare almost annihilated them all. The planet was devastated before they came to their senses. Peace was finally settled by enacting the Writ of Neutrality. In the simplest terms, they agreed to leave each other alone. By that time, barrenness and genetic abnormalities were catastrophic, not to mention that a quarter of the population sustained some kind of physical injuries during the war.

"From necessity, major medical and technological advancements followed. They developed one of the top medical treatment programs in the galaxy for trauma, reconstructive surgery, and in gynecology and fertility issues. We used some of their ideas to develop the technology to transport frozen embryos across space and propagate Earth's flora and fauna on other planets.

"Despite these advancements, it's a hard place to be poor, even in the Imperial City. Work crews pay little, provide no benefits to workers, and access to education and medical treatment is limited."

Gibbons droned on, oblivious to the apparent boredom of his audience. At the back of the auditorium, Cadet Benjamin Houston jumped slightly at a sharp jab from his roommate's elbow.

"For God's sake, Houston, wake up."

"Why, who the hell gets sent to Bengar?" Houston leaned forward and stretched his muscular, six-foot frame. "I'm a soldier, not a diplomat. I'm going Fleet."

One

Ninallia dressed in the dark, careful not to disturb her mother, Vicori. In the next room, she found her aunt sitting at the table, head bowed, with tears on her cheeks. Aunt Rese's tall, graceful figure was slumped with grief, and her fine-boned, handsome features were puffy from crying. Her once elegant hands were now rough and scarred from the harsh chemicals she used on the cleaning crew. A cup of tea shook in her unsteady grasp. Ninallia understood the tears—there wasn't enough money for rent, food, and medicine for Vicori. She wrapped her arms around her aunt.

Rese was leasing a two-room apartment in a poor neighborhood when she took in her young, widowed sister and child. It was supposed to be temporary, but that was ten years ago.

"I'll find work, Rese. I can quit school. I will join a work crew. I'm almost grown, and I'm a strong girl."

Rese freed herself from Ninallia's embrace and stood. Her gaze darted toward the room where her sister lay. "No child, you have to be seventeen to apply for work on the cleaning crew. I promised your mother you would finish school. It would kill her to see you on a work crew."

"Will our creditors wait two years?"

Taking Ninallia's face in her hand, Rese straightened to her full height and looked down into her eyes. "Enough! I will deal with the creditors. Have some porridge. I need you to go to the market for me." She reached for a bowl, her eyes red and heavy with tears.

"I'm not hungry," Ninallia lied. She regretted the sharp

tone and touched her aunt's shoulder. "There are always samples at the market. I can eat those."

Rese lowered her eyes and handed Ninallia a meager list and a few coins.

As Ninallia walked along Market Street, familiar sounds and smells lifted her spirits. A well-dressed woman with a large basket of fruits and vegetables crossed the street ahead of her. A boy jostled the woman as he ran by, and two large figs fell from the basket onto the dusty street. The woman didn't notice, nor did she turn back to pick them up.

Ninallia hurried toward the figs, anxious to reach them before some careless person stepped on them and they became useless. She made it and added them to her basket. Aunt Rese loved figs. These would make her a fine treat.

"Thief!" The woman's shrill voice sounded an alarm.

Ninallia took the figs from her basket and held them out. "They fell in the street, lady," she stammered. Tears stung her eyes. True, but also true, she intended to keep the figs for herself.

The woman looked down her nose at Ninallia's shabby clothes. She grabbed the figs. Her lips curled disdainfully. Dirt from the ground covered part of the smooth skin. "I don't eat dirt." She turned and threw them into the gutter. "Give me your basket, girl. What else have you stolen? We don't need your kind here. You eat samples and steal produce without a thought for the merchants."

Other shoppers began to stop and watch the scene. Mento, the baker, hurried from his shop. He placed his large frame in front of Ninallia. "Leave the girl alone; she's an honorable child. Don't blame her for your carelessness."

The woman stalked away, and Ninallia covered her face in shame. The story of her dishonorable action was sure to reach Aunt Rese before she arrived home. Mento patted her shoulder, then laughed as he dusted off the flour. He was a kind man and one of the best bakers in the Imperial City. His cakes and pastries drew customers from all over the city.

"Come into my shop. I have fresh pastry." Mento coaxed her away from the curious crowd.

The aroma of baking tickled her nose and made her mouth water. Bread, fresh and golden brown from the oven, cluttered the shelves. Pastries, flaky and filled with luscious fruit and decadent chocolate, were displayed on silver and glass plates along the counter. Mento nodded toward the pastries. There was never a shortage of samples in his shop. She bowed in thanks and selected a small piece of chocolate pastry, popping it into her mouth and holding it there with her tongue to savor the sweet, velvety chocolate oozing from the flaky crust. It was bliss.

"Try the fruitcake; it's a new recipe," he suggested, holding out a large sample.

He waited expectantly as she tasted the cake and clapped her approval. It was delicious. The blend of fruit and nuts in a buttery cake was sure to become a favorite throughout the city.

"How are Vicori and Rese?" Mento emphasized Rese's name, his round cheeks brightening with pink.

"Mother is sick, but Rese is well and sends her thanks for your generosity," she answered.

This made Mento's large face beam with happiness. He was sweet on Aunt Rese and often gave them day-old bread and cakes. Ninallia gazed around the prosperous shop. *Why doesn't Aunt Rese marry Mento? That would solve our problems.* The house above the bakery was snug and warm. A worrisome thought crossed her mind. *Would Mento welcome his wife's ill sister and her niece into his home? Was this why Aunt Rese hesitated?*

It was time to bid him goodbye. He placed gifts of bread and pastry into her basket. She nodded her thanks again, unable to find the words to thank him enough. Outside, the street was quiet. People returned to their shopping, and so must she. Ninallia shook her head. If she were not poor and hungry, she would not have dishonored herself by trying to pick up those figs. She must convince her aunt and her mother that she was old enough to go on a work crew, at least until her mother recovered. Perhaps the best way was to find a position and take it.

Across the street, a section of the wall was designated for memos and job openings. It was covered with posters and fliers. Wouldn't hurt to see what was there. She started across the street to read the postings, only to find herself in the path of a transport speeding above the street. The driver blared a warning, and she jumped back. The air streaming from the sleek metal transport bus almost ripped the basket from her hands. Several passengers laughed at her carelessness. Ninallia shook her fist at the transport. *One day, I will ride the transport from the north to the south or east to west in the Imperial City whenever I want.*

She perused the job offerings posted on the wall. Very few papers giving details on how to apply for the jobs remained. A notice for the position of dumas caught her attention—the need for paid surrogate mothers was great. After the war and chemical plagues of the past, many women were barren. She gasped at the figures offered for this service. The pay was many times higher than any work crew would offer.

The notice stated requirements for the dumas position: "A woman must be eighteen years or older, fertile, and genetically free of abnormalities."

She almost screamed her disappointment. I cannot wait three years. These are lean times, and many in the Imperial City need work and housing. We will be living on the street.

There was a harsh laugh beside her. An old woman's voice said, "A fertile body and a clean scan are a valuable commodity, no? Keep yourself pure, child."

Ninallia blushed, grabbed a slip attached to the notice, then jammed it into her pocket.

~ * ~

The morning sun began to burn away the dense fog that shrouded the Imperial City of Obantu, revealing in the distance the towers of the Golden Palace. This brought both a blessing and a curse to a fugitive from the classroom. Ninallia might be seen and reported, then a conference between her esteemed teachers and aunt would follow. However, the light did make her journey less dangerous. She quickened her pace, navigating the intricate spider web of streets and alleys in the ancient capital with care. One wrong turn could take her from streets lined with posh shops and eateries to dangerous streets where no lone female was safe, even during the daytime.

Ninallia rubbed the advertisement torn from the public notice wall. It crinkled in her pocket. She tried to squelch the hope building inside her. There was little chance she, a girl in her early teens, would be chosen by a wealthy couple to be their surrogate, but she was determined to try. She experienced her monthly woman's flow, her scans were clean, and there were family legends of nobility in her heritage. Many nights she listened to her mother and aunt talk of royal blood in her family's history. Being a dumas offered them hope, a chance to escape poverty. She might even restore her family honor. Her family was once prosperous, though not wealthy. Aunt Rese's closet held a few reminders from that better life. Sadly, she was forced to sell most of them in recent years.

Without credits for transport, it would take hours of walking to reach the address on the slip. Ninallia's left eye began to itch, but she forced herself to ignore it to keep from smearing her makeup. She tugged at the simple gown that came from Aunt Rese's closet. The gown was more appropriate for an interview than her well-worn school tunic, though truth be told, it hung off her narrow shoulders.

Ninallia ignored the blisters on her feet and continued

walking. She considered taking off the ill-fitting shoes but realized this would ruin her hose. She felt foolish. *Why didn't I wear my own shoes?* At a large intersection, she paused and reread the directions, smiling to herself when she saw the final street come into view. After taking the left, she stood before her destination to adjust the sagging dress and smooth the braids in her dark hair. She climbed the steps, took in a deep breath, and then knocked.

The door swung open, and a large square-faced woman stared at her. The woman's broad shoulders and full skirts blocked the view inside. "Can I help you?"

"I am here to interview for a dumas position. I have a clean scan." Ninallia's voice trailed off under the woman's frown.

"Dumas applicants must be eighteen. Come back when you are older." The woman began to close the door.

"I have royal ancestry on my mother's side." Ninallia felt her future slip away as the woman shook her head. The door shut before she could say anything else.

Dejected, she turned to begin the journey to her aunt's small home across town. Without the credit for transport, another long walk lay ahead.

"Come here, child," a gentle voice called from the door.

Ninallia whirled and raced back to the door. A woman stood there dressed in an elegant silver and blue silk gown. *Was this woman noble or upper class?* Ninallia could not tell. To be safe, she greeted her by saying, "My Lady?"

The woman studied Ninallia. There was a sharp, intelligent mind behind her gentle eyes. She patted Ninallia's shoulder. "You say you have royal blood?"

She fumbled in her pocket and found the disk with her medical records. "Both my mother and aunt say it is far back in our line. I am clean and fertile."

"You know a dumas must be eighteen."

Too embarrassed to explain, Ninallia hung her head. *If I*

wait three years, Mother will be dead. Before then, we will be living on the streets and begging for food. There isn't much left to sell. With Mother ill and not working, Aunt Rese can't pay rent and buy food much longer. There are too many creditors to pay. Ninallia tried to hold back tears as she turned to leave.

"I serve high-born clients. The purity of their dumas is more important than her age. One prefers royal blood."

Ninallia lifted her chin as hope coursed through her. She dared a smile at this woman.

The woman returned the smile as she took a small card from her pocket and held it out. "I am Madama Ector. I own a private dumas hostel and procure surrogates for the highest clientele in the Empire. Everything at my hostel is very proper, and my women receive the best treatment. Come to this address tomorrow. If you carry royal blood, I may be able to use you."

"Yes, Madama." Ninallia grasped the card. "I will be there."

Madama Ector turned toward the door. Ninallia almost missed her final admonition. "A dumas must be neat and clean. However, you do not need to wear makeup."

Ninallia watched her benefactress, the card clasped in her hand. She almost missed the small credit chip on the corner. She opened her mouth to ask Madama Ector about the chip. The door closed before she could. Ninallia stroked the chip and slipped the card into her pocket.

On the way home, she swiped the card at a public access terminal and gasped at the amount on the chip. One hundred credits were a huge sum for her family. *Doesn't Madama know the card's value? Why would she extend me such a generous amount?* Ninallia pressed the cash button. She scanned the area to make sure no one watched as five twenty-credit coins were dispensed.

Even in a safe neighborhood, it wasn't wise to carry a large amount. Ducking into a public toilet, she placed each credit coin into a separate location in her clothes and shoes. *What if Madama Ector wants the money back or demands I do something dishonorable to earn it?* She decided not to spend the credits until after tomorrow's interview. The coins hidden, Ninallia stepped back outside and headed home at a brisk pace.

At home, where the sour smell of illness filled the cramped apartment, she heard Vicori's raspy breathing come from the next room. Aunt Rese sat at her table nursing a cup of weak tea. Her face was lined with worry and weariness, but she raised a hand in greeting and managed a smile.

"How is she?" Ninallia asked.

Aunt Rese's hands trembled. She dabbed at tears. "No medicine."

The hidden credits weighed heavily on Ninallia, and her determination failed. If she was rejected, she would find a way to repay Madama Ector. Taking out forty credits, she said, "This should be enough for both the healer and the medicine."

"Where did you get this money?" Aunt Rese was dubious. "Have you shamed us?"

Ninallia shook her head. "I have applied for an honorable job and have been paid in advance." She dared not tell her aunt about the job for fear Rese would forbid her from performing the duty of dumas.

Aunt Rese studied her face for a long time before taking the money. She relaxed and filled Ninallia's bowl with leftover stew before going for the healer.

~ * ~

About an hour later, Rese returned to their tiny apartment with Healer Taborn from the neighborhood clinic. His skills were excellent, and he was well-known and admired in the poor community. His services were cheaper than most, and he was the only healer who made calls to the southern slums of the Imperial City. He could have grown wealthy as a private healer, but chose to provide care to those who could pay less. He looked around and nodded at the scrubbed floors and clean counters. He would shake his head but not condemn them for waiting so long to seek his help.

The fabric of his long green healer's robes rustled as he passed Ninallia. He closed the door to the smaller chamber while he examined her mother. Ninallia listened to his quiet voice and the much weaker voice of her mother answering his questions.

The healer's face was grave when he returned to the front room. He accepted Rese's offer of tea, making a slight grimace, probably at the weak flavor. "She has the wasting lung disease. The medicine will help her, but to get well, she needs to be in a sanitarium for treatment."

Ninallia gasped. *A sanitarium will cost much more than one hundred credits.*

They thanked him and paid for his visit. Rese took some of the stew to Vicori, while Ninallia put on her cloak and went to find an apothecary. It was several blocks away, almost to Market Street. When she returned home, she placed the medicine along with fresh milk and fruit onto their small table. Fewer than half her credits remained. She set them in a small cloth bag under her mattress.

For the first time in weeks, Ninallia slept through the night without waking to the sound of her mother's labored breathing. The medicine was working. Aunt Rese helped her sister to the main room in the morning, and the three shared a small breakfast of hot mush and fruit.

Ninallia tried to decide how to explain her upcoming pregnancy. She could hide it for a short time, but Aunt Rese and her mother would notice in a few months. Being a dumas was an honorable thing. If she were older, they would no doubt be proud, but for now, it must be secret. "I have to go to my employer today. If I keep this job, I can help pay for food and medicine."

Concern darkened her mother's face. Aunt Rese stroked her sister's hair. "It is okay, Vicori, Ninallia is a good girl. This will be an honorable position."

"But she must finish school," protested her mother.

Ninallia took her mother's hand. "If I keep this job, it will be a good thing for our family because I can finish school at night and send you credits. I promise to write you often."

This seemed to satisfy Vicori. She motioned for Ninallia to come close. Taking her daughter's hands in hers, she kissed them. She whispered a prayer, "May the Spirits guide your path, protect you from all harm, and return you to my heart."

It was an ancient blessing. Aunt Rese placed her hands on Ninallia's head as she added her own silent prayer. Ninallia brushed away tears. She hugged them tightly before she left for her appointment with Madama Ector.

Two

The Andorian jungle closed in, rife with predators. Colonel Benjamin Houston spotted at least five soldiers surrounding him, and they weren't his men. He wiped sweat from his face and switched the communicator on. No need for radio silence now.

"Colonel Houston," a voice hissed in his ear.

"Brandon, check, it's an ambush. Get the hell out of here. Don't wait for me. I'm done."

"An ambush? Where are you?"

"Get my men the hell off the planet." Sweat was making his trigger hand slippery. If he made a run for it and gave the Andorians a fight, his men would have a chance to get out alive. His own death was certain. Crashing through the underbrush, he opened fire on the Andorians. They returned fire.

Houston, a trained soldier and black ops officer, managed to dodge and evade death for a few precious minutes. The blast tore through him like a blast of lightning, ripping him apart in a million directions. The pain lasted less than a minute, then nothingness engulfed him.

Houston came to with a start. He had blacked out in the regeneration tank again. He longed to return to the oblivion of unconsciousness. Pain and regret pressed in from every side, drowning him in sorrow.

"Colonel Houston, move your legs," a disembodied voice commanded.

The reality of his surroundings came back into focus. He felt the breathing mask over his mouth and the thick fluid supporting his weight in the regeneration tank. He began to lift his legs in a rhythmic motion.

"That's good, Colonel. You must stop dwelling on the ambush. The mission was a success. You're alive."

"Two of my men died on Andoria. Their lives were wasted. There were no hostages."

"The captured soldiers led officials to the Vice President of Andoria. Thanks to you, his planned coup failed."

Houston closed his eyes and gave himself over to the regeneration fluid. His legs continued to move up and down in rhythm. He was tired of discussing the ambush and his "feelings." *What does this psychologist know about my men? What does he know about me?*

The regeneration session ended with soft music as the fluid swirled around him. Houston's brain regained some semblance of control. He tried to remember how long he had been recovering on Bengar. Days turned into weeks, then months.

Brandon and Edwards found what was left of him and risked their lives dragging him out of the jungle. Skipper and Johnson, two other soldiers, didn't make it back to the ship. They died trying to provide cover for the rescue. Once back onboard the spaceship, Houston was placed in stasis and transported to the nearest high-level medical center. It was on Bengar, a neutral planet in the same star system.

He'd lost an arm, part of a leg, and was the recipient of an artificial heart-lung capacitor. He was alive, but his military career was over. Slowly, he began to sob. Two of his best men, his friends, died to implicate one minor politician on an unimportant planet—unimportant to the League of Seeded Worlds at least. Here he was, what was left of him, on an even less important planet. *Why didn't I die? I did die; they just didn't let me stay dead.*

"Negative thinking won't help your recovery, Colonel Houston. I have told you to expect an almost complete recovery. Your new heart and limbs will function with more than adequate power," said Healer Bannoff.

The fluid drained from the tank, and the weight of Houston's body was supported by his muscles. Every muscle screamed at the imposition. He welcomed the pain. "Can I have a drink?"

"Water, yes."

The reply elicited a muttered profanity from Houston.

"We discourage stimulants at this stage of your recovery; our records do show you have a mild alcohol dependency."

"What the hell?"

"A glass of wine with your lunch," the healer acquiesced.

Houston grunted as jets of warm air dried the remaining fluid from his body, which felt thicker than water. The sticky residue reminded him of sweat. He always wanted a hot shower after—even a shower while strapped in a chair for support.

"You have two messages, Colonel. Would you like them forwarded to your quarters?"

Houston shook his head as he was assisted into the wheelchair and steered toward his rooms at the Bengarian Medical Center.

He did not want to read well-wishes from his men. He should have died.

Three

Spirits bless me and guide my path to success, Ninallia prayed as she turned toward the market street again. This would be the second day of school she missed in less than a week. The absence couldn't be helped. She walked until her aunt's building was no longer in view before retrieving the card from her pocket to check the address. The credit symbol on the small square card blinked. She hurried to a terminal and slid it into the reader. The account showed another one hundred credits on the card.

With disbelief, she stared at the amount. She couldn't bring herself to cash these out. After boarding the transport, she handed the driver one of her remaining credit coins to take a transport bus to Madama Ector's establishment. The address on the card was unfamiliar, but the driver assured her it was in one of the wealthiest areas of the Imperial City. She thanked him and took an empty seat.

As the transport weaved through busy streets and increasingly posh neighborhoods, she fought the temptation to lean out the window to gawk at the wealth on display in shop windows and buildings. With a whoosh of airbrakes, the transport stopped.

The driver pointed to a multistory marble and stone building surrounded by rich lawns and shrubbery. "Madama Ector's establishment."

Could he be right? Ninallia checked the address again before climbing the steps to the door. She touched her simple shift dress. It was clean but well-worn, certainly not the fashionable gown of a wealthy girl. Even before her knock was answered, she was embarrassed by her lack of proper clothes for such an establishment. Dear Spirits, this is not a good sign.

A woman with a wide, pleasant face opened the door. The crisp blue and white robe belted at her waist proclaimed her the housekeeper. She smiled expectantly and waited for Ninallia to speak.

"I'm here to see Madama Ector," Ninallia stammered to break the awkward silence.

"Come in, child. They're waiting for you." The housekeeper stepped aside to allow Ninallia to enter.

"They?" she voiced the thought unintentionally.

"Healer, of course, and the client's representative are here." The housekeeper answered and didn't appear to think the question odd.

Ninallia wondered how much of Madama Ector's business the woman learned by answering the door and managing the household. She followed the housekeeper down a hallway carpeted in plush golden brown. Ornate picture frames hung on pale ivory walls, displaying images of historical figures and even the faces of some nobles she recognized. Her gaze drank in the wealth and beauty of her surroundings. Even the air was redolent with the scent of expensive leather and freshly polished wood.

The housekeeper stopped before a room where the heavy wood of the door muted the sound of the voices inside. The housekeeper knocked, and the voices inside quieted.

"Come in," Madama Ector's soft voice answered.

Ninallia hesitated as she stepped into the room. The rich, wooden floor was covered by an exquisitely woven carpet. Her eyes widened in wonder as she stared at the expensive rug. How could she step on something so beautiful after walking outside? She noticed shoes left by the door. Rich people did this to keep dirt from the street from getting inside their houses. She slipped off her shoes, thankful her stockings were clean and without holes.

"Ninallia, isn't it?" queried a thin man. The angles of a minister's tricorn hat elongated his already thin face. He studied her features. "Well, she has the right coloring. Her eyes are very unusual. Very few people have a combination of violet eyes and ebony hair."

"Yes, I noticed the resemblance when I met her at the dumas hostel. She resembles our client enough to be a sister or daughter." Madama Ector raised a delicate cup to her lips. "She claims royal blood through her mother. This appears to be true, through a minor indiscretion of the emperor's great-great-grandfather."

Ninallia could feel a flush rising. What should she do? She lowered her gaze and contemplated the pattern on the rug, feeling the texture through her thin hose.

"She's young," commented the white-robed healer. Unlike Healer Taborn, his costly robes and golden chains proclaimed his status. This healer serviced only wealthy customers.

"Purity must be unquestionable," the minister responded. A highbrow and prominent nose gave his face a haughty appearance, although his smile was reassuring.

Unperturbed, the healer addressed Ninallia. "Are you aware of what you are doing? Have you ever had a woman's examination before?"

"Yes, Healer, I have. There's a clinic in my neighborhood. All the girls in my class were examined. I am clean and fertile." A nagging fear formed in her stomach. *What if this is more than a dumas position? What if these clients want a sex slave or concubine?*

Madama Ector seemed to read her mind as she said, "I run a very honorable establishment. You will be treated well here. Our women never meet the clients or even know their names."

Ninallia didn't intend for her sigh of relief to be quite so audible—it was, and it seemed to lighten the mood in the room.

"You will go with the healer now, child. We maintain an examination room here. It may not be pleasant, but it will be over quickly."

Ninallia bowed, and the healer rose. She followed him from the room and was relieved when a female assistant joined them in the starkly furnished exam room. Closing her eyes, Ninallia lay back on the table, then felt a small prick as blood was drawn and the exam began.

"A virgin. Everything appears healthy." The assistant spoke with a clipped accent, and Ninallia wondered where she might be from.

The healer was gentle and thorough in his examination. After he finished, she dressed and waited anxiously for him to return. He tapped at the door before entering. His smile was reassuring.

"I've known Madama Ector for many years, and she is a very good woman. I must take your blood sample to my office for analysis. My recommendation will be dependent on those results, but I don't think we have anything to worry about. The housekeeper will see to your lunch, and I will return in a few hours with the results." He reassured Ninallia before leaving.

Her stomach growled at the mention of food. Her meager breakfast of grain mush and tea that morning was gone. The housekeeper was waiting outside the exam room. "Kitchen's this way. There'll be leftover roast sandwiches and some fruit and cheese today. Cook baked a berry pie, and she might cut you a piece of it."

Ninallia imagined what this woman would say if she sat at their table at home. When there was meat, which was seldom, it was always stringy, nearly-tainted discards from the butcher.

She spent the next hour in the kitchen eating at a small wooden table and listening to the cook and her assistant banter. She couldn't help gobbling up the tasty meat and cheese. The cook laughed and offered her more, even refilling her mug with fresh milk.

"Madama's girls are not allowed any alcohol, not even light ale," she explained, and set a large slice of berry pie in front of Ninallia.

The crust was warm, flaky, and the berry filling was rich and sweet. She almost swooned at the decadent flavor.

Left on her own after the meal, she followed the sound of feminine laughter to an open window overlooking a walled garden. The garden wasn't huge, but it was larger than any in her neighborhood. In its center was an oblong-shaped pool where several young women in various stages of pregnancy were swimming. Other women were laying on mats beside the pool, naked in the sunshine. She couldn't imagine being able to swim nude as these women were doing.

"No men allowed here, except for the healer and an occasional client." The housekeeper walked up quietly and touched her arm.

Ninallia was startled into an involuntary yelp.

The housekeeper laughed. "The healer is back, and Madama is ready for you." There was no indication of her mistress's decision.

Ninallia turned and followed the housekeeper to the drawing room. Madama Ector was alone, her face shining with excitement. She waved Ninallia in while dismissing the housekeeper with a nod. "Come in, child. We can celebrate a most lucrative deal."

"So, everything is okay. I do have royal ancestry?" She always doubted the family stories, at least some. No doubts remained now as Madama Ector's smile broadcasted her pleasure.

"Oh yes, more than we hoped for. Your father must have come from Nariland, because there is also… never mind. Healer Ession has given you a clean bill of health, and the insemination has been scheduled for early next week."

Ninallia caught her breath. *So soon?* The sooner the better, she supposed. She imagined the joy on her aunt's face when she dropped enough credits on the table to pay off her family's debt.

"Come, let me show you to your room." Madama Ector rose in one fluid motion and walked past her. "You will, of course, want to send word to your family. There is a communications port in your room."

Ninallia hung her head. Few families in her neighborhood could afford a connection to the communications network. She assumed she would be going back to leave her aunt the chip with the credits as payment for her mother's care.

"Ah," said Madama Ector, as she seemed to grasp the situation. "You must write them a note. It can be delivered before nightfall." She paused, then added, "I will advance enough credits to provide for them in your absence. You, my child, are a very lucky girl. We are receiving three times the normal rate for your services, and our normal rates are not cheap."

Awestruck, she followed Madama Ector up a marble staircase and down a carpeted hallway. The luxury was overwhelming. She never imagined such a house, much less living in one.

"Most of our girls share rooms, but I thought you might enjoy privacy."

The room was decorated in aqua tones with flowered curtains and rich, dark wood furniture. A glass door opened onto a balcony complete with a small table and two chairs. In the closet, five or six silken gowns hung above matching slippers.

Confused, Ninallia stammered, "Someone has left her clothes."

"Judging your size was hard, because what you're wearing is too large and the tags are faded. I think they'll fit." Madama grinned impishly. "It was fun sneaking a peek at your clothes while you were with the healer."

Ninallia had only dreamed of fine garments. The gowns were grander than anything she owned. The real silk shimmered in the light, and the room smelled of fresh flowers from a bouquet arranged in a pale vase on the dresser. It was like stepping into a world where she was transformed into a princess. The wonder of it brought tears of happiness to her eyes.

Madama Ector seemed pleased with her reaction. She pointed to a door leading to a private dressing room and toilet. "I'll leave you to settle in and try on your new things. Marta will come up later to get your letter. If there is anything you want her to bring from your home, give her a list."

The minute Madama Ector closed the door, Ninallia raced to the closet and took down one of the gowns. The material rustled softly in her fingers. The deep purple and white pattern was the most beautiful material she could imagine. *How can I wear something this fine?* She removed her simple shift and slipped into the gown. Its belt shimmered with color. The fit was perfect. Ninallia spun in circles before the mirror, admiring her finery.

Still wearing the gown, she sat at the writing table and composed a letter to reassure her aunt and mother. She tried to think of anything she might need. By the time the housekeeper, Marta, arrived, she had written two pages to her mother. Without explaining her "job", she reassured them she was safe and doing a good thing.

Marta placed a tray of tea, fruit, cheese, and sweet biscuits on the table. She took Ninallia's letter. "I have to go to the market. It may be late when I get back. Supper will be served at 6:30 in the dining room, unless you want a tray in your room."

Ninallia could only gape at the food. It was the middle of the afternoon, and she was still full from eating such a large lunch. On the tray, there was more food than her family ate in a whole day. She couldn't believe Madama Ector provided this much.

Marta laughed. "Madama likes the girls to eat well. It's good for the babies." She took the list from the writing table and slipped from the room, leaving Ninallia gaping at the food.

After selecting from the assortment, she bit into a sweet biscuit and walked onto the balcony. Below, a larger garden and a high fence separated the Madama's property from her neighbors.

After finishing, Ninallia enjoyed a hot bath and even washed her hair. She dressed again in the beautiful gown. The tiny bow on the slippers matched the darkest color. After checking herself in the mirror yet again, she headed downstairs to find the dining room.

"You must be a new girl," a soft voice called behind her.

Ninallia turned to see a tall, broad-shouldered woman with a plain, friendly face. The cut of her gown emphasized the well-rounded stomach of pregnancy.

"I'm Irinia, this is my third time working for Madama."

Ninallia was surprised. This was not one of the young women who had been swimming earlier. Irinia appeared to be in her thirties.

"I'm a good breeder and come from a hearty bloodline. My clients requested me again. All their children will be full brothers and sisters. My husband and I have two children of our own. He takes care of them while I am here."

Ninallia took in this deluge of information. She didn't know what she should say. "I'm Ninallia, and this is my first time to serve as dumas."

"I can tell you aren't more than fifteen or sixteen. You're too young for the public dumas hostels. Madama is strict about age rules, so you're lucky or special for her to make an exception in your case."

Ninallia wanted to tell this woman how grateful she was to Madama Ector. She followed the older woman into the dining area, where several women were already fixing plates from a large buffet table. Ninallia tried not to gape at the food. There were meat pies, roast fowl, and a platter of baked fish. Irinia began to fill a large plate with meat, vegetables, and breads. Ninallia followed, taking smaller portions. After introductions, she ate and listened to the lighthearted conversations going on around her. Madama Ector did not seem to mistreat her girls. They ate as much as they pleased and appeared to be very happy.

Later, after putting away the few things from home, Ninallia slipped into the large bed and snuggled under quilts and spreads. She was soon asleep.

~ * ~

The first test results were in—she wasn't pregnant. Even though Madama assured her the insemination seldom took the first time, Ninallia was afraid. *What will happen if I don't conceive? Will I have to repay Madama for everything, plus the credits Aunt Rese and mother are spending?*

"Why the gloomy face?" Irinia asked with a laugh. "It took me three times for the first child, and I already birthed one of my own. Sometimes it takes several tries; Madama isn't going to put you out."

"But what if I don't get pregnant? I could never pay her back." Ninallia stared down at her plate. The delicious food was tasteless.

"Did Madama Ector say you must pay her back? There's never any guarantee a woman will conceive." Irinia set her own fork down and patted Ninallia's arm. "Give it some time. The healer says you are fertile. Stop worrying and eat."

Ninallia wanted to hug the older woman. She wanted her own mother and aunt. She put a bite of the meat pie into her mouth and chewed. It was rich and delicious.

Four

Ice clung to the Temple's spires. Its reflected light was lost in the blowing wind before it reached the ground. The snow stopped at daybreak. Sisters and Brothers hurried between the buildings, keeping their hoods pulled tightly against the blasts of wind-blown snow as they hurried about their duties. The Temple City of Uban was frozen and isolated for almost half of the year, and the members of the Order, acolytes, and their servants were accustomed to harsh conditions.

Tegani, Sister of the Order and instructress of acolytes, fought her way against the wind. This confrontation had been brewing for some time. My Lady of Wisdom, as the leader of the Holy Order was known, overlooked her request once again. This could not be a simple oversight. Tegani made her desire for a mission outside the Temple City known many times. All Sisters and Brothers were given one outside the city once during their time of service. It pained her that Sister Hellith, who was years younger and whom she trained, was given the mission Tegani requested. My Lady would listen.

Shaking snow from her robes, Tegani bowed deferentially to an older Sister and climbed the stairway to the meeting chambers of My Lady. Taking in a deep breath before entering, she bowed low. Agreil, My Lady of Wisdom, sat contemplating the Pool of Knowledge. Tegani waited for her to acknowledge her presence.

"Sister Tegani, your mind is troubled." The old woman's tone held a note of disappointment, but her gaze never left the large ebony bowl containing the pool.

"Yes, My Lady. I do not understand why I have not been sent on a mission outside Uban. Am I not worthy?"

The old woman looked up. "You are one of our most gifted Sisters. Your work with acolytes here in the Temple City is outstanding."

"Why have I not been sent on a mission?"

"Your work here displeases you?"

"No, My Lady. I feel a mission outside the city will make me a better Sister."

A male voice queried from a corner, "How old were you when you came to the Temple City?"

Tegani turned to see First Brother Arturon, My Lady's assistant and the next in line to rule the Temple City, standing by a window. The man could be almost invisible when he chose.

"I was five when my mother gave me to the temple," Tegani replied. She liked Arturon. He was one of her favorite instructors.

"You have never been outside the city?"

"No, Brother," she answered. *Why is he asking me these questions when he already knows my answers?* She waited while My Lady again studied the pool.

My Lady turned to Arturon. "Gather what is needed to test and train acolytes outside the Temple City. One of our Sisters will have need of them."

Many years of training and deep respect for My Lady prevented Tegani from stamping her foot in exasperation. "My Lady, my mission?"

"Your time is not yet, Tegani. Study patience; it will give you solace. If you need something to do, help Arturon with his chore. The messenger must leave before the heavy snows set in." With a nod of her silver head, she dismissed them.

"Not yet? It must be soon, My Lady," Arturon said as he bowed to her, his words barely loud enough for Tegani to hear.

"Where is the package going?" Tegani asked when they were outside My Lady's chamber.

"I don't know. I wish she would tell me more," Arturon answered. They walked in silence for a time, then he added, "If anything were to happen to me, I think she wants you close by."

As an instructor of acolytes, she never considered herself in line to be My Lady. Always, Brother followed Sister and Sister followed Brother in the line of ascension. My Lady of Wisdom and the Father of Wisdom always possessed the gift of Sight. Her own gift was an ability to affect objects with her mind. She trained for many years to develop her skill and would spend many more to perfect it. The implication of Arturon's words took on a more personal meaning.

She regarded her friend and mentor with concern. "You are not well?"

"I am in good health, Sister, and hope to serve as Father of Wisdom, though I pray the Spirits not for some time."

Relief filled Tegani. She couldn't imagine the Temple City without Arturon. Their first stop was at the small shop that carried sacred oil. As they came out, the wind picked up and pelted them with ice. Arturon grabbed her hand and pulled her out into the street as he did when she was a young acolyte.

"Come, let's hurry. We can have some hot tea and soup for lunch," he said.

When they returned, the messenger was waiting with orders from My Lady and the destination. After helping to pack the items, Tegani returned to her quarters and sipped hot tea before her own fire. She had lived in the Temple City for twenty-five years, and she was thirty, after all. *If My Lady does not send me on a mission in the next year, I will take a sabbatical and visit my homeland. My parents are gone, but I have two stepsisters and their families. Perhaps I will find a mate and settle outside the Temple City.*

Many Sisters and Brothers chose this less isolated path

of service. In this way, they benefited the Temple and their homelands.

Five

Night claimed the Imperial City of Obantu. Merchants closed their shops and hurried home to their families. The weather was chilly with the first taste of winter's breath. Clouds darkened the pale light from the moons of Bengar. Inside the Imperial Palace, the Emperor Rhealgar and Empress Cynthy celebrated the recent news from Madama Ector.

The empress opened a small box, finding a silver ring set with fire opals. "My husband, you honor me when no honor is due."

"You will raise my son to be a great man, a worthy emperor to follow me."

The empress smiled. She loved this man. When she was proven barren, he could have dismissed her as many emperors would have.

"How far along is the girl?" he asked, stroking her hand. "When will we have a son?"

"Just far enough along for the tests to run true," she answered. "Madama sent word today. How the healers know the girl carries a son this soon is beyond me."

A servant entered carrying a tray of wine, cheeses, and an assortment of candies she loved. She and the emperor pulled apart.

"We will serve ourselves." The emperor dismissed the servant.

Cynthy took a sip of tea before speaking. "I am so happy. I want to shout the news to everyone so they can share our joy."

"Our dealings with Madama Ector and the birth of our

son must be a closely guarded secret for now. He must be born, and his paternity proven, before anyone in the court learns of his existence."

After sharing a glass of wine and eating many of the delicacies, Cynthy rose and bid her husband good night. She bent to kiss his hand, and he whispered. "Come to me tonight, my dear one. Let us celebrate together."

The assassin found them together in the emperor's bed, asleep in each other's arms. His blade was sharp, and his movements were swift. Neither roused before slumber became the final sleep of death. He slipped from the Imperial Palace and disappeared into the darkness.

As morning dawned, the screams of the emperor's personal groom woke the palace. The guards stationed outside the royal bedroom all night were put in chains. The emperor's nephew and heir, Lord Hanoree, ordered the ringing of the bells and called the nobles to assemble.

His solemn face was broadcast on communications networks throughout the empire. Hanoree declared his love for Emperor Rhealgar and assured the people that he would avenge the death of the royal couple. He wept copiously and decreed that bells should be rung within all areas of the Empire for three days. Shock and mourning spread throughout the city.

~ * ~

As the bells continued to ring, customers hurried home to mourn the death of the emperor. Beliani wiped down the bar and studied her husband. He was shaking.

Often agitated after a job, Ricol was frantic. "You got to listen to me, woman. I need you to listen."

"I'm listening."

"If anything happens to me, you need to run. Get to the League. You'll be safer there."

"What have you done?" She took his arm.

Ricol shook off her hand. "Made us rich is what I've done. Didn't I promise as much? You remember what I said." He gave her a quick, hard kiss and strode from the bar.

Six

The ringing of the bells shook the Imperial Palace, the Imperial City, and the Empire. Ninallia covered her ears and ran from her room into a common area of Madama Ector's dumas hostel. All the women housed at the hostel crowded into the room, their anxious chatter adding to the din of noise.

"Is the city under attack?" asked Irinia. Her baby had been born, and she was soon to leave the hostel. Madama Ector required the babies to spend the first two months with their mothers if possible.

Ninallia had been at Madama Ector's for four months. Nothing like this happened before. The bells were making it difficult to think. Everyone was frightened.

"There has been a death at the palace. We are in no danger here. Please go back to what you were doing." The firm voice of Marta, the housekeeper, stilled the panic in the room. "Madama Ector will return with news soon."

Something in the housekeeper's face worried Ninallia. She went to her room and caught the end of the Royal Nephew's speech. She could not believe the news. The Imperial Palace was on lockdown after the assassination of the emperor and empress. Memories of images of the beautiful empress posted throughout the city brought tears to her eyes. The luxury of her room and clothing seemed wrong.

"There you are!" Madama Ector startled her.

Ninallia turned and saw Madama staring at her from the doorway. There were tears streaming down her cheeks. Ninallia rose and started toward the older woman.

Madama Ector turned and shut the door with such violence it shook. She raised one hand to stop Ninallia. "You have to leave. Get out!"

Ninallia shook her head. "I don't understand. I conceived. I haven't lost the child."

Madama Ector pushed her toward the closet. "You don't understand. It is the emperor's child you carry. It was to remain a secret. They will find me and come for you."

Ninallia stood frozen in shock. Words and questions flooded her mind. They would not come out. She stared at Madama. How could she be carrying the royal heir?

Before her mind could focus, Madama was shaking her and screaming, "Run, you silly child! They will kill you and the heir if they find you here."

She stared into Madama Ector's eyes, absorbing the fear and panic bubbling behind the tranquil color. "Home?"

"Of course not! If they can find you here, they will find your family. Go somewhere and hide yourself until the child is born."

"Where?" Her question was unheeded as Madama Ector thrust a small bag of garments and a pouch heavy with credits into her hands and pushed her toward the open balcony window.

Thrust into the night, Ninallia clutched the garment bag and ran. *Is Madama Ector a madwoman? Would such a fine man as the Royal Nephew harm anyone, let alone an infant?* Ninallia slowed her pace, shaking her head. *Of course, he would. He wants the throne for himself, no matter what he says.*

She ducked into a public toilet and opened the bag. Tears fell. None of the fine clothes she loved were spilled out. These were servants' clothes and not too clean. They would have to do. She changed from her gown into the new clothes. She looked in the mirror. The poor young girl of a few months past stared back at her.

As she walked back onto the street, she faced a new dilemma. Madama Ector was generous with credit chips, but a lone girl could not approach an inn or hostel at night without raising notice and comment. Ninallia slept in an alley hidden behind some bins. It was smelly and cold.

When morning light woke her, she rose from her hiding place and brushed the worst of the dirt from her clothes. She bought a hot beverage and a meat roll from a vendor and ate as she walked toward the outskirts of the city. She almost collided with a young boy who was running ahead of his mother. Ninallia stopped. The boy was a few years younger, but he was almost her height and weight. He smiled and bowed in apology. She nodded back.

A plan formed in her mind as she moved through the crowded city street. Anyone trying to harm her would be seeking a young woman carrying the emperor's heir. They would not be looking for a boy.

After turning down a street of shops, she began her transformation. *I must not appear to be a poor boy, or merchants will question the credits he carries. He cannot be wealthy or noble born, or they will question his lack of servants.* She purchased clothes suitable for the son of a middle-class merchant. She would call herself Naro. Her imagination took over, and after a day of wandering the streets buying supplies, she felt ready to don her disguise.

The boy's attire fit loosely and would hide her pregnancy as the baby grew for a while. Shaving the sides of her head and plaiting the rest of her hair in a long braid finished the transformation. Naro could travel alone without comment. He could sleep in a hostel and eat at any inn in the city. Heading along the busy street, she sought a hostel to spend the night. She was eager to have a good meal and sleep in a bed.

She walked awkwardly down the street, trying to imitate a boy's long strides. The clothes were comfortable, and she was getting used to the shoes. The hair was another matter. Every day or two, she would need to shave the sides to maintain the style, and the intricate braid wasn't easy.

The proprietor of the modest inn smiled as she entered his establishment. "Good day, young master. How may I help you?"

Ninallia let her hand touch the pouch holding her credits. "I am traveling to my uncle's home in the northern mountains."

"A long journey, young master. How may I assist?"

Ninallia was thrilled that the innkeeper was fooled by her disguise. "This is my first time in the Imperial City, and I plan to spend a few weeks here before I continue my journey. I must arrive before full winter."

"We have the perfect room for you," the innkeeper assured her. "Will you want meals as well?"

She responded with a polite nod. "Breakfast and dinner." She followed the innkeeper up the stairs to a small guestroom.

Seven

The bells ceased clanging, and a wary silence engulfed the Temple City. News of the death of the emperor and empress frightened people, even in Uban, which lay far from the Imperial City and outside the Empire. My Lady summoned Tegani to personal attendance. Instead of performing her duties as instructress of acolytes, she sat in My Lady's room waiting. She concentrated on a meditation crystal as a heated debate raged between My Lady and Arturon. He paced, his long braids swinging their onyx beads angrily. My Lady stood, her gray braids touching the floor. Her pale eyes remained calm.

"And what makes you think they won't attack the Temple City?" Arturon demanded.

"They aren't stupid enough to violate the Writ of Neutrality and go to war with the Seven Kingdoms," My Lady reasoned.

Tegani listened in silence as the two argued back and forth. Arturon was more upset than she had ever seen him.

My Lady raised her hand. "Enough! Once we have the girl in the Temple City, there is nothing Lord Hanoree can do."

"So, who is this girl? Where can I find her?" Arturon asked.

"Not you, Brother, it is Tegani's time."

"But, My Lady, I have never been outside the Temple City. How will I know what to do?" Tegani dropped her pretense of meditation. A simple mission where she could see something of the world was one thing; this was much more dangerous.

"You are more capable than you know." She stepped toward Tegani and embraced her. With surprising speed, My Lady took a pair of shears from her pocket and cut the bottom half of Tegani's braids. Tiny beads woven into each braid spilled across the floor. "The Royal Nephew must never know the Temple Order is involved. What you must do has to be done in secret. Many Sisters and Brothers stand ready to assist you when they can."

Tegani fell to the floor and covered her face. Cutting off the braids happened when a Sister disgraced themselves. They were dismissed from the Order and cast from the Temple City. It was a thing of shame.

Arturon lifted the sobbing Tegani to her feet. His expression spoke louder than his words. "My Lady, I cannot stand in agreement with what you are doing."

"Then don't stand against me, Brother. I love this Sister like my own daughter. If there was another way, I would choose it."

They let Tegani cry out her pain, giving her a glass of wine when the worst of the tears were shed. There were many questions churning inside her. She didn't know where to begin. The time for her mission outside the Temple City arrived and came with a terrible price. She would appear to be stripped of her position as a Sister and dishonored. Few would know the truth. My Lady pressed a single page of instructions into her hand.

Tegani covered her head to hide her shame as she hurried to prepare for the journey. In her room, she removed the remaining beads from her hair, adding them to those retrieved from My Lady's floor. Before she could focus on what she must do, Tegani painstakingly counted the beads. She sighed. They were all there. She placed them in a jar and sealed the top. Loosening a brick on the side of her fireplace, she placed the jar in a small hole where she kept her few valuables. She replaced the brick and used paint, salt, and flour to make mortar and filled in around the brick to conceal the spot. It wouldn't last for years, but if she wasn't back in a few months, she was dead anyway, so it wouldn't matter.

She scrubbed her face clean of ornamental makeup and trimmed her hair before twisting it into a common knot.

Sixteen hours left her no time to grieve and barely enough time to study what was written about the mysterious woman who carried the royal heir. My Lady's note did not even tell the woman's name or age. She was to contact Madama Ector, a mother of dumas in one of the Imperial City's wealthier neighborhoods. This Madama would be able to provide information and perhaps help.

Eight

Houston mentally controlled his prosthetics—increasing his speed on the treadmill. He ignored Healer Bannoff's warning that he needed at least three or four more months to acclimate his new heart and limbs. Houston was eager to escape this sanatorium and leave this remote world. Though recovered sufficiently to be allowed small amounts of alcohol, he could not drink enough to escape the memories of his last mission. Sweat trickled down his face and neck as he pushed himself.

A buzz sounded, and the door to the clinic's gym slid open. A voice Houston never expected to hear again greeted him. "Not bad for an old man. Are you ready to escape this place?"

The greeting caused a jolt of surprise, and the new heart skipped a couple of beats. Houston gasped and grabbed the handrest for support. The treadmill stopped, shifting his weight even further onto the rail. He struggled upright. "General, I'm glad to see you, sir."

Healer Bannoff rushed past General Evans and took Houston's arm to steady him. "You see, General, I told you the colonel is not ready. It will be months before the heart is functional without monitoring. Your plan is impossible."

Houston pushed away the healer. "I'm okay, Banny. The shock of seeing the old man here crossed a few wires. Why don't you leave us alone for a bit?"

Healer Bannoff, who despised being called Banny, huffed disapprovingly as he left the gym.

"Can we talk here?" General Evans asked. He patted his pocket where he kept cigars and shrugged apologetically. They were confiscated upon arrival at the clinic. The healer insisted even the smoke from "safe" synthetic tobacco would have a negative effect on Houston's new heart-lung capacitor.

There were mirrors in the clinic. Houston knew he didn't look like the same man. He was thin and pale. Hell, he looked like death warmed over. Standing straight, he tried to walk with his old gait. The general wouldn't travel this far for a social visit. There was a mission. Something important must have happened. Damn the news blackout in this place.

General Evans began as soon as the doors to Houston's room closed. "You heard the bells a few days ago?"

"Yes, caused quite a disturbance. I asked what the excitement was, and they told me there was a death in the royal family. There isn't much direct communication here. No current news or entertainment to disturb the healing process."

The general continued, "This facility isn't in the Empire. The murder of the emperor and empress has caused an uproar all over Bengar."

Houston whistled sharp and low. The assassination of the emperor was reason enough for the League of Seeded World's concern and action. The general must have a mission in mind, but Houston wasn't sure what he could do without his team for backup. Hell, he wasn't even sure he could go grocery shopping without help. "Got a smoke?"

"Not anymore," the general groused. "I wouldn't give one to you if I could. You look like hell. What have you lost, fifty pounds?"

"Thirty-five, and I was fat before. All I need is sunshine and fresh air."

The general patted his pocket and sighed again. His voice grew low and serious as he said, "We've come into some valuable information, and the League wants you to act on it. Earlier this year, the empress hired a high-class dumas to provide an heir. According to our sources, the dumas has reported she is pregnant."

"Poor girl," Houston said. "She won't last long."

"Right, League Command wants us to get the woman and the heir off Bengar. Nowhere here is safe. If you are up to it, you are to locate her and get her to the Kingdom of Romar, and from there off planet. After things settle here, the League will announce the heir is in their custody and negotiate terms."

Houston laughed. "On a strange planet with over sixty million people, you want me to find one pregnant woman and take her to the League."

"Right, I knew you would understand."

"What if she doesn't want to go?"

"That would be a very big mistake. We're pretty sure the Royal Nephew is behind the murders. If the palace has the same information we have, she's as good as dead if you don't find her first."

"You're talking about a complicated rescue. I take it you haven't assembled my team?"

The general looked down at the floor.

"I thought not. In case you haven't noticed, I can't pass as a native. I'm too tall, and my coloring is wrong."

The general shook his head. "No, your team is not here," he said, then answered Houston's concerns in order. "You'll be on your own. The Imperial City is very multicultural, and with a few minor alterations, you can pass for one of the natives of the Southern Kingdom. They run tall and muscular. Years of living off the sea, I suspect. Healer Bannoff has agreed to let us use his facility to handle the skin and hair adjustment. The effects won't be permanent. They have state-of-the-art eye tinting here. No one will be able to tell you don't have silver eyes."

Houston flinched. He specialized in disguise work. No matter how many times he used them, he was never comfortable with wearing contacts. He hated having anything done to his eyes.

The general coughed and avoided looking directly at Houston. "If you are not up to this, I'll understand. It is short notice."

Houston didn't know what to say. It was short notice, and he was weak, but there was no one else. "I'll do it. I'll be ready tomorrow or as soon as the healer can get the work done."

The general clasped Houston's hand and pumped his arm hard. At Houston's gasp, the general loosened his grip and mumbled an apology.

Nine

Trying to contain his excitement, Hanoree paced the length of the royal throne room. All his plans were working. The assassin's work was done, his own death accomplished, and his body disposed of.

"There is nothing to lead this back to me," he said aloud to the empty room.

He longed to wear the Imperial Crown. His imagination spun fantasies where he led the Empire through a time of terrible grief before humbly assuming his rightful place as emperor. To make these dreams a reality, he planned to leak information tying the deaths of the emperor and empress to the Temple Order. He would launch a crusade to lead the Empire to victory over its enemies.

A soft chime announced a visitor to the royal chamber. Hanoree rose from the throne and drew his face into a somber expression. "Enter." He relaxed when his most trusted aide, Lord Varick, entered.

With uncustomary curtness, Varick dismissed the servants who followed him into the royal chamber. When they were alone, he handed Hanoree a small slip of paper.

He opened it and frowned at the single name written there: *Madama Ector*. "What is this? Who is Madama Ector?" He hated it when Varick played these guessing games.

"Madama Ector is an expensive mistress of dumas, my lord." Varick paused. "My sources report the empress employed her services. There is or will be an heir."

Hanoree inhaled sharply. It tested his will not to fall to the floor screaming. After the first flush of shock, rage began to fill him. Nothing would stand between him and the throne. "Does anyone else know?"

"No, my lord, the Empress Cynthy was very discreet. I have Madama Ector's name, but not the name of the dumas."

"Bring me this Madama Ector and secure all the women in her care. I will have this woman and her child." Hanoree slammed his fist onto the table. "Go!"

He knew Varick was loyal, but the tiny smile on his lips told Hanoree the man enjoyed his small moments of power too much. It would be easy to deal with him once he located this Madama Ector and her women.

Hanoree tried to maintain his composure as he prepared to greet the Nobles who formed the council that would decide if he was worthy of the throne. The Council of Nobles never ruled against the hereditary succession, but he did not want to risk offending them. It would be disastrous for any of the Nobles to learn of his interest in Madama Ector.

~ * ~

Six hired men, dressed in uniform, filed up the steps of Madama Ector's fine house. Lord Varick was leading them, although no one would have recognized him in the robes of a Priest of Elden. He knocked on the door, and when the housekeeper opened it, he could tell something was amiss. The woman was almost hysterical, her eyes were red from weeping.

"You've come," she said between sobs. "She's in there."

The place was too quiet. Varick followed the housekeeper to the door of what appeared to be the Mistress's receiving room. Madama Ector's body lay on the floor, a note clutched in her hand. Remains of a large fire smoldered in the fireplace. He rolled the body over, and her sightless eyes stared up at him. He smelled the odor of poison. Lord Hanoree would be furious with him.

Varick glared at the housekeeper and demanded, "Where

are the women?"

The housekeeper scrubbed her face with her hands. "Gone. Madama sent them away two days ago. Dismissed the servants, too, except me and the cook. I knew she was upset, but none of us expected this." She burst into a torrent of sobs.

He motioned toward his men, and they hurried through the house, searching for anything to identify the women who lived there. The rooms were empty; even the beds were stripped for washing.

"Where are the women?" roared Varick.

"Gone, Master. Madama paid them and sent them home. Told them to have their children and live in peace."

"Where are the records?" He glanced at the smoldering ashes in the fireplace with a sickening realization of failure.

Hanoree would have his head for this. The drawers of the desk were open and contained nothing. The housekeeper was being held by one of the men.

Varick raised a hand and slapped her across the face. "How many women were staying here? I need names."

"Names, yes sir, I can give you names. There were twenty girls, and a lively bunch they were." She described the girls.

"Last names, too. There must be thousands of women called Renalla in the Empire."

"Oh, Master, Madama Ector was very strict about names. The women were known only by their first names, and none spoke about where they were from. Our clients were very important. They wanted things kept confidential. If you want the last names of the girls, I can't help you."

Varick was an intelligent man. He realized this woman was telling the truth, and if he tried to beat information from her, it would, without a doubt, be false. He decided to use a different tactic. Smoothing his face into amiability, he motioned for the housekeeper to have a seat.

"I am afraid your mistress has been involved in something dangerous. We are with Imperial security. We need your help in locating the women who lived under Madama's care. They may be in danger."

The housekeeper straightened. "Yes sir, I'll do what I can. I am a loyal citizen."

He patted her shoulder. He brought a pad of paper and a pen to the table. "You're a smart woman; you will be fine. Write down everything you remember about each one, describing anything you think will help us identify these women: their appearance, how old they are, what did they sound like? Did you notice an accent?"

"Oh, I can help you. I took care of those girls myself. I knew them better than anyone here." The housekeeper seemed to unwind as she listed the women, stopping every few to count.

The guards removed the body and sent away the local police.

"There were twenty women staying at the hostel," the housekeeper said. "Do you want the names of the ones who have birthed their babies?"

"Not now, I will let you know later. I want you to know you are doing a good thing, and there will be a reward." He placed a hundred-credit chip on the table but kept his hand on it.

The housekeeper bent with renewed vigor to her task. Soon she handed him four pages, neatly written, describing each woman living at Madama's.

"Thank you, mistress." Varick smiled and motioned for his men to get going. "Tell me, has there been anyone else here in the last few days? A visitor Madama met with you didn't recognize?"

The housekeeper pursed her lips for a bit. "No, she stayed in her office alone. I thought she was having personal problems."

"We are leaving now, but I will be back. If you remember

anything at all..."

"Oh yes, sir. I would do anything to help you find those poor girls and make sure they are safe," she answered, walking with Varick to the door.

~ * ~

The grief of Lord Hanoree appeared genuine. His tear-stained face was on every communications port as Ninallia watched the daily newsfeeds. *It would be simple to go to see such an honorable man and explain.*

She spotted the housekeeper at a small eatery with outside tables. She took a seat nearby and eavesdropped, hoping it would be possible to return to Madama Ector's. Soon, the housekeeper was joined by a woman Ninallia recognized as one of the women who worked in the kitchen. Both women were haggard and upset.

"I can't believe it. Madama would not kill herself. Why would she kill herself? She was a wealthy woman. I won't believe it." The cook wiped her eyes.

"I saw the note myself, and it was in her handwriting," the housekeeper said. She glanced around and lowered her voice to say, "Why do they want to know about Madama's girls? She sent the girls away and burned the records. Imperial officers have been asking questions. What can I say? I am the housekeeper. I never saw any of the files. Madama handled them personally."

"I don't know," the cook answered. "Maybe one of the girls was into something bad. Maybe Madama was involved in something illegal."

"I won't believe it. Madama Ector was a good woman. She treated those girls well. I never heard of one complaint, not one."

Ninallia hid her shaking hands under the table and pretended to study the menu. She suppressed a squeak as the waitress's approach startled her.

"I'll have white ale, eggs, and bread." Remembering she was passing as a boy, she added, "Can you bring a big slice of honey cake?"

The housekeeper and cook continued to talk, but she stopped listening. Tears wanted to pour down her face, but she fought them back. Madama was dead. Had she killed herself or been murdered by someone trying to find the emperor's unborn child?

A sudden fear came over her. *What if the Imperial Soldiers discover who I am? Would they find Mother and Aunt Rese and kill them? I must warn them.*

After finishing her meal, she made her way to the old neighborhood. No one she knew appeared to recognize the boy walking down the cobbled street as Ninallia. She drew near and noticed there were no curtains in her aunt's window. She circled the building and climbed the back steps with a mounting sense of dread. It was empty. Her mother and aunt were both gone. Heart pounding, she raced back down.

~ * ~

Lord Hanoree stormed around his meeting chamber. He was furious that he could not interrogate Madama Ector, but her suicide confirmed his fear that a true heir to the emperor would be born. How did the empress manage that coup without anyone in his network learning of it?

"Here, drink this, my lord." Varick handed him a glass of wine.

Hanoree sipped the wine, confident that Varick added the correct amount of sedative.

"From what this housekeeper reports, the first of the possible babies won't be born for months. By my own calculations, the earliest the royal heir could be born is five or six months off. Three women can be eliminated from the list." Hanoree began to feel the effects of the drug and smiled. *Varick knows when I need something to unwind. I should give him a minister's position when I ascend the throne. He shook his head. But, it's too bad I have to kill the man. Loyalty like his should be rewarded.*

"We don't have the time or luxury to wait until the baby is born and have the child tested," Varick commented. "It would be better to track down these twenty women and kill them, all of them."

Hanoree agreed. It would be so. In the back of his mind, he began to doubt himself about Varick's fate. Perhaps he did not need to be killed. He was brilliant, ruthless, and a loyal aide.

Hanoree shook himself. Varick knew too much. Knowledge gave him power over his master, and that could not be tolerated. Soon, he would deal with the man. Soon.

Ten

Houston checked the address on the com screen on his wrist. The house was large with a marble and stone façade—a home suited for a minor Noble. Whoever Madama Ector had been, her house spoke of wealth and taste. After learning that she sent the women away before committing suicide, it was probably pointless for him to be staking out the place. He was here because, when one doesn't have any leads, one must start somewhere. He was almost at the point of giving up and telling the general to get him off this frigging planet. There wasn't any coffee, and his disguise itched. He watched the housekeeper come and go as the long evening meandered into night. Houston fought the urge to go find a bed in a local hostel. Well-honed instincts were telling him this was the place he needed to be.

A slender figure walked past the Madama's hostel before slipping behind the next house. Alert for any movement, he headed to the other side. Oh yes, the woman, and it was a woman, crossed the street and was approaching Madama's house. She pushed open a back window and climbed in. Silent as a cat from years of training and missions, he followed.

As he drew closer, he tried to decide what to say to her. She would be scared and wouldn't trust strangers. *Why would anyone in her position come back? She must know she isn't safe here, or did she?* He checked the voice-activated translator, satisfied it was working.

Inside the house, he could see the woman going through what appeared to be an office. Her back was to him as he moved into position. Before he could grab her, she whirled around and, in one smooth action, reversed the tables. She was standing behind him and holding a weapon to his neck. *What the fuck?*

"I'm a friend," was all he could think to croak. The metal of the weapon nudged further into the back of his neck. "I know about Madama Ector, the emperor, everything. I can help."

She gave him a shove in the back, and he stumbled. "League spy! What are you doing here, and how do you know about Madama Ector?"

Houston had a bad feeling. His eyes widened at the sight of the beautiful woman holding a weapon in very steady hands. She stared at him. Something told him this was not the dumas he was looking for. "I believe I'm doing the same thing you are, trying to find a pregnant woman who used to live here. We need to locate her before she is killed."

The woman slid the sleeve of her robe up, revealing a multicolored pattern tattooed on her arm. Houston clicked a picture with the camera imbedded in his right eye. He blinked again and sent the image to the computer identification system.

In less than five seconds, a tiny voice spoke into his transmitter earbud. "Sister of the Order. The Order is a semi-religious group located in the Bananok Kingdom. It has its own independent city and is politically neutral. The Sisters and Brothers of the Order are highly trained in mental and physical abilities. They can be dangerous."

He eyed the weapon aimed at his recently installed and very expensive artificial heart. She was dangerous. He doubted either this Sister or her Order were politically neutral. "You're not the dumas."

"No, and you are not Bengarian. What business is this of the League?" she demanded.

"The League does not support murder or the takeover of the Empire. We know she carries the heir, and I have been sent to get the woman and the heir off planet to safety."

She huffed in disgust. "Are your leaders stupid enough to believe anyone in the Empire would support an emperor who was raised by the League?"

She asked a very astute question. Houston was silent for a minute. He didn't think she was going to shoot him, not if he kept her talking. "What does the Order have to do with the Empire?"

"Everything on Bengar concerns the Order. What do you know about the woman?"

Houston was getting tired. His heart-lung capacitor was beating erratically. He backed to the wall and slid down into a sitting position. He glanced up at the beautiful woman. There was a puzzled look on her face. He held up his hand. After a few minutes, the heart resumed its normal rhythm, and he could speak. "I know she is pregnant and is carrying the heir to the late emperor."

She nodded. "Unfortunately, too many sources seem to know this. Madama Ector was dead because too many people did. I am here to find Madama's records. There must be something, some clue to help identify this woman who carries the true emperor."

Houston asked, "Wouldn't the authorities already have taken everything when they searched?"

"Yes, if they found it."

He could have launched himself at her and disarmed her. Instead, he studied the fine-boned face with those incredible eyes. She frowned.

"The housekeeper gave the authorities a list of the names the women used and their descriptions." Houston didn't know why he was telling her or how the general acquired the list.

"You have it?" Excitement shone in her eyes. When he patted a pocket, she smiled. It was the kind of smile that could light up a room.

"Partners?"

"I believe we can work together. Where are you from?"

"Houston."

She looked at him with confusion.

He reached out a hand. "I'm Colonel Benjamin Houston."

She nodded again. "I am Tegani, senior Sister of the Order. May I see the list?"

~ * ~

The smell of the human, Colonel Houston, affected Tegani's senses in ways she couldn't understand. She was trained to suppress emotions and physical reactions, but something penetrated her guards. She bit the inside of her cheek hard; the pain helped her focus. There were twenty names on the list and brief descriptions. Not as detailed as the housekeeper provided the authorities, but sufficient. She read each name and description.

Finally, she pointed to one name. "This one, her name is Ninallia. She is a girl of fifteen. Purity would have been important to the empress. Another clue, and an important one, is the girl's physical description. The dark hair and violet eyes are common in the Northern Plains people. The empress, whose coloring was similar, came from the northern part of the Empire."

Houston stepped closer. His nearness sent a wave of energy flooding Tegani's senses. She stepped back and handed him the note. "Ninallia is not an uncommon name."

Tegani was not much of a telepath. Her gift was one of affecting physical objects. She was far from the Temple City and in need of help if she wanted to find this girl. There were Sisters and Brothers living in the Imperial City.

She focused her mind and sent a short message: *Name: Ninallia. Age fifteen.* It would be relayed until it reached My Lady. She panted from the effort that sending always caused those who pushed the limits of their gifts.

"Are you okay?" Concern furrowed Houston's brow.

She smiled. As a human, never having seen anyone

sending, this must seem very strange. She tried to imagine how it appeared to him. The frozen, vacant expression and rapid breathing might appear to be a seizure. "Yes, I'm sending the information we found."

His reply was interrupted by a sudden noise at the front of the house. Someone else was there. She concentrated. The door closed, and the lock clicked. "Out the window before they find us."

She headed toward the window, turning to see Houston sitting and staring at her in an odd way. Was he ill? She then realized he had never seen anyone manipulate matter before. "It's called telekinesis on Earth. Let's go!"

He struggled to his feet and moved toward the window. Tegani jumped and landed in the alley behind the house, stepping to the side in time to avoid being smashed by his heavier body. He landed nimbly with his weapon drawn. She closed her eyes and concentrated. The window slid closed and locked. He whistled as he turned to the left and headed down the alley.

When they were away from the house, he grabbed her arm. "There is a small café over there. I don't know about you, but I'm hungry."

She was starving. Using her mental powers always left her drained, plus her legs were aching. "I need to eat too."

After a few minutes, they were seated at a table in a corner of the café. It was small, crowded with students and other late-night customers. The scent of roasting meat and ale filled the air.

They were a normal enough couple. He was a tall, muscular man from the seacoast, having a late supper with an attractive woman. She caught a glimpse of herself in a window and turned away. The pain of her shorn braids was fresh, though she understood why the Order could not publicly acknowledge her mission. Her thoughts were interrupted when the waiter approached to take their orders.

"Do I smell fresh mountain goat?" she inquired, smiling at the waiter. It was her favorite meat in the Temple City. When the waiter nodded, she continued, "I'll have a roast sandwich with strong jarri sauce, a mug of black ale, and maybe a sweet pie later."

Houston looked at the waiter and smiled. "I'll have the same, but you may go ahead and bring my pie."

The waiter hurried off to place their order and bring back their drinks. He set a pitcher of the dark, fragrant ale and two glasses on the table and said, "Your food will be out soon."

"You did some trick with the locks and window. How do you do that?" Houston poured two glasses of the ale and slid one toward her after the waiter left.

"It's my gift. It is my area of training in the Order."

"How long does it take to learn?"

"If it is your gift, it takes most Sisters ten years of training to develop the skill. It takes a lifetime to master it. If it is not your gift, telekinesis is almost impossible to learn."

Two platters with large slabs of meat and bread arrived, and they grew quiet while eating. The sauce was perfect, bringing a touch of heat to the dish. They were discussing another pitcher of ale when the waiter approached, bowed, and then handed Tegani a small piece of paper. "From the lady by the door."

She whirled and saw the back of a woman dressed in dark robes leaving. She recognized a fellow Sister of the Order instantly. The robes, intricately beaded braids, the way she walked—all spoke of Temple training.

Tegani unfolded the paper and read the message: *Ninallia of Rishual, daughter of Vicori from the village of Shunni. Last known address is in the southern slums of the Imperial City. 215 Runnel House Row # 10.* She slid the note across the table.

Houston smiled and raised an eyebrow. "Let's meet here in the morning and go to the girl's address."

A good suggestion. Suffering from lack of sleep, Tegani agreed to rest and meet at the same eatery in the morning to scout the girl's neighborhood.

Eleven

Houston stood for thirty minutes in front of the café, cursing his stupidity. Of course, she'd lied. The fact that Tegani was beautiful with an innocent face meant nothing. He raised a hand and hailed a personal transport. After barking out the address, he sat back. He felt like choking her. His temper cooled by the time the transport arrived in the poorer section of the city. In truth, he might have done the same thing if his hormones weren't reacting to her.

Tegani stood near a fruit stand and stared across at an apartment building. He walked up and took her by the arm. "I thought we were working together."

"I decided to get an early start," she said. "The apartment is empty. Her family fled after the emperor's murder."

"Why are we here?"

Her head jerked to the side, and a finger rose to her lips. She pointed at a boy walking past the apartments. His clothes were too fine for this area, and his walk was stilted. "That's her," Tegani whispered.

With the speed of a jungle predator, Houston closed in on the figure as Tegani hurried close behind. One couldn't snatch someone off the street, even in this neighborhood. Well, apparently, he could and did. He grabbed the girl and yanked her into an alley. His hand was clamped over her mouth.

Tegani dashed after them and spoke rapidly to the struggling girl. "Ninallia, it's okay. We're friends. We mean you no harm." She repeated the refrain for the third time.

The girl stilled, then delivered a vicious kick to Houston's non-artificial knee. He grunted but held on.

Tegani raised an arm. The sleeve fell open, revealing her tattoos. "I'm a Sister of the Order. I have been sent to help you."

The girl collapsed into Tegani's arms. Her sobs shook the thin body. Tegani patted her back and shared a look with Houston. The girl's disguise was effective. If her training had made her skilled at watching for signs, they might have passed over the young boy walking in a seedy area of the city.

The trio exited the alley. In case she tried to bolt, Houston kept his arm around the girl's shoulder. Tegani noted she thought that was unnecessary. The girl seemed relieved to have found help at last.

"How did you find me? How did you recognize me?" The girl turned toward Tegani as if Houston's presence was unimportant.

"Let's leave and find a place to rest." Houston hailed a personal transport.

Tegani frowned and whispered, "No one in this neighborhood would have enough credits for personal transport. We should find a public station."

"I am a well-to-do businessman visiting the Imperial City. I have plenty of credits."

The transport arrived, and the trio got into the private aircab.

"Your destination, good sir?" the driver queried.

"A family hostel, please. We are not from this city and were dropped off in this unfortunate area. Nothing here is suitable for my family."

The driver rubbed his chin. "How much can you pay?" His question was directed toward Houston, who was likely perceived as the husband and father.

"Nothing is too grand for my wife. A small, quiet place in one of the better areas of town would be perfect. Perhaps one with a view of the Imperial Palace."

The driver smiled. "I know just the place."

The transport wound its way through the city as the driver pointed out sites of interest. They arrived at a small, elegant inn with a view of the palace gates in the distance. Houston paid the driver and tipped generously. The driver looked at him strangely as he drove off.

"Let me handle this. We do not tip here," Tegani said as they walked up to the door. "It is the custom for women to take care of these things. It would be odd for you to arrange them."

He nodded while he and Ninallia fell in line behind her. Houston reminded himself to think of the girl as the boy she appeared to be. If he didn't, her disguise might be blown.

Tegani walked up to the door and knocked. The door was opened by a uniformed servant. She didn't wait for the servant to speak. "Tell your mistress I wish to inspect your best rooms. We have traveled a long way and were lost in this great city. Be quick and fetch your mistress."

Soon, a plump woman in voluminous robes hurried toward them. "Come in, mistress. I am sorry my stupid servant left you standing at the door." She eyed the trio with eagerness.

"We need a room for a few days. We want something with a private bath and a view of the palace."

"All our rooms come with a private bath." The woman's voice was haughty. "Our front rooms have a view of the palace, and the back rooms overlook Imperial Park."

"May we see a room? Show us one of each, please. I prefer the palace, but I'm sure my son would enjoy watching the horses. I believe there is an excellent stable, a gift from Earth."

"Yes, they were a gift to the late emperor on his coronation. Rest his soul in the Mists."

Tegani and the others lowered their gazes and murmured agreement. The landlady opened the door wider, and they followed her down the hall. No one spoke of credits. He figured if one asked, one probably couldn't afford to stay there.

The room facing the palace was on the second floor with a balcony. It was large and had two beds, a seating area, and a separate bath. She looked around and nodded. Next, they climbed to the third floor and walked down a carpeted hallway to the end. This room was larger and furnished with the best in antiques. The balcony provided a view of the Imperial Park. The view was breathtaking.

"We'll take this one," Tegani said, her voice hushed as if in awe. "We will send for our things."

Twelve

Ninallia slept curled next to Tegani. When she closed her eyes that night, she felt safe for the first time in many days. Her feelings of safety evaporated the next morning. She woke early from hunger and decided to go downstairs and check out the breakfast options. When she arrived on the first floor, she was greeted with a sight that made her want to race back upstairs. There were Imperial soldiers in the hallway.

The hostel mistress was flushed with anger. "I run a very respectable place. I tell you, there is no girl fitting your description here. I will not disturb my patrons at this hour."

"I'm afraid we must insist," growled the taller of the men.

"I'll get my parents, mistress," Ninallia said, turning and going back up the stairs. "My mother will not be pleased at being rousted from her sleep."

On her way to the room, she was met by Sister Tegani, who demanded, "Where did you go?"

Ninallia tried to catch her breath so she could speak. A couple came down the hall, so she nodded toward the room.

Houston appeared sleepy and relaxed. He stretched, wearing only his pants, then scratching his chest. In the forest of tiny spikes, random gray hairs stood out against his dark skin. "I told you she went looking for food. She didn't eat last night."

Ninallia glared at them. "Imperial guards are downstairs asking about me. We have to go out the back."

He shook his head. "That's what we don't need to do. They will be after a lone woman, not a married couple with their son. It's better we go down; we can leave later."

Tegani said, "I agree. If we run, they'll know there are three of us, and your disguise will be useless."

Ninallia saw the truth in what they were saying, but she was terrified. What if one of the men could tell she wasn't a boy? What if they seized them all? She helped the Sister into her outer robes and followed them down the steps.

"Keep your chin up. You're a spoiled young boy. Don't act afraid, or they will think we have something to hide," Sister Tegani said over her shoulder.

Houston crossed his arms and looked menacing. Sister Tegani went up to the soldiers and berated them. "My husband is a very important man, and our credits are good. Why are you harassing this fine mistress and disturbing our peace?"

"We're sorry, my lady, this is Imperial security business. We have to check visitors." He glanced at Houston and Ninallia. "You and your family may go, mistress. Sorry to have disturbed you."

Other patrons of the hostel were being rousted and brought down. Tegani marched back up the stairs, followed by Ninallia and Houston.

"I'll send you a breakfast up at no charge," called the mistress of the hostel.

Once inside the room, Ninallia was consumed with a fit of giggles, and tears streamed down her face.

"No giggling. Remember, you are a boy." Sister Tegani laughed.

Soon, Tegani and Houston discussed what to do. Sister Tegani maintained they should stay in the city until the spring thaw. Later, they could head for the Temple City. Houston wanted to get Ninallia off planet as soon as possible.

"I would like to see the…" Ninallia stopped. The news feed was broadcasting the deaths of two young women. She recognized their faces. They were two of the women from Madama Ector's hostel. Tears of sadness trickled down her cheeks.

"You knew them?" Sister Tegani asked. She placed a hand on Ninallia's shoulder as she nodded in misery.

How many more people were going to die? There were ways to end a pregnancy. If Ninallia were no longer carrying the heir, the Royal Nephew might leave her in peace. Somehow, she knew aborting the baby wasn't the answer. Madama Ector willingly gave her life to protect the royal heir.

There was a small knock at the door, and Ninallia jumped. When Tegani opened the door, a young girl stood in the hallway with their breakfast. "Enjoy this with the compliments of the house and our apologies for the disturbance this morning."

Tegani gave the girl a credit chip. Their tray contained pastries, fruit, cheese, bread, and strong tea.

As they enjoyed the meal, Tegani and Houston agreed it would be safest to leave the Imperial City. Sister Tegani suggested they travel toward the Temple City and stop for the winter in a small town at the foot of the Great Mountains.

For the next two days, Tegani and Houston gathered supplies while keeping their ears open for news. The Royal Nephew was spinning a story of collusion and betrayal. He blamed two neighboring kingdoms for planning the assassination of the late emperor. He even hinted at other, more ominous villains.

At the end of the week, Ninallia and the others boarded an early transport train headed south of the Imperial City. She watched the city speed by. Houston appeared to be dozing in the seat across from her, and Sister Tegani was reading.

As the Imperial City disappeared behind them, the view was filled with smaller towns and villages. Ninallia felt safer the further from the Imperial City they traveled, forgetting she was supposed to be a boy. She squeaked in alarm when there was a loud crash outside their berth. After a simple breakfast, she relaxed against the seat and soon drifted off.

She woke to Tegani shaking her gently while Houston retrieved their bags from the overhead. Ninallia yawned and stretched as she got to her feet. After hours of sleep, her body was stiff. She was also sick.

Covering her mouth, she ran for the bathroom. Waves of nausea wracked her stomach. She threw up her breakfast and what seemed like the last three days' meals, too. Afterward, she felt better and opened the door. Tegani stood there with a concerned look on her face.

"I'm okay. It's morning sickness."

Tegani patted her shoulder. Ninallia was slender and could hide the pregnancy for a while yet, but knew one day deception would no longer be an option.

Thirteen

"We have eliminated twelve of the women from Madama Ector's hostel. Eight appear to have vanished. Someone must be helping them." Lord Varick voiced his theory, echoing Hanoree's worst fears.

"You think the Order is involved?" Hanoree demanded.

"It is logical. Who else has the power and connections to get these women out of the Empire? Has to be the Order."

Hanoree agreed. "I want the Temple City surrounded. I want to know who goes in or out. If the Order is harboring our fugitives, I will level their city."

"What about the Writ of Neutrality?" Varick poured a glass of wine and added Hanoree's drug of choice, more today because of his anger.

"There is no agreement with the enemies of the Empire," Hanoree said, taking the glass and downing the contents. Wine and opiates surged through his system. He calmed, and a heightened sense of his own god-like abilities filled him.

"Get My Lady of Wisdom on my communicator." He drummed his fingers across the surface of the empty glass.

In minutes, the serene face of My Lady filled his screen. "Greetings, Most Noble Hanoree."

"Greetings, My Lady of Wisdom. We are seeking a woman in connection with the assassination of our beloved emperor and his wife. The Empire requires your help in this matter."

"How can we help you? We are iced in at the Temple City this time of year."

"We are aware of your weather, My Lady. It has come

to our attention that this woman may seek sanctuary. She is an enemy of the Empire, and anyone giving her sanctuary will be regarded as our enemy as well."

"We have taken in no refugees. Do you have reason to believe she is headed here?"

"I have reason to believe many things. As a long-time member of the Writ of Neutrality, I am calling on the Order to abide by that agreement. Failing to do so will result in unfortunate consequences."

Anger flared across the face of My Lady. "Be careful who you threaten, Hanoree. Your actions may produce the very thing you fear." The communication abruptly ended.

Thinking, Hanoree sat back. The Order would be a powerful enemy. He needed an equally powerful ally. Who better than the League of Seeded Worlds? He would need to request support from the League, but not go empty-handed. What would entice them to support him should a war between the Empire and the Order break out?

"Put me through to the League. I want to speak with their top official on Bengar."

Soon, his screen was filled with the face of Senior Ambassador Hollins. She smiled. "Lord Honoree, it is good to see you again. Let me repeat my condolences on the death of your uncle."

Honoree replied, "We are in shock, Madam Ambassador, but life goes on. We are seeking those responsible."

"I am sure when the Council of Nobles declares you emperor, your people will be in capable hands."

"Thank you. It has always been my vision to bring the Empire into the future. My late uncle did not see the advantages of becoming a full member of the League of Seeded Worlds. We have not benefited from its guidance. I want to work with the League to bring trade and prosperity to the Empire."

Her smile broadened. "How may I assist you in making this vision a reality?"

"The Empire has many enemies. At present, there is someone who claims to carry the heir to the throne. There are those who say the empress hired a surrogate before her untimely death. If this is true, the Empire will rejoice. However, since this woman has disappeared, there is no way to verify her claims. I have offered her safe conduct and housing until the child is born. If a test proves this is indeed the royal heir, I can act as guardian and advisor until he is of age."

Hanoree was confident in his skill at sounding sincere and honorable.

"Why do you think she has not come forward?" Hollins asked.

"Either she is a fake, or she has been fed lies and is afraid. I fear that if this is the heir, certain enemies of the Empire will take the opportunity to brainwash mother and child."

There it was, Hanoree accused the Order. No one else possessed their mental powers.

"You will personally guarantee the safety of the heir and surrogate?"

Honoree smiled into the screen as he lied, "Of course, this is the possible offspring of my beloved uncle."

When the meeting ended, Honoree congratulated himself for planting doubt against the Order into the minds of the League. He presented himself as a truly progressive leader, willing to usher the Empire into the League.

Fourteen

Sister Tegani noticed Ninallia's pale face. Morning sickness was not unusual, but the girl was barely more than a child herself. She must be encouraged to eat more so the baby inside her would grow strong. She looked exhausted, too, and the stress of the situation was taking a toll on all of them. Wintering in this village would be a much-needed respite. They would travel on to the Temple City in a few months.

There was a knock, and Tegani heard Houston rise to answer the door. Would he never learn? Men did not answer doors. She got to her feet and walked toward the front of the small cottage they had rented.

He was standing there. Whoever knocked was gone. She frowned in confusion. He handed her a small envelope, addressed to the Sister of the Order.

He shook his head. "How do they know where we are?"

"I don't know." Tegani took the envelope. Inside was a small electronic message. *How had My Lady managed to send it in the dead of winter?* She couldn't imagine what her friends there were thinking as she slipped the small chip from its protective sleeve, using her thumb to unlock the chip's message. If anyone else tried to gain access, the message would have been destroyed.

My Lady's troubled face was projected onto the nearest communications screen. "Tegani, I trust the girl is well. All is not safe here in the Temple City. Communications from Uban are being monitored. Hanoree's men have surrounded the city. It is not safe for anyone to enter. You must take the girl and hide her until the child is born. I leave it to you to find a safe place.

Everyone in the Order is being watched by Hanoree's men. It will not be wise for us to have further contact. May the Spirits guide you."

"Damn!" She heard Houston curse behind her.

Tegani echoed the sentiment. What My Lady did not say, Tegani understood. It was shocking. The Writ of Neutrality was in danger of being breached.

"That does it. I'll get in touch with the general and get the three of us off this planet."

She shook her head. "No, the reasons for not turning Ninallia and the child over to the League haven't changed."

Houston asked, "So, what do you plan on doing? We can't stay here and wait for Hanoree's men to come and kill us."

"Take refuge somewhere else." Tegani concentrated, using years of training to focus.

One name and place emerged, dragged from her memory. Lady Sayeri, half-sister to the late empress, had been married off to a wealthy merchant when she became pregnant out of wedlock. She was ostracized and hadn't been seen at court for many years. Tegani tried to remember more. Lady Sayeri's husband was from Madori, the smallest kingdom on Bengar and famous for its wealth and lawlessness. She explained this to Houston.

"What makes you think she will help?"

"Lady Sayeri has no fondness for the Empire, and she may prove loyal to the Order. She spent a year in training at the Temple City. It has been a long time since she paid homage, but she took the novice oath."

Their conversation was interrupted when Ninallia came into the room, pale as a ghost. Her hands were holding her stomach. She looked at Tegani and said, "Help me."

Houston caught Ninallia as she slumped to the floor, his eyes wide in alarm. Soldiers weren't trained to deal with women in labor. "Is she going to lose the baby?"

She helped him get Ninallia to a couch where she could lean back. There was a sheen of sweat on the girl's face, and it was distorted by pain. Tegani, almost as panicked as Houston, knew little about pregnancy. Something was very wrong. "We have to find a healer."

If the girl miscarried, Tegani's mission would be a complete failure. Hanoree would get away with murder and be declared Emperor.

She placed a hand on Houston's shoulder. "Go to the center of the village and ask for a healer. There should be one living somewhere near."

While he was gone, she spoke to Ninallia in a soft tone and taught her a breathing exercise—anything to distract her from the pain. Houston returned in an hour, leading a silver-robed healer. The man stopped when he saw what appeared to be a boy lying on the couch in pain. It was clear he was expecting his patient to be a young pregnant woman.

"Help her," Tegani said. The words were not meant to be a command, but they were effective.

The healer got to work. He opened his bag while Tegani wiped Ninallia's head with a cold, wet cloth. He drew blood and gave her a dose of medicine.

Ninallia made a face as she swallowed the bitter liquid. The healer listened to her heart, then put the instrument on her stomach. "You're about three months along. This medicine will help, but I want you to stay off your feet as much as possible. You almost lost your baby."

She relaxed, the pain seeming to lessen already. "Will I lose my baby?"

The healer smiled at her. "I don't know. You're young and healthy." He indicated her clothes and shaved head. "I don't know what's going on here, but you must avoid stress. It's dangerous for you and your child."

Tegani paced behind the healer. Should she try to explain the deception? Would he report them to the authorities as soon as he left? "When will she be able to travel?"

The healer shook his head at her disapprovingly. "The girl was close to a miscarriage. The next time could kill both of them."

"What if we travel in a train car with a bed?" she asked, more to ease the tension than for an answer. They were leaving no matter what the healer advised.

"That might help, but she must get plenty of rest and keep her feet elevated as much as possible. The next month is critical."

The healer handed Tegani two more vials of the medicine to halt miscarriages, some vitamins, and a small book on pregnancy care. "This book explains the importance of diet and rest and how to manage the symptoms of pregnancy. See that she reads it."

Tegani smiled and handed him enough credits to more than cover his cost. She hesitated when she realized her purse was now almost empty. She could count on the Sisters and Brothers of the Order to provide more, but didn't want to overburden them.

After the healer left, Ninallia reached into a pocket and brought out the remaining credit chips from Madama Ector. "I don't know if the account is closed or if the credits can be traced." She handed them to Tegani. "It's from Madama. I used some credits in the Imperial City, but nothing since."

Tegani shook her head. "They might be traced. We'll keep those for an emergency. It's too dangerous to use anything traceable to Madama Ector."

She listened as Houston used the communicator to search for train schedules. Every train leaving the Empire ran through the Imperial City. That was where they didn't want to be. After weighing several options, he booked passage on a train going to the coast. They could take a ship to a neighboring kingdom and get passage from there.

Tegani nodded. "When does the train leave?"

"Not for twelve hours. The girl can rest. We can pack."

She settled Ninallia on the couch with her feet elevated before preparing a light meal of eggs and toast. She added nourishing herbs to the eggs and just a little cheese.

Ninallia began reading the pregnancy book, but soon drifted off to sleep.

~ * ~

Ninallia woke with a start. She was on the couch. Tegani was packing two large trunks. *When did we get trunks?* The events of the evening before came back to her. Her hands stroked her stomach. She felt no pain, but there was no morning sickness either. Was her baby still there? Overwhelmed by a flood of emotions, tears spilled down her cheeks.

Sister Tegani hurried to her side. "What's wrong? Are you in pain again?"

"No." Ninallia's voice sounded as if she barely possessed the energy to get the words out. When she started to stand, her legs wobbled. She fell back onto the bed, staring at Tegani with alarm.

"That's the medicine. It makes you slow and weak, but also helps you rest. Do you think you can eat?"

The nausea was gone, and Ninallia realized she was hungry. She nodded. Tegani adjusted her on the couch, making sure her feet were elevated before going into the kitchen.

"Where's the man?" Ninallia asked.

"He is sleeping. He bought the trunks and supplies. We will wake him in time to get to the train, another hour, I think."

Ninallia leaned back again. She trusted Tegani. A Sister of the Order could do many unusual things, and she wanted to be as strong and smart as Tegani. "Sister, do you think I might one day go to the Temple City and learn the ways of the Order?"

Tegani turned. The expression on her face was hard to

read. "I don't know Ninallia; the mother of the emperor will have many duties at court. Perhaps, if you have a gift, you can be trained to use it." Her answer was thoughtful and carried a note of sadness.

"Will you train me?"

Tegani set the bowl of cooked grain onto the table. "Eat now; we will see if you can learn anything later."

Ninallia took the bowl and shoveled the warm cereal into her mouth. She smiled at Tegani, understanding from the Sister's reaction that there was no way the Empire would allow her to study at the Temple. Ninallia began spinning fantasies that she would become a Sister, and no one would ever be able to hurt her or frighten her again. Tegani could teach her the ways of the Order.

"I can read your aura. That will tell if you can be trained." Tegani took the empty bowl and then picked up Ninallia's hand. "You have a strong aura, but I cannot tell your gift without testing."

Houston came into the room, and Tegani placed two more bowls of food on the small table. After they finished eating, she washed and put away the dishes.

~ * ~

The transport arrived, and Tegani busied herself helping Houston load their belongings.

"I can walk," Ninallia insisted when Houston picked her up and started for the transport.¬He ignored this protest and carried her.

The driver raised his eyebrows. Tegani was quick to explain. "Our son is ill, and we are going to a master healer in the south. Pray the Spirits we arrive in time."

The driver's expression softened, and he remained silent for most of the trip. When Tegani handed him her credits, he shook his head. "For the young sir. Good speed on your journey, and Spirits blessings."

She felt guilty for cheating the man from his fare, but she honored his gracious gift.

"A Sister must learn to obey those who are senior in the Order." Tegani smoothed the blanket. She stroked the girl's flushed face. They were risking both mother and child by traveling, but what else could they do? Their compartment was small with pull-out beds. Tegani opened one, added a blanket, and settled a protesting Ninallia in, raising her feet with pillows from the other bed.

She sat on the seat across from Ninallia and glanced at her watch for the third time. Where was Houston? There were only a few minutes before the train departed. Where was he?

~ * ~

In the station, Houston was hoping to buy sandwiches and fruit for their lunch. There was no food car on this train, and they would need to eat something before they arrived at the port. His communicator buzzed in his ear. A welcome sound. He had questions and needed to let them know Hanoree was having the women from Madama's hostel killed. "General?"

"Yes. I take it you have contacted the girl."

Houston heard tension in the general's voice, and he answered with a noncommittal sound.

"Ambassador Hollins has made an agreement with Lord Hanoree. If she turns herself in, he guarantees her safety. If the child is indeed the son of the emperor, he will serve as the child's regent and turn over control when the heir comes of age."

"You believe that bastard?"

"It doesn't matter what I believe or what you feel. The League has negotiated a deal. Stay put. We will pick you up. You should be off planet in twenty-four hours."

Too stunned to speak, Houston didn't answer. The girl was as good as dead; the Sister too.

"Houston, do you copy me?"

"Yes, sir. I understand."

"Good. The Empire is offering a lot of concessions to their trade restrictions. This is important."

The general signed off, and Houston stared at the train. The last call whistle blew. Could they make it without him? If he joined them, the League would track them, meet the train, and take Ninallia into custody.

Wincing, he yanked the implanted communicator from his ear. There would be hearing loss. The League would no longer be able to trace him, but he was cut off from their help, including credits. This would mean a court-martial. He let out a sigh of resignation. He was washed up as a League officer anyway.

Houston pitched the earbud onto the back of a truck, leaving the station. With minutes before departure, he ran across the street to a credit machine. He withdrew an obscene amount of credits before the League got wise and closed his account. He could hear the boarding call being repeated over and over.

Come on, he willed the credit machine. Credits clanked into the tray. He stuffed them inside his robes and ran for the train. Squeezing his big frame between the closing doors, Houston boarded the train as it was preparing to lift off.

~ * ~

Tegani peered through the window. She couldn't see the boarding area from her window, because they were on the wrong side of the train. She leaned back in frustration. *Where is Houston?* The last call for boarding clanged, and he was not on the train. Spirits willing, they could make it to Lady Sayeri without him. She felt the gentle tug as the train started to lift off.

"Your man?" Ninallia asked cautiously.

Tegani was about to say Houston was not her man, at least not in the way the girl's tone suggested, when the door opened, and his large frame entered, taking a seat beside her. He was breathing hard, and Tegani spotted a trickle of blood on his right ear. "Are you okay?"

He swiped at the blood and said, "I didn't get the food, sorry."

"There's a thirty-minute stop in Hakona. It's a larger city and should have a larger station."

He loosened his outer robe. Hakona was four hours away. Their small breakfast would have to hold them a while longer.

"The Sister was afraid you left us," Ninallia spoke up. "I think she was going to cry. You shouldn't scare her."

He glanced at Tegani. "My apologies, I was trying to get credits, and the machine backed up. I almost missed the train. I would never desert the Sister or you."

"Sleep, girl, you don't want to lose the baby." Adding to her embarrassment, Tegani's voice sounded harsher than she intended. She did want to think about her attraction to Houston. There was something dangerous about the man, but also something very honorable. Even in merchant's clothes, he looked like a soldier.

"Will you teach me more? I want to know how to be a Sister of the Order?" Ninallia's voice sounded young and pleading.

Tegani smiled. "If you rest now, I will teach you the novice's prayer. It is the first thing a Sister learns at the Temple."

Ninallia pulled the cover up to her chin and closed her eyes. Tegani and Houston sat in silence. After a while, she got up to find the toilet. She walked down the corridor between the compartments. One door was open, and its occupants were listening to a news report. When she recognized the voice of the Royal Nephew Hanoree, she slowed.

"I promise you that I will find those responsible for the murder of my dear uncle," his silky voice proclaimed. "My only desire is to serve the Empire and guard against our enemies, no matter who or how powerful they are." He went on to imply that those enemies included the Order, though he stopped short of implicating them in the murder.

She held herself together until she made it to the women's lavatory. She closed the door and burst into tears. My Lady and her other friends there were in danger. Hanoree was ready to attack the Temple City to get his way. The Order was peaceful—there was no army or military defenses protecting Uban. She washed the tears from her face.

"Spirits protect them," she prayed.

When she returned to the compartment, Ninallia was asleep, and Houston was reading a newssheet. "Hanoree is threatening the Order. I think he may invade the Temple City."

"That idiot."

"Will the League step in and force him to abide by the Writ of Neutrality?" Tegani asked.

A troubled expression crossed his face. "I don't know. There's something I didn't tell you."

She listened in alarm as he described his conversation with the general. "Doesn't your ambassador know Hanoree cannot be trusted? You would be signing Ninallia's death warrant."

"I told him Hanoree is a madman. I removed my communicator, so they won't be able to track us."

Tears of gratitude flooded her eyes. He could have turned them in or walked away. *Thank you* seemed to be inadequate. "Spirits bless you. You could have left us, and maybe you should have."

Houston made a dismissive sound and returned to reading. She leaned back and closed her eyes. She was tired. The rhythm of the train and Ninallia's gentle breathing soon lulled her to sleep.

The train was arriving at the station when a loud announcement woke her. Tegani realized she was leaning against Houston with her head nestled against his shoulder. She sat up and apologized. He laughed and asked what she wanted from the station.

"Food!" Ninallia piped up from her covers. "I'm starved. I would love something cold to drink too."

Houston grinned at Ninallia. He gave Sister Tegani a nod and left their compartment.

"Is there a bathroom on this train? I think I'm going to burst," Ninallia asked.

They made their way into the corridor. Tegani grabbed her arm when she almost entered the women's room. "Son, open your eyes," she scolded.

Ninallia dropped her hand. A woman stood in the doorway across the hall. Ninallia entered the men's room, while Tegani waited outside, praying to the Spirits that the girl would not pass out. She looked at the woman. "My son has been sick. His mind is not well."

The woman clucked in sympathy. "You've seen a healer?"

"Yes, he advised us to see a master healer. The boy is our only child."

"Spirits keep you," said the woman and closed the door to her compartment.

Ninallia emerged and took Tegani's arm for support. "The place was filthy. It's my punishment for this disguise."

They laughed and walked back down the car and waited in anticipation for Houston's return.

~ * ~

Houston made a production of unwrapping each item to reveal their treats. First, there were the rich fried meat pies that the city was famous for, and bottles of a soft, sweetened tea. After these were downed, he reached into a smaller bag and brought out slices of spice cake wrapped in clear parchment. The creamy icing oozed from the wrapper.

There was a sharp knock at the door. Ninallia jumped

back into her bed, clutching her piece of cake, and pulled up the covers.

Tegani answered with Houston standing behind her, blocking view of most of the compartment.

"What do you require?" she asked civilly. Her expression was not civil. It screamed *Why are you disturbing us?*

"Identity check, mistress. Where did you board?" the guard asked.

"In Halivo. We've a sick son, and the healer is sending us to the master healer of the area."

Ninallia coughed and moaned.

"Now you've woken him." Tegani's voice resounded with indignant fury.

"I'm sorry, mistress. We have to check passengers."

"Mama, who is there? I am thirsty and hot."

Houston stepped aside and revealed Ninallia in all her glory. Her cheeks were stained with cake icing, and the sweet tea made a damp sheen on her forehead. Tegani stood in silent admiration. The girl was smart. She also used tea to slick down and emphasize the shaved sides of her hair.

The station guard froze. He eyed Ninallia and asked, "Is he contagious? We don't want the fever in this town."

"How should I know? Our healer is an old fool. We're taking our son to the master healer."

Tegani held out their boarding tickets from Halivo. The guard nodded. He did not touch the tickets.

"Sorry to disturb you, mistress, and Spirits keep your son." The guard hurried on to the next compartment.

His reaction sent Ninallia into a fit of giggling.

Tegani administered a sharp pinch and said, "A Sister of the Order masters her emotions before they master her."

The half-smile on Tegani's face softened the rebuke, and Ninallia smiled and said, "Yes, Sister. I am young and will learn."

Fifteen

Ninallia walked next to Sister Tegani along the trash-littered streets of Nabbul, hiding her fear by commenting on the buildings and people. Rivulets of foul-smelling water ran along the side of the street. It was a busy port town known for its freight ships, alehouses, and whores—not sanitation. She judged it was not the place a family would book passage on a ship. Houston soon came back to join them.

"Not many passenger ships stop here to refuel. We'll have to book passage on a freighter," he reported.

The stench of dead fish and oil from the wharf hit them as they continued walking along the street leading to town. Ninallia's stomach did a dangerous lurch, and she hurried to the side of the road and threw up.

Several men standing around began to laugh and jeer. "The sissy boy is already seasick. The smell of the ocean makes him ill."

Houston smashed his fist into the man's face. Before his friends could come to his aid, a large net came loose and landed over them. They fell into a tangled knot. Houston shot a grin at Tegani, and she winked in return. The Sister's face was pale from the mental exertion. She grabbed Ninallia's arm and walked toward a nearby hostel. Houston fell in line behind her.

Tegani inspected his bruised knuckles. "You shouldn't have done that. We want to stay here without drawing attention from security."

"Me? What about the net? You're lucky they didn't fall into the water and drown. How would you explain their deaths to Imperial security?"

"Me? I don't know what you mean. I was nowhere near any net." Sister Tegani tried to sound innocent.

She and Houston laughed. Ninallia moaned that she needed to sit down, bringing a somber note to their expressions.

~ * ~

"We need a room for tonight and maybe tomorrow. We're seeking passage to the Gabbarni Kingdom." Tegani leaned on the counter, her neck craned to look up at the tall figure of the innkeeper. He was even taller than Houston and massively built.

"Why do you want to go there? The Empire is twice as grand." The innkeeper grinned down at her.

"My sister lives there, if you must know. We're going for a visit. She's never met her godson." She nodded toward Ninallia.

"You don't look like you're from Gabbarni." The innkeeper was apparently enjoying baiting the attractive woman at his counter, or maybe he was baiting her glowering husband, who was standing by the frail-looking boy.

She snorted. "Of course, I don't, you stupid man. My sister ran off with a foreigner."

The innkeeper roared with laughter. "You and your fine family will have my best room. Right this way."

They followed the innkeeper up a flight of stairs, where he opened the door to a room at the end of the hall. *If this was his best room, and this is the largest and best hostel in the city, I'm glad we won't be staying long.* Tegani handed him credits and secured a promise that he would find them suitable passage. When the door was closed, she stripped and shook out the bed covers. The sheets appeared to be clean, but the stale odor of drunken sailors hung in the room. She threw open the windows, breathed in the air blowing in from the wharf, then closed them again.

"Relax, we'll only be here for the night," Houston replied.

"I'd rather not catch the fever."

Ninallia collapsed across one of the beds.

"I'll find us some supper," offered Houston. He left the room, closing the door before Tegani asked him to bring back clean towels.

She shed her robes and managed to get clean in the small bath, drying off with the least stained towel. The delicious smell of fish stew and fresh bread greeted her as she came back into the main room. The food was spread on the small table like a banquet. A bottle of wine on one side.

"Can I have some wine?" asked Ninallia.

"No," Houston and Tegani said at the same time.

"There's a bottle of juice. The waitress says there will be fresh milk in the morning. A local dairy delivers here at six," he added.

~ * ~

The innkeeper gave them bad news at breakfast. "There won't be a suitable ship for passage available for two days."

Tegani was disappointed but reasoned that the time would give Ninallia a chance to recover. The inn might be a dump, but the cook was excellent and ran a clean kitchen. Tegani peeked in and found a sleek, modern, and spotless place. A friendly waitress informed them that the cook liked to use local, fresh produce and dairy products, and, in fact, the quality of the food drew customers to the inn. They enjoyed a hearty breakfast before heading out.

They strolled along the docks and town square, looking at the sights. It didn't have much to offer tourists. The economy was primarily based on the shipping industry, warehouses, and shipyards—not known for their picturesque qualities. The stench of saltwater, oil, fish, and offal was everywhere.

As their group turned back toward the inn, a group of men stepped from between buildings. "There he is."

There was the sound of a blaster, and Houston turned,

drawing his weapon as he fell. It flew from his hand and hit the ground. Tegani rushed to him as Ninallia dove for his weapon. She grasped it in both hands and fired toward the men.

"Hey, you're going to kill someone. We're using a stun gun," one of the men shouted.

"Well, I'm not playing, and this is a real blaster." Ninallia fired off two more blasts. Her aim wasn't good, but it was close enough to send the men scattering.

"Help me get him inside," Tegani said. Each grabbing an arm, they lifted Houston and dragged him into an empty storage building, locking the door behind them.

Ninallia touched Houston's chest. He didn't appear to be breathing. "Is he dead?"

Tegani loosened his robes. The stunner shouldn't have been fatal. The men intended to incapacitate him and rob them. There was no way they knew he had an artificial heart system.

"Help him!" Ninallia urged.

"I don't know how. I'm not a healer." Tegani's mind was frozen with fear. "The mechanical system keeping Houston alive is much more sophisticated than a lock."

Ninallia placed her hand on Tegani's arm and shook it vigorously. "I've seen you do more than locks. You can do this. You have to try."

The words penetrated Tegani's panicked thoughts, giving her confidence. Closing her eyes, she pressed her hands to his chest. The mechanism was still. Tegani sent a small jolt of energy into the heart capacitor, and it responded with a small beat. She tried again, and his heart began to beat weakly but stopped when she stopped. For a moment, the heart beat on its own. Focusing her mental energy and willing the heart to function, she tried again. As he gave a huge shudder and drew in a breath, she collapsed across Houston's chest.

Soon, Tegani began to stir, weak but unharmed from the

exertion.

"I knew you could do it," Ninallia congratulated her.

"Do you smell something?" Houston struggled to his feet.

The scent of fuel filtered under the door.

"We know you're in there. Hope you can take some heat." There was drunken laughter.

Houston looked around at the boxes and shipping material. Once the fire got under the door, this place would burn quickly. He didn't see another door or even a window? "Got any ideas, Sister?"

Ninallia said, "What about fighting fire with fire? Do you have anything that will explode?"

He gave her a nod and a slight smile. Tegani thought Ninallia was smart, an asset on any mission. He handed Tegani a blaster and a smaller one to Ninallia. Taking one of his weapons, he fiddled with it until it jammed. The warning light began to flash, and it emitted a high-pitched squeal.

After removing the safety, he tossed the blaster next to the door where the smoke was filtering into the unit. "Get down and be ready to run, shoot at anything that moves."

The explosion shook the building and sent the door flying out in a cloud of dust.

"Run," Houston shouted.

He led the way, aiming at the men surrounding them. At first, they seemed too surprised to return fire. A shot almost caught Ninallia, and Houston rushed to pull her close and shield her with his body.

Tegani continued to aim shots toward the figures. Sirens squealed, and the men scattered instead of firing back. Houston motioned for Tegani to return. "We can't afford to be questioned."

~ * ~

Back in their room, Tegani cleaned their scrapes and cuts before applying healing cream. A new layer of stains soiled the towels.

Houston's face was pale, but the attack seemed to have energized him as he barely sat still.

She said, "I think we should stay in the room until our ship departs."

Ninallia washed the smoke and soot off her face. She ran her fingers through the sides of her hair. They would need to be trimmed before they got on the ship. She made a promise to herself. *One day, I will wear fine robes and gowns again. No more boys' clothes, even if they do make movement easier.*

Their evening was uneventful, which was what Ninallia needed because the day's attack exhausted her. She curled up in the blankets on her bed and tried to sleep. Tegani was asleep beside her, and Houston was quiet on the next bed.

She could tell he wasn't asleep. There was definite chemistry between the Sister and Colonel Houston. Ninallia couldn't understand why they didn't act on it. Sisters weren't forbidden to marry or take lovers. Maybe it was because there was something dangerous about Houston—dangerous and foreign.

Sixteen

The Bella Star was a large freighter with sleek lines and massive armory. These were modern times with aircraft, space travel, and treaties, but the Berini Sea remained rife with pirates. No ship carrying a valuable cargo sailed unarmed.

Moving like a well-oiled machine, the crew loaded freight being transported out of the Empire into the ship's large cargo bays. There was a joke circulated in the port city that the captain was more interested in the cleanliness of the cargo bays than she was the personal hygiene of her men. This was pretty much true. Whatever the goods, if they were transported by the Bella Star, they were delivered on time and in excellent condition. No dents and cracks in shipping cartons, and temperature-sensitive items were handled appropriately. The captain's prices were high, but those with quality freight were more than willing to pay the price.

Houston led the way up the boarding ramp. Tegani and Ninallia followed a porter pushing their supplies. Tegani stepped up ahead of Houston and said in a firm voice, "We'll see the captain now, please."

One of the deck crew swung round, and Houston stepped aside to avoid getting hit with the box he was carrying. "Captain's busy. We're all busy."

"If you'll be good enough to point us in the direction of our stateroom, we'll get set up."

"This isn't a passenger ship. There's one stateroom besides the captain's." He nodded toward the front of the ship.

Tegani motioned to the porter, and they headed toward the stateroom.

"Ho, mistress. Are you the family that booked passage on my ship?" The voice was friendly and feminine.

Tegani turned. Her gaze moved up and up. This was the tallest woman she had ever seen.

The woman extended a large hand. "I'm Captain Joanani, and this is my ship."

Remembering the innkeeper's assurance that the captain's father owned the largest private fleet in the Empire, Tegani bowed. Something honest and wholesome about the captain's manner made Tegani like her at once. She took the large hand. "Pleased to meet you, Captain. We're glad there was room for us on your ship."

Houston and Ninallia seemed to be laughing at a private joke as they caught up to the two women.

Tegani gave them a quelling glare. "This is our captain. Her family has been in shipping for over two hundred years."

"Pleased to meet you, Captain," said Ninallia.

The captain gave Houston an appraising glance. Ninallia frowned.

Tegani watched her a moment, then they all followed the captain. Their room was large by a ship's standards, but felt cramped. There was a bed, a bolted-down table and chairs, and a fold-down, single bunk built into one wall. Houston wouldn't even be able to stretch his legs on that.

When Ninallia opened her mouth, Tegani silenced the girl with a glare, afraid Ninallia was about to volunteer to sleep on the bunk. That would have embarrassed Tegani. She looked around. Dim natural light filtered in from a small porthole that was so high she would have to climb on a chair to see out. Not a chance of that either, since they were bolted.

Finally, Ninallia stretched on the normal-sized bed and declared herself ready for a nap.

~ * ~

"Of course, I know the empress's half-sister. I'll have a large shipment of her wine on the return voyage. They can't get enough of it in the Imperial City's restaurants." Captain Joanani smiled. "If you want to visit her, I recommend you stay on board until we reach the Port of Davondi."

"Why?" Tegani asked. She sat across the table from the captain, who had invited them to dinner on their first night onboard.

"It saves three days overland freight, and we can refuel. It's an extra day onboard, but worth it."

Houston, who appeared to be enjoying a steak grilled rare, nodded. He'd cautioned against telling the captain their destination, but Tegani trusted Joanani.

Ninallia wanted to try some wine. The captain even came to her defense. "The boy's half-grown. A glass of wine won't hurt him."

"I'm his mother, and I say he gets no wine until he's older." Tegani shot Ninallia a message that made her blush.

"My wife's father was a drunk. She is afraid the gene carries down," explained Houston.

The captain turned to Tegani. "My apologies to you, lady. A mother's word is law."

"Can I walk around the ship and watch the loading?" asked Ninallia.

The captain frowned.

"You'd get in the way. Why don't we unpack and begin your lessons?" Tegani interrupted.

"Yes, Momma. I'll go begin unpacking now." She bowed to the captain and thanked her for the dinner, and headed back to their cabin.

The captain laughed. "I've never seen a boy so eager for schooling."

"My wife is a great motivator. She bribes the boy." Houston

finished his glass of wine. The captain winked and refilled his glass.

"There is nothing wrong with rewarding diligent study. The boy may inherit his grandfather's business one day," Tegani said.

He changed the subject by asking the captain to describe the ship's armory and why it was necessary on a cargo vessel.

"I thought I spotted a military man. Imperial Army?"

Tegani rolled her eyes. "My husband ran away as a boy and joined the League."

The captain whistled. "Having a League soldier on my ship will be an honor."

"Ten years ago, I got wounded at Minino. They sent me home to recover, and I never returned to duty."

~ * ~

They walked back to their cabin. Houston asked if Tegani thought it was wise to be training Ninallia. "You know there is no way the Empire will let her go to the Temple City."

"The empress's half-sister spent a year in the Temple, as many Nobles do in their youth."

He glanced sideways and cleared his throat. "She was an unimportant relative. If Ninallia lives, she may become the regent."

Tegani shook her head. "That is for the Council of Nobles to decide. I don't see them placing an untrained teenager in charge of the Empire."

They found Ninallia waiting in their cabin. She was anxious to begin her training as a Sister.

"You must first understand I can't properly train you without testing. The best I can do is the basic exercises novices learn."

Ninallia sat on the bed. "I know I will be a Sister. It's like a vision, and I can see myself doing it."

"Well, empty your mind," Tegani said.

"But I thought you were going to teach me to be a Sister of the Order."

"I am. The first thing you must learn is to empty your mind of everything." Tegani used the tone she always used on novices—firm and commanding, not harsh.

"That should be easy; her mind is empty anyway," teased Houston. When she and Ninallia shot him almost identical scowls, he raised his hands in surrender. "Okay. I'll go talk to the crew and leave you two to your work."

As the door closed, Ninallia turned to Tegani. "Why does he get to go talk to the crew, and I can't?"

"Don't worry about Houston. We'll begin your first lesson. Empty your mind."

Most novices found this harder than they imagined. Whenever they managed to almost get there, memories and random thoughts invaded. A mother's smile or someone's kindness filled the empty space and brought them to tears.

Ninallia opened her eyes and hit the table in exasperation. "I can't do it."

Tegani laughed. "I didn't say it would be easy. You're giving up after what, fifteen minutes?"

"I'm not giving up," Ninallia said and closed her eyes again. She concentrated and was silent for the next hour. She felt the room go quiet. She couldn't hear Tegani breathing or the hum of the ship.

"I did it!" Ninallia shouted.

"Yes, you did," said Tegani in amazement. It took most novices days to master the skill. "Now practice until you can empty your mind at will."

There was a knock at the cabin door. Tegani answered, and the door opened to admit a crewman carrying a small crate.

"Captain sent us to make a quick run before we left the

dock. She said your son would need these." He set the crate on the table and pried open the top. Inside the crate, bottles reflected the cabin light in several colors.

"Fizzies!" cried Ninallia, clapping her hands in excitement. The fruity carbonated water was obviously a favorite.

~ * ~

"Incoming, Captain, incoming fire. Pirates in the area." The warning booms clanged. The clatter of the crew rushing to man the armory sounded on the decks and ladders.

Houston jumped up from his bed and drew his weapon. "Stay here. I'll see if the captain needs help."

"We can help. Tegani can stop the shells," Ninallia said.

Tegani stared at her in surprise. She shook her head. "I cannot stop them. No one can. Houston is right, we should stay here. We would only be in the way."

"But, if you concentrate, you could explode the shells before they reach the ship or send them back on the pirates," Ninallia insisted.

Tegani gave the girl's shoulder a shake and said, "That's not the way my gift works. We might get in the way and endanger the crew."

Chastened, Ninallia said meekly, "Yes, Sister. I'm sorry."

She got back onto her bed and pulled the pillow up around her.

The Berini Sea was the third largest body of water on Bengar, behind the great Caserian Ocean and the Sea of Destiny. Four Kingdoms and the Empire itself had coastlines on the Berini Sea. Over the centuries, squabbles and wars over control of the shipping lanes in the Berini Sea cost millions in lives and credits. Because of treaties and agreements, the sea was declared open territory, and the Empire and other kingdoms were limited to less than ten miles from their coast. Piracy was supported by several governments and cargo ships were armed to survive. The sailors who manned the freighters in the Berini Sea were a tough lot.

~ * ~

Houston climbed to where the captain was directing her men and watching for incoming. She nodded as he approached.

"Can I help?" Houston returned her nod. He squinted as he looked past her to the sea. This could be an ordinary pirate attack, or it could be more. Someone might know they were on board.

The captain gave him an appraising look. "I could use someone to handle the aft gunnery. Do you have any experience with short-range missiles?"

"A bit," he answered with a grin.

The captain looked toward the aft section. "It'll help if I don't have to split my focus. We're trying to set up communications with the pirates to see if I can talk them down." Her voice wasn't hopeful.

His senses ratcheted to full alert. "Do these pirates have aircraft?"

"Sometimes, not often."

He gave her a knowing look that was returned. It was always best to prepare for the worst.

"Incoming aircraft! Ready on the aft," the first mate shouted.

Houston raced forward and commandeered a weapon. He muscled the weapon frame loose and aimed it skyward, then fired a burst into a low-hanging cloudbank. The sky lit up with an explosion, and the attacking aircraft spiraled down.

More missiles were fired and landed in the waters around the ship. There were no hits, and he began to hope the worst was over. A sudden barrage of fire sank those hopes. The ship took a hit, knocking out three guns and killing one of the gunners.

The captain ran to where Houston was feeding more ammo into his weapon. "I need you starboard. I think they will strike there next."

"Do you have any long-range weapons?" he asked. "We need to be able to strike from beyond their range."

"I have a shipment of long-range armor-piercing rounds. Unfortunately, we don't have anything to fire them."

He nodded. "If you'll bring me those, I can remove the inner chamber, and this will fire them. It won't hold up long, but it will get the job done."

"Okay. I'll go with your call."

"Take your ship further out of their range. Give me ten minutes to set up."

The captain signaled, and a sailor ran to tell the helm. "Can you read the trajectory of incoming?"

She rattled off coordinates from her radar.

Three more missiles whistled by before Houston was ready. He watched the sky and noted the arch of the next incoming. He adjusted the weapon and fired. A direct hit. The explosion could be seen in the distance. Cheers sounded all over the deck. Sailors were slapping each other on the back and wiping perspiration off their faces. Others hurried to examine the damage.

The captain's grin spread across her face, transforming it with childlike glee. "So, you were in the League army? You're good."

"Space Command and ground-to-air combat."

"So, what's a League colonel doing on a third-tier planet like Bengar? You can ditch the Marumbi kingdom farce. The disguise would fool most people, not me. I've lived there, and something about you doesn't fit."

Houston, a veteran of many missions and without his disguise being spotted, stared at the captain. "Let's say it's an important mission, and it's a need to know situation."

The captain laughed and touched his arm. Houston picked up on her interest and would have enjoyed her company, but for some reason, he felt like that would be betraying the Sister and the girl, even if it was betraying a pretend family. "I'll go and check on my wife now, Captain."

"Did you blow up the pirates?" asked Ninallia.

"I think we landed a few hits. They thought better of the attack and gave up. I don't think the attack was anything unusual. They were after the cargo, not us."

With excitement, she told Houston about what she'd been doing. "Tegani has been teaching me to focus. I'm pretty good at emptying my mind, and she says she can teach me to send a message."

He quelled his skepticism and congratulated the girl. What he wanted was to take a shower and sleep for twelve hours. He listened to her and answered Tegani's questions, then gave them a brief description of the battle.

"I think Houston needs to sleep now. Why don't we see if there is something to eat in the galley and let him get some rest?" Tegani said.

~ * ~

The smell of gunfire, blood, and smoke was heavy on the deck, and crewmen were hurrying to repair the armory. The ship itself suffered minor damage. As they walked by, the sailors got quiet. Tegani heard them whispering about League agents and Houston's amazing accuracy.

The galley was crowded with men who were fresh from battle, and their adrenaline-induced excitement hadn't quite dissipated.

Tegani made her way toward the serving line. They were free to have meals served in their cabin, but with the recent attack, she didn't want to impose. She and Ninallia could eat what the crew was eating and take Houston back something. He would be hungry when he woke.

Thick stew served with bread, fruit, and a dark, sweet cake

looked and tasted wonderful. It was a man's meal, and Tegani wondered how the captain kept such a trim, muscular figure if she ate like this every day. Would be hard to resist.

The sounds of pleasure Ninallia was making as she devoured her stew would have done any growing boy proud. What was the girl now, maybe three months along? There was a slight thickening of her slender waist, hidden by the robes. Later, the pregnancy would be hard to hide.

She finished everything on her platter and was eyeing Tegani's cake. When she caught Tegani's eye, she blushed. "At first, the thought of food made me sick, but now I'm hungry all the time."

"There's no law against a growing boy having seconds," Tegani said, nodding to the serving line. "In fact, I think it's expected."

Ninallia grinned and carried her tray back up to the line, returning with a smaller portion of stew and another piece of the cake. This time she ate the cake first.

Tegani asked for a tray to be sent up to the room for Houston and thanked the cook.

"I think I ate too much," Ninallia moaned as they climbed the ladder to the deck where their cabin was.

Houston was sprawled on top of the bunk, snoring. His face was smooth and pink from the recent shave. Somehow, he seemed very vulnerable.

Ninallia grinned and tiptoed past his bed to the lavatory. There was a full mirror on the back of the door, and she stripped off her robes and posed, pushing out her belly. Tegani smiled.

Seventeen

"Rumors! All you bring me are rumors. The Order is helping the woman. There is a League agent with her. You can't even guarantee this young girl, Ninallia, is the one. There are six other women who are missing." Hanoree was at the point of manic rage. He was acting as regent, but the other Nobles were watching everything he did or said.

"But my lord, someone has to be helping her. I think it is safe to assume the League and the Order have their fingers firmly in this pie. Our records show an agent of the League was on Bengar for medical treatment, and there is no record of his transport off planet."

"Why haven't you found them? I expect results, not rumors."

"Yes, my lord. I have been waiting on your permission to question a senior Brother of the Order living in the Imperial City."

"You have him in custody?"

"He is in custody not far from here," Varick assured him.

"See what he knows. Make sure we cannot be linked to whatever accident befalls him. We must send a message to My Lady that I am serious."

"Yes, my lord, it is as you wish. I will give you a briefing later today."

"I am counting on you. Do not fail me." Hanoree glared at Varick. The threat of retribution might bring better results than a promise of reward.

~ * ~

"I have no knowledge of Madama Ector or any of her dumas clients. I don't understand why you are detaining me. I assure you that I will complain to the Order, and there will be repercussions." The Brother's voice was cracked, as were his lips. He had been abducted, beaten, and interrogated.

Varick knew Brothers were sworn to an Oath of Honesty, and he would have given these people any information he possessed. He could not give any information he did not possess.

Still, he continued, "Was the Order in any way involved in the death of the emperor?"

"No! My Lady had great respect for the emperor. She would not condone a violation of the Writ of Neutrality."

"Who does the Order suspect in the murder? What do they know?"

The Brother ran his tongue across his bruised lip. One eye swelled. For Varick, the question assured the Brother would not live to report to the Order.

"If I had any knowledge of the murder, you would have it straightway. I would not protect a murderer. I would not support an imposter."

"He's telling the truth," said the interrogator.

Varick agreed. "I believe you are correct. Make his death quick. If you can make it seem like civil unrest, do so. We need to stir up the people against the Order."

The interrogator turned. There was the slightest movement of his hand, and one of his men stepped forward and slit the Brother's throat. It wasn't a clean kill. The Brother struggled to breathe as blood gushed from the wound. No professional would do such sloppy work.

Varick turned away in disgust. He would have preferred the executioner wait until he was no longer in the room.

"Did you see, my lord?" Varick pointed to the screen as he spoke to Hanoree.

"The man knew nothing. Either the Order is not involved, or you selected the wrong Brother to interrogate. Make sure his death is recorded as random violence." Hanoree sipped a second glass of drug-laced wine Varick had prepared earlier. "We shall see how long it takes My Lady to hear of her agent's death. If I am correct, it won't be long."

~ * ~

"I demand to know what happened to Brother Angonius," My Lady said without her usual calm. Her face was florid.

It was all Hanoree could do to contain his smile. "I am sure you have read the same reports I have, My Lady. Brother Angonius worked in the most dangerous areas of the city. Unfortunately, his body was found in an alley. He was robbed and killed."

My Lady answered, "Brother Angonius was known in that area. He lived there for many years and never carried large sums of credit."

Hanoree shook his head. "I share your grief. We are doing everything we can to apprehend those responsible. Unfortunately, there is rising sentiment against the Order. Many of the uneducated believe the Order was responsible for the death of their emperor. The Order tends to involve itself in many things that are not its business, which is always a dangerous policy."

"You have no idea how dangerous your polices are about to become." My Lady's voice hissed across the communicators. She leaned into her screen as if coming through it to grab Hanoree. "The Order is a dangerous enemy, Hanoree. You have crossed the line."

Hanoree laughed. "My Lady is becoming neurotic. Remember, old woman, who has your city surrounded."

"You dare threaten the Temple City, Hanoree? You are a fool."

"I am the regent of the empire, and you should watch how

you speak to me."

My Lady's eyes narrowed. Her lips drew together in a grimace. The communications screen exploded, sending pieces of clear plastic into the room. The blast threw Hanoree back. He guffawed until he saw the shard of glass in his arm. One of his guards lay on the floor with a piece of the screen through his throat.

"What happened?" My Lady's voice had become silky and deadly. "We lost visual communications. I hope there isn't a problem."

"I'll see you dead, you old witch," Hanoree shouted as security rushed to treat his bleeding arm.

Varick stood frozen, staring at the glass and blood splattered in the room.

Hanoree shouted orders, ignoring others who could overhear his words. "Round up as many Brothers and Sisters of the Order as you can find. I want them expelled from the Empire. I want those other women found and killed!"

~ * ~

My Lady buried her head in her hands. She was shaking with grief and rage. "What have I done?"

"It appears you have declared war on the Empire," Arturon replied.

My Lady slapped her hand on the table. "Not with the Empire, with that murdering snake, Hanoree!"

"For now, My Lady, he is the Empire," Brother Arturon cautioned.

My Lady wiped her face and forwarded a warning to members of the Order living in the Empire. They were not safe. She was sure Hanoree would waste no time rounding them up. Well, let him try to find them. By morning, no Brother or Sister would remain in the Empire.

"Has anyone heard from Tegani?" Arturon asked.

"She is on her way to Lady Sayeri's estate."

A faint flush crept up his face even as a slight smile touched his face. Sayeri had trained at the Temple city when Arturon was a young Brother. She was a willful and unpredictable woman. He had been fond of her.

"Get me a League official on the communications line. I do not want to speak to Ambassador Hollins. Who's the top League official in this quadrant?"

"Governor Bashari. He is on Rijellon. He oversees the entire quadrant. Bengar isn't part of the League."

My Lady said, "I want you to talk with Rom Ellino, too. If Hanoree finds our refugees, I want it to be as difficult as possible for him to get them extradited."

"Rom Ellino is unreliable, My Lady," Arturon warned.

My Lady smiled. "Not so, Brother. He is a man who can be bought. Make sure the price is right. His kingdom is small, but they have the most dangerous weapons on Bengar."

"Indeed, they do, and Ellino may love nothing better than to start another great war."

My Lady agreed. "Yes, Hanoree will hesitate to invade his kingdom to retrieve our little mother."

"You're playing a dangerous hand." As was his wont, Arturon continued to play the devil's advocate. After a few minutes, he said, "Governor Bashari is on the line, My Lady."

She waved Arturon away and straightened her robes before greeting the governor of the space quadrant. She wanted to be at her most persuasive. "Good evening, Governor Bashari. I was hoping that you could help…"

"Ambassador Hollins is a fool. I've warned her about dealing with Hanoree on more than one occasion. She is convinced she's negotiating a new treaty with the Empire. I think she wants my job."

"So, you understand my dilemma. The Temple City is a

place of peace and order. We are not armed. Our Brothers and Sisters throughout Bengar are largely unprotected."

The governor asked, "If it comes to a trial, do you have proof Hanoree was behind the assassination of the emperor?"

My Lady's lips twisted as she admitted, "Not yet. I have people working on getting proof. It won't be easy."

"Well, let me make it easier. The League can and will enforce a no-fly zone around the Temple City. I have the locations of Hanoree's men in your area. If they try to launch an attack, we'll give them something to think about."

My Lady wanted to dance for joy, and later she would. She thanked the governor and signed off. Having accomplished all she could for now, she wanted to contact Tegani but was afraid of giving away her location.

~ * ~

Arturon faked a smile as he greeted Ellino, dictator of the Madori Kingdom.

"You want me to side with the Order against the Empire?" Ellino said. "The Order doesn't use weapons, while on the other hand, the Empire has a powerful army."

"We aren't opposing the entire Empire, only Hanoree as emperor. You have to agree he is dangerous," Brother Arturon replied.

"I'm dangerous, too, but you're not offering a fortune for my head."

"No one said anything about Hanoree's head. We want to prove he murdered the emperor and have him convicted before he is executed."

Ellino snorted. "My Lady is a cunning old bird. I will keep her secret and protect this Sister Tegani and whatever prize she is hiding from Hanoree. You are offering enough credits to finance my army for a year."

Ellino would enjoy pulling one over on one of his arch

enemies, perhaps even helping in Hanoree's downfall. It was a good deal. However, he might choose to hold Sister Tegani and the girl for ransom.

Arturon made the bank transfer and signed off. He always felt like he needed to take a bath after dealing with Ellino.

He was glad Tegani and the girl were seeking refuge with Lady Sayeri. He remembered Sayeri from her time in the Temple City. He had been a young man, a new and somewhat cocky Brother. She was a spoiled and willful girl, as much a child as a woman. They were both young and thought they were in love.

Sayeri's family summoned her home to the Imperial City. He continued to rise in the Order. He had thought of her often, but neither tried to contact the other. Later, he learned that she was involved in a scandal and married off to a rich merchant or something, disappearing from the Empire and his life.

My Lady's voice brought him back to the present. "We've done what we can from here, Brother. The governor sent word that a League agent seems to have joined forces with our Sister. I hope he is trustworthy."

"Sister Tegani has been trained well to recognize deceit, My Lady. She would see through a traitor. Are you sure we have the right girl?"

"I think so. Tegani will be able to tell us if the vision is true."

"You didn't tell her the vision, My Lady." Arturon poured them both wine. The day had been stressful.

"Of course not, she would try to make it happen. This way, the vision will prove itself."

Arturon turned to go, wishing they could at least warn Tegani. He watched My Lady. He wouldn't hazard a guess at her true age. Today, she seemed ancient and frail, yet he knew her to be a powerful force and a wise leader. He prayed to the Spirits that when his time came, he would serve as faithfully.

Eighteen

Hanoree glowered at the group of Nobles. They were convened to discuss his ordination as regent, but they were more concerned with the relationship between the Order and the Empire.

"I will not vote for a violation of the Writ of Neutrality," Lord Nebron said firmly, and several other Nobles assented.

"The Order has broken neutrality. They are behind the murder of my uncle, the emperor." Hanoree stood to his full height and crossed his arms.

"I have seen no proof of their involvement, and the League has sent a warning that it will defend the neutrality of the Temple City by establishing a no-fly zone."

"What! They sent a message to you. I met with Ambassador Hollins, and she shares my suspicions."

"Well, the governor of this quadrant doesn't, and he is recalling the ambassador."

Hanoree swallowed hard. *Damn that witch. My Lady of Wisdom indeed.*

The querulous voice of the eldest lord present demanded, "Do we need men surrounding the Temple City?"

The room was silent, and the Nobles turned to Hanoree. He fought to control his anger, using a deferential smile to mask his true feelings. "Yes, I believe we do. I have hesitated to bring this before the Nobles, but I will soon have evidence of the Order's interference. They have helped a suspect and a witness evade capture and escape the Empire. I have spoken with My Lady, and she refuses to cooperate with Imperial security. These criminals may be trying to find sanctuary in the Temple City."

Murmurs of concern and outrage filled the room. Lord Nabili raised his arm, and the room gradually silenced. "You have evidence you wish to present before the Nobles? We are ready to appoint you temporary regent, but not if you continue to bring the Empire to the brink of war."

Hanoree feigned surprise. It had taken these fools long enough to challenge him. He bowed. "I promise you my motive is to find justice for my uncle, the emperor. When I have proof, I will present it to you. My news will shake Bengar and reveal how traitorous the Order is."

He kept his composure civil. Varick stood behind him and gave him support. When the Nobles filed from the chamber, congratulating Hanoree on his appointment, he threw a glass against the wall in a fit of temper. "Do they think I will be a puppet emperor?"

"They are fools, my lord, but we must be wary. My Lady has played her hand. Now it is your turn."

"I want a Brother or Sister of the Order to confess to being involved in the murder or in covering up for those responsible."

"It will be hard to manage, my lord. The Order seems to have fled the Empire."

"They have not left the Empire. They are hiding like the vermin they are. Find them. Bring them in. They can be persuaded to confess their sins."

Varick retreated as Hanoree began to formulate a fictional scenario: *The Order hired a woman to pretend to carry the emperor's child. They sought to place an imposter on the throne, so they could control the Empire. My Lady was behind the plot to expand the influence of the Order.*

Nineteen

Lady Sayeri ran her estate far better than her late husband or his father. She amassed a fortune in the wine and beef trade. Earth cattle thrived on the rich grassland found in her area, and she seized the opportunity to buy a herd when they were imported from the League.

Her husband died in a fever that swept the kingdom ten years after they were wed, leaving her with a young daughter. Years later, her daughter ran off, so now she was raising her grandson. Peterno was the joy of her life.

Sayeri looked from the window of her sprawling villa. Her wine and cattle business ran smoothly without her nowadays. This gave her time to spoil her grandson and enjoy her hobbies of botany and painting. Sometimes these overlapped, like the painting she was doing of the rare roses she grew in large hot houses on her estate. She loved mixing the colors to get the exact shade. Every wall in the villa was covered with paintings. She gave many away as gifts, and an art gallery in the Imperial City offered to do an exhibition of her work if her royal status could be advertised, but she declined.

She reacted to the news of her half-sister's death with her usual stoicism. She admired Cynthy, but they were not raised together. The emperor was a good man and ruler, but neither supported her when she turned up pregnant as a young woman. She was married to a much older merchant and left her life at court behind. Her marriage had been no love match, but in time, she grew to care for her husband and his homeland even more.

Peterno came running, carrying a small kitten. "Look,

Nana, the babies have opened their eyes."

"Mama cat will scratch you for picking him up, Peterno. Put him back."

He frowned and studied the kitten. Peterno reminded her so much of his grandfather.

"Don't you want to paint the kitten, Nana?"

"Not today. You put the kitten back, and we'll see if cook has some sweets for us in the kitchen."

"Cook has a pie; it's for supper." Peterno smiled.

Her grin matched his. She whispered conspiratorially, "The pie is for supper, but there's honey cake. I think it even has nuts."

Peterno clapped his hands in delight.

Not much later, the two were settled on the couch in the great room, enjoying the honey cake and fresh milk. There was a soft ping, and Sayeri set down her plate to answer her message.

It was a short text. Sister Tegani, of the Order, was requesting a meeting with the Imperial Lady Sayeri. Sayeri paused, staring at the message. No one referenced her title, not for many years. She received enough information from the Empire to be concerned for her own safety. What could the Order want with her after so many years? She looked at her grandson sprawled across the rug, playing games.

Better to be forewarned of any dangers than to be blindsided. She sent her acceptance and noted the meeting on her calendar.

A sense of unease invaded her world. Hanoree couldn't think she harbored any aspirations to the throne. Her life was good, and she would fight to protect it.

~ * ~

Tegani followed the housekeeper into an elegant waiting room. Being kept waiting for forty-five minutes was not an auspicious omen. There was no reason for Sayeri to love the Order and reason enough for her to hate the Empire. That was why Tegani came alone. If Sayeri refused to help them, they would leave the kingdom before the Empire could reach them.

The years had been kind to Sayeri. She was tall with an ample figure, honey-colored hair, and tawny eyes. Life on a country estate suited her.

Tegani approached and bowed as was custom when greeting royalty. To cut through a world of explanations and formality, she bared her right arm to the elbow, exposing the tattoo of the Order. This was the universal sign of a Sister in need or distress. She was asking Sayeri to pledge to help her before hearing her plea.

Sayeri frowned and studied the Sister in silence. After what must have seemed like eternity, Sayeri bared her left arm. Her tattoos told Tegani she was loyal to the Order. She cleared her throat, then said, "I'll hear you, Sister, and pledge to do you no harm for now."

The beautiful, wild young royal who spent a year in the Temple City when Tegani was a child had matured into a cautious woman. "Spirits bless you, Sister, and I thank you for your kindness," she answered.

"I think I remember you." Sayeri indicated for Tegani to sit. The room was formal, the chairs overstuffed and ornate.

"I was a small child when you were there," Tegani said, shifting in the chair. *Were these things designed to make visitors uncomfortable?*

"Of course, I remember now. You are little bright eyes." Sayeri's face relaxed into a genuine smile.

"Little bright eyes?" Tegani was confused.

Sayeri laughed. "Arturon gave you the name. You were such a tiny thing when your parents left you at the Temple."

Tegani blushed. It was strange to hear Arturon's nickname for her.

"How stands Arturon?"

This was more than a query about his health. It was a request to know his status as a member of the Order. Tegani was surprised that Sayeri, being a Sister, even a lapsed Sister, was ignorant. "Arturon is First Brother and stands beside My Lady."

Sayeri nodded. She seemed very pleased at the news. "Would you like some tea?"

Tegani accepted and steeled herself for more formality.

"What brings you to this kingdom and to my door for aid?"

The question was direct, and Tegani was thrown off guard for a few minutes. "I have your word that if you cannot help, you will never repeat this?"

Sayeri lifted a brow, then agreed.

Tegani explained her mission and, over tea and forty minutes, she brought Sayeri up to speed.

Her face darkened when Tegani talked of the assassination and her belief that Hanoree was responsible.

"He's always been a snake in the palace waiting for an opportunity to strike."

Tegani told of Hanoree's threats against the Temple City.

A flicker of panic crossed Sayeri's face. "He wouldn't dare. The City must be evacuated. Arturon and My Lady must hide."

"You know they cannot flee. They would not leave the others to die."

Sayeri shook her head. "Where is the girl?"

"Waiting on your word, mistress." Tegani bowed again.

Sayeri grasped her arm. She held the tattoos side-by-side. "There is no mistress, only Sisters and Brothers in the Order."

Tegani smiled. The training Sayeri received at the Temple had taken root. She offered to send a transport to pick up Ninallia and Houston.

"I'd better go myself. Houston might be difficult if he isn't sure everything is safe."

"I have a healer I trust. I'll contact him," Sayeri offered.

"A healer?" Tegani turned back to Sayeri.

"You have a pregnant girl with you. Unless you're a midwife, we're going to need the services of a healer."

Tegani felt herself blush. Sayeri must think her a fool.

"Go bring this girl and the soldier. I will call the healer and tell the cook there will be three more for dinner."

Tegani's ride back to the hostel, where Houston and Ninallia were waiting, gave her a chance to relax. They would be safe for now. They could stay with Sayeri until the baby was born. Later, they could petition the Council of Nobles for a paternity test to establish the child as the late emperor's son.

Ninallia and Houston rented a game cartridge and were engaged in a realistic space battle. It wasn't a fair match given his experience. It appeared Ninallia was having a wonderful time being a teenager.

"She is going to let us stay there?" Ninallia asked, her head tilted.

"Yes, and she knows a healer who will make sure the baby is okay. When is your due date?"

"In the spring, I think. After everything, I don't remember the exact date."

"Well, the new healer can tell us. How long has it been since you learned you were with child?"

"I took pregnancy tests three times. The final test about three months ago was positive."

"The birth could be from the end of March to the middle of April," Tegani said. "We want the baby to be a few months old before we notify the Council and travel back to the Empire." She prayed to the Spirits that they could stay hidden from Hanoree for six or seven more months.

"Can I dress like a girl again?" Ninallia asked. She rubbed

the shaved sides of her head, clearly anxious for it to grow back in.

"We'll ask Lady Sayeri. Remember, we are in hiding."

Ninallia's face fell, and tears filled her eyes. "They won't come here, will they? Couldn't we tell them I lost the baby? I could join the League fleet school and go into space."

Tegani stared at Ninallia. If life were that simple, they could go home in peace, but Hanoree would be emperor.

"I don't want anyone else to die because of this," Ninallia continued. "Couldn't I get rid of the baby?"

This was not the first time they discussed this, but Ninallia's tone was more serious this time. "Isn't the welfare of the Empire worth more than your safety? Don't you want justice for those who have died?"

"I want my mother and my aunt. I want Madama to be alive. I wish I had never met her; then she would be alive."

"You don't know that; she would have found another dumas. The empress wanted a son, and the emperor needed an heir."

Ninallia's head hung down like a dog bereft of its last bone.

"This won't last forever. After the baby comes, we'll return to the Empire, and you will live in a palace."

"I will?"

"Where else would the baby emperor live? He'll need his mother to take care of him and teach him how be a good man."

A smile brightened Ninallia's face. Her moods shifted quickly, a combination of youth and hormones.

~ * ~

Tegani smiled as she leaned back in the transport. Houston closed his eyes. She did too and whispered a prayer of thanks to the Spirits. Sayeri was a wealthy, powerful woman and a Sister. She was loyal to the Order; her tattoos still showing. Tegani, responsible for Ninallia's safety, now felt it was more of a shared burden.

Tegani opened her eyes at a squeal of delight from Ninallia.

"Oh, my Spirits! Are those horses?"

"They sure are. I believe those are appaloosas," Houston said admiringly. Having been in space for twenty-five years, he was also relishing the sight of the Earth animals. Not many alien worlds were compatible with Earth's fauna, Tegani knew.

"Can I ride one?" Ninallia asked Tegani.

"Not until after the baby is born." She watched as the herd of horses disappeared behind them. "It could be dangerous."

Ninallia sighed. Probably thinking that carrying a baby was a lot like being in prison. There seemed to be endless rules and restrictions. If it looked like fun, it was forbidden. She turned back to the window.

~ * ~

There was confusion concerning the sleeping arrangements. Sayeri's housekeeper assumed Tegani would be sleeping with Houston.

"Mistress Tegani will require her own room," Sayeri said quickly, and, after an embarrassed apology, another room was readied.

Houston and Ninallia left to explore the estate, leaving Tegani to unpack her personal things. Three robes of the Order, two shifts, and a few underthings did not take up much room in the large dresser. She should not wear the robes, but they were all she had with her, and her only clothes for most of her life. There was a knock at the door.

"Come in." She turned as the door opened.

Sayeri stood there with a package in her hands. "I'm sorry I forgot this earlier. This package came for you, and I put it away. It slipped my mind."

"But no one knew we were coming here. We didn't even

know until a few weeks ago."

"The letter said I would receive a visit from a Sister, and I was to give you this." Sayeri handed her the package. At Tegani's startled expression, she gave it a shake. "It's not a snake."

Tegani laughed and took the package. It was heavy and seemed to be packed securely. When she saw the elegant spidery script on the label, she froze—this was from My Lady. She unwrapped the package, and inside were the things she had gathered in the Temple City: scented candles, a bottle of sacred oil, a small ceremonial bowl…everything a Sister would need to test and train a young applicant to the Order. There could be no misunderstanding now. My Lady intended for Ninallia to be trained as a Sister.

"You're going to train the girl? Is she gifted?"

The answer to both questions was yes. How gifted remained in question. Tegani had never known a novice to master the basics faster than Ninallia. "I believe My Lady has seen it to be so."

"Ninallia will need the skills you can teach her to survive at court, providing we can get her there."

"You'll have to help us both. I know nothing of court etiquette," Tegani admitted.

The only thing she knew about life at court was that the Imperial court could be a treacherous place for the unwary. The dangers there were real, and it was the one place she would not be of any help to the girl, having never been to a court of any kind. The social protocols would be as alien to her as they were to Ninallia, maybe more so. Houston would be of no help; he was a soldier.

"I see," Sayeri said. "When do you expect to be ready to present the child as the emperor's heir?"

"I don't know. I'd like to have proof of Hanoree's involvement and an independent paternity test proving our case."

"She seems an easy student. I think I can turn her into a court lady by the time we need one," Sayeri said.

She had been away from the Imperial court for many years, but likely was familiar with the players, and her sources of information seemed to be good.

"Spirits bless you. I pray we have not brought trouble your way for nothing."

"Trouble can be good, I was getting bored." Sayeri laughed.

Ninallia entered the room. Both Tegani and Sayeri stared at her. "What? Do I have something on my face?"

Laughing, Tegani said, "Sayeri will teach you court etiquette. How to dress and act is very important in those circles. She will be able to tell us who our friends are and who to avoid."

"May I stop dressing as a boy and shaving my head?" Ninallia pleaded.

"Yes, I don't want the healer to see you like this. Come with me. I have something I think will do for now."

~ * ~

Excited at the chance to be a girl again, Ninallia took Sayeri's hand and started from the room.

"Don't prance like a colt, child," Sayeri scolded. "Hold your head up and walk with pride. You are to be the mother of an emperor."

Ninallia slowed and tried to match Sayeri's walk. Her hips refused to make the correct swishing motion, and she almost stumbled.

"We'll work on it." Sayeri held one of Ninallia's hands up for inspection. "You'll need a manicure and false nails too, at least until yours grow."

Down the hall, they entered a room. It looked as if it had not been used in years. The burnished wood furniture was quality, but there was dust everywhere, and the room smelled musty.

Sayeri sighed. "I tell the housekeeper to keep things in order in here, but she lets the dust build up."

She opened an ornate wardrobe with at least two dozen beautiful gowns hanging inside. Many of them looked as if they were never worn. "I think these will almost fit you. They were my daughter's things. She won't be using them; she's been gone for over three years."

"I'm sorry." Ninallia's soft heart was touched.

"Oh, she's not dead, child. She ran off with a trader when Peterno was a baby. We haven't heard from her in a long time." Sayeri shook her head. "She always was a wild thing."

Ninallia sighed. She felt much better taking over the clothes of someone who ran away than a daughter who died young. The gowns were beautiful, ranging from simple to semi-formal. She slipped into a simple blue gown. It was a few inches too long; they all were. After a few minutes of trying on items, she noticed there was a smaller section of robes and dresses. As she looked at these, she realized they were maternity clothes. She looked at Sayeri, who smiled and nodded for her to try those on too.

"You're such a slender girl; you won't need those until the last couple of months. My daughter was like me. She filled out like a melon early."

Sayeri picked three gowns easy enough for the housekeeper to fix by hemming the bottom. The others she would send to the seamstress for alterations. "There's nothing suitable for court, but they will be good enough for here in the country."

Ninallia could not imagine them being unsuitable for court. They were beautiful.

"Now, let's wash your hair and see what can be done. I think you're too young to wear wigs."

After a vigorous shampoo and a heavenly smelling conditioning treatment, Sayeri got down to business. She studied

Ninallia. "Your hair is curly—what do you think of cutting it short in the Banoilian style and having curls all over? It won't take long for the sides to grow long enough to match, and I think it'll look lovely with the shape of your face.

Ninallia agreed, and soon Sayeri was snipping away at her hair. The result was indeed flattering. Ninallia had seen one of the entertainment stars wearing a similar cut last spring.

Eager to learn how to send and receive messages like a Sister, she asked for a lesson after she finished getting the new hairstyle.

Tegani, who joined them, sat back in a comfortable chair. "First, you have to empty your mind."

"I already know how to do that."

"All our talents begin with that. You must master it before anything else. Once your mind is clear, focus until you can see the face of the person you want to contact. You must hold your mind empty except for that face, and then you think their name and wait until they answer. After that, it is much like a conversation, only here and instead of here." Tegani touched her temple and then her lips. "See if you can reach Lady Sayeri when she is in the garden."

Sayeri stood and nodded. "Give me a few minutes."

After a few minutes, Ninallia focused, but it took a few tries before she could hold her mind empty while picturing Sayeri.

Finally, Sayeri answered, "Ninallia? Goodness, child, you have a strong voice. Softly, please."

Ninallia was so excited that she immediately lost the connection. Sayeri's voice had sounded as if she were standing right behind her, speaking softly in her ear.

~*~

Houston barely recognized the girl when he greeted them at lunch. Gone was the pale, young boy in loose robes. In his place was a young lady with short, cropped hair and delicate features. Ninallia twirled in the gown, letting the green and gold fabric catch the light.

He bowed formally. "It is a pleasure to meet you, my lady, Ninallia."

"I'm not a lady," she said, laughing.

"I beg your pardon." Sayeri interrupted their play. "As the mother of the future emperor, you are the first lady of the Empire, and no one outranks you until a new empress is crowned."

Ninallia ducked her head. Sayeri's tone held more than a small measure of reproof.

"Knowing your place in the Imperial court structure is the key to success or failure there. You will be the highest-ranking woman there. Don't forget, and don't let others forget it either."

Ninallia straightened in her seat and met Sayeri's eyes. She lifted her chin and gave a small bow. From what he'd seen, this approximated a video of the late empress greeting dignitaries.

"Much better. Now, do you think you can do it with all of the noble ladies scowling at you?"

Ninallia pursed her lips. "Yes, Sayeri. For my son, I can do it."

Tegani said, "I hate to interrupt the lesson, but the food smells delicious and is getting cold."

They were sitting to eat when a small boy ran into the room. He ran up to Sayeri and climbed into her lap. He turned and looked at the guests. "Hello."

"This is Peterno, my grandson. He needs to work on his manners, too."

He gave her a hurt look and bowed his head.

Tegani cocked her head, studying the boy. After a few minutes, she looked at Sayeri in amazement.

"He looks like his grandfather, doesn't he?" Sayeri said dryly, around an amused smile.

Houston looked at the two women who seemed to be discussing a secret. When neither said anything else, everyone began eating.

Peterno's governess hesitantly came to the door. Her face was flushed with embarrassment. "I'm sorry, Lady Sayeri. We were napping."

Sayeri hugged her grandson and sat him down. "Go on now and be a good boy. You must stop running off."

The governess scooped the boy up into her arms, where he laughed and squirmed.

"She spoils him too much," said Sayeri. "The entire staff does. His mother ran off when he was still in diapers, and now he rules my whole estate."

The love and affection in her voice were clear.

"This is the best meat I have ever eaten," said Ninallia. "What is it?"

"We have several herds of League imported beef cattle. I sell most of the meat, but I always keep plenty for my household. This is a sirloin roast."

"Yes, it is," said Houston with apparent pleasure. He finished two large slices and was using some of the fresh bread to sop up the juices from his plate.

"One of my neighbors has imported pigs and chickens. They're good, but more like some of our native animals in flavor."

When he and the others were served after dinner drinks, Ninallia had a bowl of ice cream made with fresh berries and rich cream. She licked her spoon and eyed the empty bowl, but did not ask for seconds. Houston hid a grin.

She looked at Sayeri. "May I be excused? I want to practice my sending."

"Of course," said Sayeri.

"If I find a true gift, I will train her to use it," said Tigani.

Sayeri added, "It can be no accident, My Lady sent one of

her most experienced Sisters to find this girl. How and why did she send the tools needed to prove a gift ahead of her? This is bordering, if not jumping the border, on interference in the affairs of a sovereign kingdom. What was the old woman doing?"

Houston agreed. "The League's concern and involvement lent credence to the rumors concerning Hanoree."

Twenty

My Lady paced around her quarters. She did not know if Tegani and the girl had reached Sayeri, but she was sure Hanoree was monitoring her communications. She didn't dare send a message via the Sisters because Tegani's location would be known and could fall into the wrong hands. Not even Arturon, her First Brother, knew their location or how vital it was that they succeed. She knew—she had seen it. Years of studying and practicing her gift proved valuable. She could see the future of the Empire and the whole planet if Hanoree became the next emperor. The disaster she foresaw superseded her vow of neutrality.

She sensed Arturon standing in her door, waiting for her to acknowledge his presence. She turned and motioned him into her room. "Come, Brother, do you have anything to report?"

"Good news, My Lady. We rescued four of the women who lived at Madama Ector's with the girl. Two have birthed their children. They have been taken out of the Empire." He smiled. "The girl's mother and aunt are safe, too. They are in a clinic in a remote area outside the Empire."

Their safety was good news indeed. The girl would be grateful to the Order for protecting them. It was also the right thing to do. My Lady smiled and offered Arturon tea.

"Thank you, My Lady. There is more. Sister Tegani and the girl are traveling with a man, a soldier wearing a merchant's garb. Our friend, Captain Joanani, says he is a League colonel."

My Lady had seen the dark warrior with Tegani in the vision. Was he a friend or foe? The vision was not clear. Was the League a friend or not? They were even more uncertain. "We must assume communications to and from the Temple City are monitored, and we can be sure Hanoree is listening. He has the technology, and his men are in place below the mountains. Use the Sister's link when necessary, but do not pass on anything concerning Tegani and the girl on our network. It would endanger the Sisters and Brothers outside the Temple City."

"Yes, My Lady, I have ordered discretion," said Arturon. "My Lady, why don't you sleep? I will stay with you and wake you for any news."

My Lady reached over and squeezed his hand. "Thank you, dear Brother, you are right. My mind is too old to function long without rest. Tegani and the girl are safe for now."

He poured tea. My Lady changed her robes and stretched on her bed in the next room. He did not turn on the communication or entertainment system. She gave a whispered prayer, thanking the Spirits Sayeri had proven a true Sister after all. My Lady wished she knew the outcome of her plans. Tegani and the girl were in sanctuary with Sayeri, and it was unlikely Hanoree could reach them there, if he even thought to look. She closed her eyes and drifted off to sleep.

The familiar call of her link woke her. A Sister was sending a message. "My Lady of Wisdom. My Lady of Wisdom. Hear us."

My Lady lay motionless, listening as Arturon responded. "My Lady rests. This is First Brother Arturon. Speak."

"Hanoree's men are everywhere. Three Brothers have been taken on their way back to the Temple City. Two Sisters are missing and feared dead."

"Dear Spirits. Yes, we have your message. Find safety if you can." Arturon bowed his head and wept. He rubbed his face on his sleeve like a crying child.

My Lady stood beside him, taking his arm. Winter was their protection. In the spring, Hanoree might advance against them despite the League's warnings. "You are the strongest sender in the city. I need you to pass on my message. I don't care if it is overheard. In fact, I want you to send it on the communication network too. I want Hanoree to hear."

Arturon closed his eyes and swallowed.

"Brothers and Sisters of the Order, we are under attack. I want you to be safe. The Empire is under the mistaken belief that we are its enemies. It has chosen to become our enemy—Hanoree has chosen. He, not the Empire, is behind this. Guard yourselves. Don't be afraid to use your gifts to protect what is right. Spirits be with you. Be careful of your messages and hold true to the Order."

Within minutes, every Brother and Sister on Bengar would receive the message. Hanoree would hear it. The League would hear. The Temple had been provoked, and its people killed. War with the Empire was imminent.

~ * ~

Hanoree had not expected the Order's response to be this direct. It was short of a declaration of war, but it pointed a finger at him. Perhaps he could force their hand by going public with his allegations that the Order was involved in the assassination of the late emperor and empress.

His attempt to get one of the Brothers to confess had failed. The Brother was stronger-willed than anticipated and died without cooperating.

Varick produced a video depicting a Brother confessing to hiring a woman to claim she was pregnant with the emperor's child. The tattoos looked original, but the Order could, if given the chance, prove the man depicted as a Brother was an imposter. After debating the risks of going public with the farce, Hanoree chose to go ahead.

He broadcast his story and made sure it would be carried planet-wide. The motivations of My Lady of Wisdom sounded dire and vague. He painted her as a power-hungry woman who wanted control of the whole planet for her religious Order. The implications of his message were that the Order's Writ of Neutrality was a farce.

~ * ~

Across many miles, the Southern Kingdom was enjoying warmth and full harvests. Tegani heard the message and shook her head in disbelief. She hurried to find the others. Houston was talking with some of Sayeri's men. He stopped and joined her, concern shining on his face.

"Where's Ninallia?" she asked.

"In the garden. She wanted to catalog the flowers."

Tegani walked to the garden. She didn't know what to say to the girl. She was carrying the future emperor, but was little more than a child herself.

At last, Tegani saw her sitting on a bench beside a large tree, and she was crying. She received the message. How, at such an early stage of training, the girl could receive a message not directed to her, Tegani didn't know, but it was plain she had. She sat beside the girl and put an arm across her shoulder.

"I don't want to be the cause of war." Ninallia leaned against Tegani.

"You didn't cause it, Ninallia. You got caught up in Hanoree's web. We hope we can use you to end it and put the rightful emperor on the throne."

"I can't believe my baby is also the son of the emperor."

"I believe he is. We'll know for sure after he is born." Tegani handed the girl a handkerchief.

"I'm such a ninny."

"You're a Dowager Empress because your son is the true Emperor of Kaydor."

This pronouncement sent Ninallia into a fit of giggles. "I'm sorry, the title Dowager Empress makes me think of an old and wrinkled woman sitting behind the emperor and bullying everyone at court.

Tegani smiled. She was glad to have lightened the girl's spirits. There might not be a war. The other kingdoms would react to the news and force Hanoree to back down. She prayed to the Spirits they would.

Twenty-One

Gloom settled over them as they watched the evening broadcast. Tegani's hands clenched. She grew very still and quiet, then spoke, "I'll tell you one thing, that was no Brother on the screen. The tattoo was close, but the lettering was wrong, and he did not speak in the right tone. Serving in the Empire is a privileged assignment, and I know most of the Brothers assigned to the Empire. They check in with My Lady twice a year, more often if there is a problem. That was an imposter."

Houston shook his head.

Ninallia studied the screen, trying to memorize the faces flitting across. She recognized Hanoree, of course. She hated him. Reporters were interviewing Nobles about the pronouncement and whether there was, in fact, a royal heir. She wrote down names as fast as she could.

"Stop," she called. "Can you back up to the last question?"

Sayeri used the remote to freeze and rewind the program in progress. She stopped at the frame of a harassed-looking Noble lady asking a question, then said, "That is Lady Patella. She inherited her seat on the Council from her late husband."

"No, who is the man standing behind her in line? The one wearing a tall hat and woven necklaces."

"Lord Nebron is a Noble from the Eastern Province. He is a good man. His grandfather, a wealthy banker, married the daughter of a Noble and bought her family's title."

"I've seen him before. I'm sure he is the one who signed the papers for Madama Ector. He saw me. He spoke to me. He can prove we're telling the truth."

"Why would Nebron be at Madama Ector's? He isn't a royal," Tegani asked.

"I think I understand. His wife is a cousin to the late empress. They were practically raised as sisters. Both women were barren. Nebron and his wife used a dumas. Perhaps they were helping the empress," Sayeri explained.

"So, he would be on our side?"

"I'm not saying he would be an ally, but Lady Nebron and the empress were close, as girls. What her husband's politics are, I cannot say." Sayeri seemed thoughtful. "It is significant that the empress trusted Lord Nebron to act in her stead with Madama Ector."

"Damn straight it is significant. It means he knew Ninallia was pregnant when no one else did. Who's to say he didn't betray them to Hanoree? They were murdered soon after Ninallia became pregnant." Houston paced back and forth.

"Let's get organized. We have a list of Nobles and dignitaries. Some were allies of the late emperor, and some are supporters of Hanoree." Tegani began to copy the list of names.

"For now, we will put Nebron on the side of the late emperor." Sayeri eyed the growing list. They played the whole broadcast again, and she stopped it on an image of Hanoree sitting at his desk and a man leaning over, handing him documents to sign. "I remember Lord Varick. He has been slithering around the court for years. It seems he has risen in status. Look at the pendant he is wearing. He is Hanoree's right-hand man."

"Wasn't he suspected to be dealing in drugs?" Tegani asked, "I remember there was an investigation."

Sayeri snorted. "Oh, there was talk of an investigation. It ended because too many of the younger set at court liked their recreational drugs. He has too much on them, and blackmail is one of Varick's specialties."

"He definitely goes in Hanoree's column." Ninallia tapped

her lips. "Who are the other people on the video? Some of the ones who aren't speaking could be players."

"I wish we could get this information to My Lady. She has resources we don't have here," Tegani said.

"Hanoree's men have the Temple City surrounded. I'm sure they're monitoring all communications," Houston said.

"If we send through the Sisters and Brothers link, Hanoree will know where we are and put them, as well as us, in danger." Tegani rubbed her hands together.

"We could use the old-fashioned method of communication. We could send a letter," Sayeri said, her face brightening.

"In the middle of winter?" Tegani tilted her head, her eyebrow raised.

"That's the best time. The Temple City is iced in, and the roads are impassable. Nothing goes in or out of the City except the winter supply drops." Sayeri voice's lowered as she said, "I think I can get a case of wine for My Lady added to the next drop. It's an ordinary gift. When she opens the crate, there will be our letter."

"What if she doesn't open the crate?" Houston asked.

"I can mark it with her symbol. Whoever takes it off the drop will deliver it directly to My Lady."

Tegani, Houston, and Ninallia worked on the message, and Sayeri called in a few favors to have a crate of her best wine picked up the next morning.

~ * ~

Ninallia stopped reading and put the viewer down. She put her hand to her stomach. It wasn't morning sickness, but she felt a small fluttering. Was she going to be sick? Realizing this was her baby's movements sent shivers of excitement through her. My son is growing inside me.

Tegani walked into the room. Ninallia was bent forward with her arms around her middle. "Are you okay?"

"The baby's moving. I can feel him."

Her delight fed the others, and soon she, Tegani, and Sayeri were laughing and talking babies. The two older women agreed they had been negligent in their preparations.

"You'll need a crib, diapers, baby things," Sayeri said. "I'll see what I have in storage."

"What are you going to name him?" Tegani asked as she got into the spirit of the discussion.

"I don't know. I want it to be a name worthy of an emperor and one honoring those who died to be sure he was crowned." She thought she sounded very grown-up.

Tegani smiled in approval, and Sayeri hugged Ninallia.

She had been through so much in her short life. *I'm never going to be the same again.*

Later, in her room, Ninallia stood before a mirror. She could see a baby pooch now. The healer said her son would be born in early April. He was growing, and she was healthy.

Sayeri was providing many things for the nursery, along with baby clothes. It bothered Ninallia not to be able to decide on a name for her son. Emperor Hashi sounded too weak. Emperor Mallor sounded too old and staid for a child. Then it came to her—she would name her son Hiroto. The name meant courage, which was the perfect name for an emperor.

~*~

From storage, Sayeri produced an antique wooden rocker for Ninallia, the only family heirloom she brought with her from the Imperial City. She put one of her servants to work, cleaning and polishing it. With more than four months until the birth, there was plenty of time to set up a nursery. This brought back many memories.

The birth of her daughter had been a special time. Hennina had been a happy baby, early to walk and talk, but always into everything. As she grew older, she became restless and rebellious. Her teens were difficult years, but Sayeri had hoped the unexpected pregnancy would settle her down, and at first it seemed to. Hennina would sit for hours and rock her son. One morning, she ran off and never came back.

Sayeri sighed. At least she had Peterno. The door opened, and two of her estate workmen brought in the crib she had designed for her grandson.

~ * ~

Tegani set the things packed in the special box from My Lady on her table. She had used these items to test many acolytes at the Temple. She lit the scented candle, breathing in its spicy aroma, and poured the sacred oil into the small ceremonial bowl. When she tested Ninallia, the results were exciting and frightening. She was amazed that the girl could receive at so high a level with her limited training. That was the first clue that Ninallia possessed the gift of mind touch. She would, with training, be able to touch almost anyone's mind, gifted or not.

Ninallia squealed with delight upon hearing this. She placed her hand on Tegani's forehead and said, "I can see you are thinking about Colonel Houston. He thinks about you a lot, especially at night."

Sayeri laughed, but Tegani turned red and snapped, "Your gift is not a joke or a game, child," as she hurried from the room.

Ninallia pouted. "I was teasing."

~ * ~

Tegani was walking in the garden with Sayeri. The green foliage and southern climate made the area a year-round retreat for drinking tea and enjoying time outside.

Peterno came running, playing with his toy air-car. He stopped and bowed to the two women in such a formal manner. He was the spitting image of Arturon. He even tilted his head in the same way when asking for a favor.

Tegani shook her head. She had not asked before. Now

her curiosity overcame caution. "He looks like Arturon… Does he know?"

"No, I couldn't tell him or anyone else," Sayeri answered.

"Why? I think he would have been a wonderful father and grandfather."

"I couldn't do it to him. He loved the Temple, and I hated the cold. I was the half-sister to an empress. It would have caused a terrible scandal, and he would have been dismissed from the Order." Sayeri's voice was soft as she spoke.

Tegani agreed with that assessment but was sad that her old friend had not met his daughter or seen his grandson. The boy looked so much like Arturon, she wondered if he shared any of his gifts. If so, would Sayeri let the boy go to the Temple for training?

She was sure Arturon would want to see his grandson, though she could not picture him and Sayeri together. What a tangle.

Tegani smiled, letting the matter drop. That problem could wait for another day. She was sure it would work itself out. Now, she owed Ninallia an apology for overreacting to her innocent teasing.

Tegani tried not to imagine a relationship with Houston and buried her feelings. He was League and would be leaving after this mission. He doubtless spent time with many women. If there was a sexual attraction, it was no proof of deeper feelings.

Twenty-Two

My Lady wrapped a heavy cloak about her. She felt the cold more and more. Perhaps it is time to pass on the mantle to Arturon and retire to a southern climate. When this crisis is over, I will discuss it with him, but now I have a meeting with a League general.

She noticed something different about her screen, a slight shimmer that wasn't there before. Her first thought was that the Empire was spying on her. She expected this but hoped her security measures would prevent it.

"Good evening, My Lady. I trust you are well." A gray-haired man in military uniform stared out from her communication screen. "I apologize for interrupting your day. What I must tell you is of the greatest importance. I have taken the liberty of securing this line."

My Lady's mood lifted. She smiled. She feared the League would ally with whichever side appeared to be winning the standoff. Apparently, she was wrong. "How may I help you, General?"

"I am not going to pretend we both don't know what's going on. I have an agent, a Colonel Houston, who is with your Sister and the girl. I need to get some important information to him."

"I would think you, not I, would be able to contact your colonel."

"The damn fool ripped out his earbud. If he hasn't ruined his hearing, I'll be amazed."

"I see. What is this message he needs to hear?"

"After the death of the emperor, the body of a known

assassin was found floating in a creek several miles from the Imperial City. The man's wife has gone into hiding. She claims her husband was the assassin hired to murder the emperor. She is willing to give us evidence if someone helps her leave the Empire."

My Lady sent a prayer of thanks to the Spirits. This might be the stroke of luck they needed. "And how will this help Colonel Houston?"

"It's more about how he can help us. If anyone can find this woman and get her safely from the Empire, it's Houston. It's what he specializes in."

"Couldn't the League get her out? There must be other men trained for these missions."

"That's true, My Lady, but Houston terminated communications, and we have lost contact. To command officials, he has deserted and is no longer a part of the League."

"So, the League can disavow any knowledge or responsibility for his actions?" My Lady was quick to understand.

The general indicated his contempt for League policy with a snort. "Houston never left a man behind. I don't plan on leaving him behind, even if it means ruffling a few League feathers."

"Our Sister is as dear to me as my own daughter." My Lady liked this general. He was not as tough as he pretended.

The general continued, "The woman is called Beliani. She works in one of the seediest bars in the Imperial City. She's looking for an out."

"Let's give her one. You can offer her League protection, and I will promise the Order's help in her escape. I don't want to think of her falling into Hanoree's hands." She felt hope growing like a spring flower.

"Neither you nor I can waltz in and escort her out. Houston might be able to get her to a safe location where the League can pick her up."

"I'll see what I can do. Our communications are being monitored." My Lady's words were thoughtful.

"We're working on securing your coms."

"Thank you."

The general had delivered his message, and My Lady was eager to put it into action. As soon as he signed off, she sent for Arturon.

"Dear Spirits, this is the answer to our prayers." Arturon's reaction was much like her own. "I will leave at once. I think I can get villagers to sled me down the mountain."

"You'll do no such thing. If you made it down, the Imperial guards would capture you. Your face is known throughout the Empire. Besides, you are the next in line to lead the Order. Think what Hanoree could do if he held you captive." My Lady's logic was sound, but she knew it chaffed at him.

"I am not without some skill," Arturon said defensively. His ego raised its head, even after serving the Order for thirty years.

Several years ago, she'd sent him on a mission to the Imperial City, so he had contacts. "I'm sure Colonel Houston is experienced in these things." She smiled. "We'll send a message to Sayeri. Use a code and pass it on the shortest link via the Sisters and Brothers."

"Wouldn't it be easier to send it direct?" he asked.

"Sister Tegani isn't much of a receiver."

"Sayeri has an incredible range. It was one of the gifts she excelled at." His voice was wistful.

"Yes, I remember now. A shame she never used it to keep in touch." She studied Arturon, aware of the romance between him and the young royal.

He was a superior sender, and he remembered Sayeri's mind well. His gaze clouded as he focused. Sending across so many miles without using the Sister and Brother network would tax his mental strength.

~ * ~

Sayeri was finishing her eggs and toast when her mind was touched with a familiar caress. Arturon?

Are Sister Tegani, the girl, and the League colonel with you?

Yes. Sayeri mouthed one word to the others: "Arturon."

Tegani gasped. "Are you sure? Can he send this far? He has to be in the Temple City."

Sayeri held up her hand for Tegani to be quiet. Ninallia ran to get Houston.

They are safe here. How stand things in the Temple City? Sayeri asked. She was trying to still the wild beating of her heart, his mental touch brought after so many years.

We are well. I have important news. Can you relay it to the others?

Yes, Tegani is in the room, and Ninallia is bringing Houston.

Good, much of what I tell you concerns him.

Sayeri felt the effort sending was costing him. How long could he keep such a link? She closed her eyes and focused on strengthening the bond and supporting it. She felt him sigh with relief.

Your Colonel Houston has a friend in the League named General Evans. He contacted My Lady with important information about the death of the royal couple.

Sayeri relayed this information as Houston came into the room with Ninallia.

"He's a good man," said Houston.

The body of the assassin washed up. No one in the Empire seems to connect the man to the murder, but his wife claims he was hired to do the job. She is willing to trade proof for safe passage to a League protected area.

Everyone was silent for a few minutes. Ninallia wrote

down the location and name before Arturon's link failed.

Take care, Arturon, said Sayeri.

You too, lady. Perhaps when this is over, I should visit Madori.

Yes. She held the link until he released. Tears filled her eyes.

"How soon can you get me passage to the Imperial City?" Houston asked.

"You mean get us passage?" said Tegani.

"You can't leave Ninallia. One of us has to stay here, and it is much more dangerous for a Sister in the Imperial City now than it is for me."

Sayeri knew Tegani would hate to admit it, but Houston was right. She would be failing in her duty if she left Ninallia, even in Sayeri's more than capable hands.

Sayeri concentrated on a plan of action. The best course of travel would be a direct transport flight, but that would lead back to her estate. She booked an airbus to the capital of a neighboring kingdom. Once there, Houston could book a flight to the Imperial City. She began to work on securing enough untraceable credits. It wouldn't do for them to be linked to her bank.

Tegani acted flustered. She was rattling off a list of things Houston would need and possible dangers in the city. Sayeri quietly signaled Ninallia, and the two slipped from the room.

~ * ~

"I hope you don't think you can waltz into the Dragon's End and take the woman out. I hear it is one of the worst bars in the roughest areas of the Imperial City," Tegani said.

Houston grabbed her and kissed her long and hard. Panting, he said, "I'll miss you too, and I promise to be careful."

She couldn't speak. Instead, she stared at him in surprise. Had her feelings been transparent? She turned and realized the others were not in the room.

She couldn't believe he had kissed her. He had no right to

involve her emotions when it couldn't go anywhere. When this was over, and if they succeeded, she would be going back to her Temple City, and he would return to the League and deal with his desertion.

~ * ~

Sayeri approached Houston the next morning. "Colonel Houston, I wonder if you would join me and a guest for a private lunch in the garden. It's a little cool now, but it should be pleasant in a few hours. We are blessed with a wonderful climate year-round, except for the rainy season in late spring."

"A private lunch?" he asked.

"We don't want to advertise the fact that Ninallia and Sister Tegani are here, at least not yet. I think it is important you meet my guest."

She had stressed the importance of his meeting her lunch guest, but didn't refer to the guest as a friend or neighbor. Was there some danger? Houston was on guard when he entered the garden later.

A small, well-dressed man was sipping wine and ogling Sayeri's ample bosom. She was relaxed and smiling, looking quite pleased at the success of the low-cut gown and heavy makeup.

"Colonel, glad you could join us. This is Manit Vol Timel. I think he may be able to help with your provisioning needs. I assure you that Timel is reliable and deals in quality merchandise."

Houston blinked. Sayeri was telling him that Timel was an arms dealer of some kind. How did she know he needed additional arms? How did she know Timel?

Timel looked him over. "What is the nature of your assignment, Colonel? Search and destroy?"

Houston poured himself a glass of Bengarian Brandy. He took a long sip before answering. "It's a rescue and retrieval mission."

"Does the party wish to be rescued?" Timel drawled. He

popped a small pastry into his mouth.

"Of course, the party has requested assistance. There will be opposition to the rescue from high places."

Timel smiled. "Sounds interesting. How large is your team? What kind of setting will you be in?"

"It's a solo mission, and it's in the heart of a large city."

"I see, covert, in and out, with as little collateral damage as possible," Timel said. "What do you see yourself needing?"

"Ammo for a C12 blaster, two military-grade revolvers, rations, some energy pills, and three gas bombs," Houston rattled off his needs. He looked at Timel and added, "and a League communicator."

"What! You didn't tell me he was working for the League." Timel turned an accusing glare at Sayeri. "The price goes up."

"Darling, who else would have the balls to go against Lord Hanoree?" She stroked his arm.

"Hanoree, that makes a difference. The beautiful empress did not deserve to die. She was an angel of mercy. I would gladly kill Hanoree myself." Timel's lips drew together in a tight line. It was evident his words came from true passion. "If the League wants to arrange this, I am your man. I thought they were like the Order, bound by their own laws and bureaucracy."

"The League will have Hanoree in court. We have to make sure they have the evidence to win," Sayeri said.

Timel raised her hand to his lips and kissed it. He looked at Houston. "It will take three days to get everything together. League communicators are surprisingly easy to come by. The ammunition you need will take time."

"Thank you." Houston was leery of trusting an arms dealer. They were as likely to sell you out as they were to help. He hoped Timel's professed affection for the late empress was genuine. "Three days will be fine."

They spent the rest of the time eating and enjoying Sayeri's fine wine. In fact, Houston was feeling a pleasant buzz when he returned to his room.

"Who was the man in the garden?" Tegani asked as he passed by her room.

"A friend of Sayeri's. An arms dealer."

She blinked. Obviously, she hadn't expected him to be honest and direct. "Is he going to help us?"

"For a price, he has agreed to provide some help. He is no friend of Hanoree."

"Nor are we. Do you trust him?" she asked.

"Sayeri is willing to trust him," he answered.

Houston headed to his room. There was hunger in her eyes. If he turned around and went into Tegani's room, he suspected she wouldn't protest. They could spend the afternoon making love and sleep in each other's arms. He reminded himself it was against League policy to get emotionally involved with the locals while on a mission. He closed the door.

Outside, he could hear Sayeri and Ninallia walking toward the house, their voices happy.

"Is the baby supposed to sit on my bladder? I have to pee again," Ninallia said in her childlike voice. On many worlds, there were laws against using girls her age as surrogates.

"Wait until the baby gets bigger and you can't bend over and pull your panties back up." Sayeri laughed. These were things women shared and bonded over.

He examined his weapons. Perhaps Sayeri knew an area where he could test fire them. The good food and easy life here were making him soft. Well, the clinic had not helped. The artificial heart-lung capacitor seemed to be working well, but would it continue to work in a stressful situation? What if he needed stimulants to stay awake?

~ * ~

Arturon stared at the falling snow outside his window. Touching

Sayeri's mind had affected him. He thought his feelings for her were a fond memory, but strong emotions threatened to overwhelm him. He never told her that he loved her, and she had married someone else. Disappointment had filled when she accepted her family's plans and never contacted him again.

He couldn't blame her. As a Brother, he had nothing to offer a woman used to living in palaces with servants at her beck and call. She hated living in the Temple City; she hated the cold.

There was a ringing of a small bell. My Lady wanted his presence. Arturon sighed and put away his memories to answer her summons.

"I want you to go to Sayeri's as soon as the first thaws begin," she said. "The baby will be born in the spring, and someone will have to certify the paternity test and christen the child."

"Wouldn't I lead Hanoree straight to them?"

"Hanoree has tightened his hold on the Council of Nobles. Our future is dark if they support Him. The time to act is now. We will say you are ill and sneak you out. They will not be able to follow you. The late emperor's DNA is on file, so you can test the child and prove there is a match."

"I don't want to leave you here alone. What if Hanoree orders his men to take the city?" Arturon expressed his greatest fear.

"One of us will be out of the city to lead an attack against his palace and rally the other kingdoms. I am too old to make the trip."

"Yes, My Lady."

Twenty-Three

Hanoree struggled with a problem. Varick was becoming too powerful and was beginning to try to direct policy. His strategic plans were sometimes brilliant, and he had made himself indispensable by providing a source of drugs and women. On the downside, he knew all of Hanoree's secrets, and that made him very dangerous. Worse, he failed to bring in the girl and her baby or kill them.

"How may I serve you?" Varick said.

"Bring me this woman who claims to carry the late emperor's child, or bring me her head."

"I am doing the best I can. There are new leads coming in. Unfortunately, no one knows her location," Varick explained.

"What new leads?"

"She has fled the Empire and is in a southern kingdom awaiting the birth of her child."

Hanoree looked up. That was something he might do. Which kingdom would he choose? Who would help him if he were this girl?

"You took care of the assassin?" Hanoree asked for the umpteenth time.

"Yes, my Emperor." Varick's voice lowered on the last.

It was forbidden for anyone be called emperor before being officially crowned. Hanoree smiled. He loved the title. The sooner it was his, the better. The drug took effect. He relaxed, feeling magnanimous. "You have been a loyal servant and advisor. What would you desire if I choose to reward your service?"

"I ask for my life, my Emperor, and to serve you. I would

also ask my estates be protected for my children."

Hanoree almost blasted Varick for false modesty, but realized the man knew his days might be numbered and was asking for his life. "I shall grant your request. You shall live and prosper as my servant. You will be the next First Minister of the Empire."

Varick blinked. Hanoree hid his smile. First Minister was the highest rank an emperor could bestow on a non-royal. The head of the Council of Nobles was higher but was always of noble blood.

Varick bowed low. "I am not worthy."

"Are we any closer to getting a date for our ascension to the throne?" Hanoree asked as Varick straightened.

"No, and I do not understand it. There is no reason to delay. Even the people have begun to get restless for a decision."

Hanoree's voice grew thoughtful as he said, "Perhaps someone is trying to delay the matter." He was not generally a pensive man. The drugs made him calm, and his mind was sharper when focused.

"That is a possibility. Someone may know the girl carries the late emperor's child." Varick strode to the table where a bottle of the best wine was standing in a bucket of ice. He picked up the bottle and pulled the cork.

"Join me," Hanoree said. "If the late empress had a confidant, someone who helped her arrange things with Madama Ector, who would that be?"

Holding a glass of wine to his lips, Varick turned. He took a slow sip before answering, "Someone we would not suspect. None of the court ladies comes to mind. They could not keep the secret. This person would have a vested interest in helping the empress."

"See if you can find a name for me. Is there anyone who might have a connection to the empress or a connection to

Madama Ector herself?"

"I will find out," Varick promised.

There was little Hanoree could ferret on his own. His wife would be able to learn if there were any rumors among the Noble ladies. Of course, his wife would need to leave their country estate and join him in the Imperial City. She would hate that, as would his current mistress.

The sound of activity outside the room made him start. Hanoree stepped down from the throne, and Varick hid his glass of wine. There was a knock at the door.

"Come in," Hanoree said, and Varick bowed and left as the visitor entered.

The current First Minister strode in as if he owned the palace. He was a pompous old man, large and loud in his advice. Hanoree never understood why the late emperor chose such a buffoon.

"Why are the Nobles dragging their feet with your appointment as regent?" the First Minister demanded.

Hanoree almost choked on his wine. This had to be divine providence. "I don't know, First Minister. It is not for me to decide in these matters. I am in mourning for my emperor."

"Admirable. The Empire cannot go long without an emperor. They are trying to consolidate their power. If they have their way, the emperor would be a puppet position."

Hanoree put his hand to his chest, his heart beating excitedly. He had not expected the First Minister to be an ally. In fact, he intended to oust the old fool as one of his first acts as emperor. The man rarely attended the council meetings and showed little ambition. It was amazing how the Spirits continued to shower blessings on him. "Don't say such things, the Nobles are honorable. They supported Emperor Rhealgar."

"If I thought you believed in the honor of the Nobles, I wouldn't support you as regent."

Hanoree laughed with First Minister and shook his hand, then he walked from the throne room with the First Minister. He made sure as many people as possible saw the two of them together and noted the fact that there was an accord there.

Hanoree parted from his guest and strolled toward a group of Nobles he had seen watching. Time to stir things up.

Twenty-Four

Houston sat upright in the back of Sayeri's transport. His route to the Imperial City was far from direct, but it gave him a chance to remain untraceable. If he were captured, it would be almost impossible to track his movements back to Sayeri and the others. He was more comfortable with his persona now, and once in the Imperial City, he could contact the League if backup became necessary.

The lush fields gave way to flatlands. The southern kingdom, located near the equator, was humid and warm year-round. In the Imperial City, it would be winter. Sayeri provided some cold-weather clothes, but he would need more. He studied the map of the Imperial City—he liked to do reconnaissance a day or two before a mission. It helped him prepare for the worst and put backup and escape plans in place.

The last leg of the journey began in the City of Tupon. His train to the Imperial City departed mid-morning the next day. Houston used the free afternoon to shop for more winter clothes and get a feel for the political climate in the Empire. He sat in a local pub, deliberately choosing a seat at the bar, eating sandwiches and drinking ale.

"I say the Order is behind the emperor's murder. They're always messing around behind the scenes. They control half the planet from their Temple City," one well-dressed man said.

His companion, a wilder-looking individual, shook his head. "What would they gain? Must be someone on the Council of Nobles, maybe all of them. Might even be Hanoree. He is parading on the news feeds like he's in charge."

The bartender sauntered over, wiping the bar. He leaned forward and asked the louder man to keep his voice down. "I don't want Imperial security closing this place."

The men complained about their right to free speech, but lowered their voices. Traders were known to like the ladies, so Houston feigned an interest in a few but left alone.

The next day, he slept on the train into the Imperial City. He wanted to be fresh when he scouted around that night. He took a transport to the rougher side of the city, got off several blocks from the bar, then walked around. The bar was in a warehouse area where workers came in and out at all hours. The streets were narrow, but there were alleys wide enough for one-way traffic. These were lined with trash cans, and homeless people were sleeping against the backs of the shabby buildings. There would be people in the alleys twenty-four-seven, or as the Bengarian time ran thirty hours a day, eight days a week.

There was one back exit to the bar, and it led into a long alley. Luckily, this alley wasn't a dead end. He timed a brisk walk down the alley and up a side street, noting a few hiding places. If this were a large Earth city, he might have found a subway system, but there were no subways in the Imperial City. Local transport vehicles hovered just above the roads or drove down them. Longer distance travelers used higher altitude lanes and moved faster, and travel outside the Empire was monitored. The nearest public transport stop was a mile from the bar, and a few private transports were parked in the area.

Houston jogged down a less seedy street, attracting little attention. It offered a handy escape route but had its own risks. A vehicle parked here could receive too much attention or be stolen and stripped. There were many variables. One thing was certain: he would need a quick getaway.

He made a cash purchase of an older transport that had been modified. It looked like a clunker but had a hot engine.

After parking it near the end of the alley in a small area where a few other vehicles braved the neighborhood, he circled the bar. Soon, there seemed to be a steady flow of people in and out.

Sauntering in, he took a seat at the bar. There were two barkeeps serving a dozen tables, and the bartender kept those at the bar supplied. The slender woman behind the bar was his target. She walked over to take his order, and their eyes met.

Beliani looked away. "What are you drinking?"

"Blue ale."

She turned and filled a glass, then set the drink in front of him. She leaned forward and whispered, "Not here."

Taking his drink and moving toward the tables, he smiled at a couple of women and chose a spot near theirs. There was something written on the napkin Beliani handed him with the ale. He unfolded the napkin and read it. *I get off at 2 a.m. Meet me in the alley behind the bar.*

"Damn." There was no way he'd sit in the bar for four more hours. There was no entertainment. After buying drinks for the women at the next table and after some minor flirting, he left.

His vehicle was still there. He walked past it and a few blocks further to an all-night market. The thin, pimple-faced youth behind the counter stiffened when Houston entered.

The youth watched him in the network of mirrors in the store. *I guess I can disguise my race and species, but military training and law enforcement can be spotted.*

Houston selected some bagged munchies and a large cup of hot tea and took them to the counter to pay. The youth kept his attention on the door. The acrid smell of fear, distinct from his general poor hygiene, surrounded the boy.

What had he walked in on? "You got trouble, kid?"

"No, um... yeah, maybe a little." The kid kept his gaze on the empty street outside as if waiting for an invasion. "These guys want me to open the safe. I told them I can't, but they're crazy. They said I better figure out a way. I know they're going to come back and hurt me."

"This is a rough neighborhood for someone your age to be running the store alone."

"It's my uncle's store. He is sick, so there's no one else. The day clerk comes in the morning and puts the cash in the safe. He has a weapon. There're less than a hundred credits in the till."

Houston's reply was interrupted by the door opening as three thugs entered. Houston walked over to a counter and looked at the merchandise.

"You got the key?" one of the thugs said.

"No, man, I told you I can't open the safe. It says so on the door."

The larger thug grabbed the youth and pulled him over the counter. "I said I think you have the key to open the safe."

One of the other boys, all underage, took out a knife.

Well, hell, Houston didn't want to get in the middle of this, but the kid was going to get cut up bad if he didn't. "Let the boy go."

The knife-wielder waved it in his direction. "You shut up. This isn't your business. I'll slice off that fat mouth of yours."

In a lightning-fast move, Houston whirled and kicked the knife from the boy's hand. He pointed a shiny black blaster at the trio. The thug holding the cashier was now hiding behind him. Houston could smell his fear. "Let him go."

The thug let the boy go and stepped out holding up his empty hands. Houston waved the blaster toward the door. The trio inched in that direction. "You boys get on home before I give your mothers a reason to cry."

They fled like the young, stupid kids they were, getting down the block before they began to bluster and shout insults back at him. He grinned at the young store clerk and removed a second blaster. "They'll be back. You know how to use a weapon?"

The boy swallowed nervously. "Sort of. Nothing this powerful."

He took a few minutes to give the kid a lesson in operating the baster and left him with a few spare rounds. His uncle must be a real dick to leave the kid alone in this neighborhood.

Glancing at his timepiece, Houston was relieved to see it was nearing time to meet the woman. He left the store, scanning the surroundings to make sure the thugs weren't waiting in ambush. Seeing that it was clear, he headed for the rendezvous.

Once in the alley behind the bar, he blended into the shadows and waited. After fifteen minutes or so, the door opened, and the woman came out. She called something over her shoulder and shut the door. She shouldered a package and looked around. Houston stepped from the shadows.

"Come on, let's go," she said, hurrying down the alley.

He followed. She was fast but stopped once to look back over her shoulder. That gave him a bad feeling. He caught up and grabbed her arm. "Tell me you didn't rob the place."

"No, hell, I own the place. I left everything in the till, and the place running like normal."

"Why are you scared?"

"Someone's been watching me. People know I was Ricol's wife. There hasn't been much of an investigation into his death, but Imperial security keeps coming in, pretending to be normal people. They stand out worse than you."

"You think they're after you?" Houston studied her.

"No, if they believed I knew Ricol's business, I'd be dead. They're watching to see if I go after the payoff. They can't find where he hid it."

They walked to the end of the alley, and he indicated the waiting car. After getting in, her body relaxed. Now she appeared younger than he first thought—late twenties, maybe early thirties, and pretty in a buxom, flashy sort of way. Her face was too thin, and her nose too sharply pointed to be called a true beauty. Her smile revealed crooked and discolored teeth.

Houston started the motor, glancing at the bag at Beliani's feet. "Is that the evidence?"

"No, it's a change of clothes and a few personal things. You get the evidence when I'm under the protection of the League."

Houston navigated the transport from the area and stopped at a small hostel where he booked a room that opened to the outside but was not visible to passing traffic. As they exited the transport, he drew his blaster. He made sure the room was secure.

"League couldn't fund a better place?" She blinked in the dull yellow light of the street lamp.

He motioned for her to enter. The room was small with two beds, a table, two chairs, and an entertainment console mounted on the wall. The assassin's wife turned on the console and flopped onto the bed with a grunt.

"We won't be here long," he replied. He did not want her to sleep yet.

"You got any stims?" She pulled a flask from her bag and opened it. The smell of alcohol filled the small room.

"Not here. We don't have time." He scanned the outside from the window. The parking area was quiet, and the yellow light of the street lamps cast shadows. Few of the lights on this side of the building were on.

"So why are we here?" Beliani stretched one thin leg, then the other.

"We'll check in with the League, and you can change." He could smell the mixture of her musky perfume and body sweat. It had been a long time since he had been with a woman, but he couldn't help remembering how Tegani smelled and the way she held her head.

"Call me Beliani," she said, taking the things he brought to change into. She looked at the wig and wrinkled her nose. "I never wear my hair short."

"Good, that's the idea."

She sighed and headed into the bathroom, leaving the door open a crack as she stripped off her work clothes and changed into the new clothes and wig.

He turned his back to the door and studied the window. When Beliani returned, he smiled. She looked very different. Short dark curls replaced her long, straight, silver hair. With most of her makeup gone, she could have passed for an average housewife.

"Yuck!" She made a face at her image in the mirror.

"You'll do well." He opened the portable communicator and turned it on. He trusted it was preset to a secure League frequency.

"Houston, have you picked up the woman?" the general answered.

"She's here."

"Do you have the evidence?"

Beliani said, "Is this the League?

"I am League General Evans."

"Well, you will get your evidence when I get the hell out of the Empire and not before." She winked at Houston, who covered his mouth to keep from screaming with frustration.

"I'm afraid I need more information. Transporting someone across the Imperial border is against League policy unless there is direct evidence their life may be in danger."

"That's what I've been telling Houston. My husband was hired to kill the emperor and empress. He did the job. Hanoree killed him to cover his tracks. Now his men are watching me. I am in danger."

"You are asking me to violate Imperial Law on your word

alone. You have proof that your husband was the assassin who killed the emperor?"

"I do." Beliani glowered at Houston, who was holding the communicator.

"What is the nature of your proof?" General Evans pressed.

She sighed as she sat cross-legged on the bed, debating how much she should divulge at this point. "Ricol and I were more than lovers. He trusted me, and I knew what he did. I didn't know he was going to kill the empress, or I would have tried to stop him. She was a real lady. Anyway, Ricol was careful. He always kept something for security in case a client didn't want to pay or tried to blackmail him. He said this hit was something big, and if anything happened to him, I was to go to the League. He said the League was the safest place for me. He also wanted you to have the proof because he wanted to get back at Hanoree. I know Hanoree killed him."

"Okay, I am willing to make an exception. Colonel Houston will escort you safely from the Empire, but you must turn over the evidence as soon as you are in League custody."

"You're going to take me off this planet?"

"No, you will be in a safe location until this matter is completed."

Beliani smiled. "Thank you, General. You won't be disappointed."

Houston signed off and did a quick scan of the room. He called the office and checked out. He and Beliani climbed into the car and lifted out of the parking area. It was going to be a long day of travel.

Fifteen miles from the Imperial City, he pulled into a deserted construction area. There was an empty vehicle waiting. The keys were in the ignition. Someone would take the rental back or dispose of it.

The new vehicle was a sporty air car, with wheels for

ground passage. He appreciated the smooth handling. They cruised along in relative silence, and Beliani was soon asleep.

Twenty-Five

In the Imperial Palace, Hanoree was awakened by frantic knocking. He cursed and donned a robe. He recognized the messenger and summoned Varick.

"Speak now," Hanoree said.

"The woman has bolted. She may know something after all."

"Where did she go? Why didn't you stop her?" Hanoree was livid.

Varick had warned Hanoree that the woman should be killed, but Hanoree had scoffed that no assassin would confide in his wife.

"She left the bar at the normal time. Instead of walking home, she got into a transport with a man."

"Did you interrogate her staff?"

"Yes, my lord, and they said she was going for a vacation with a new man, somewhere with sun and casinos."

"And you didn't follow her?" Hanoree's voice was low.

"It was sudden. She never mentioned a trip or a new man. When she didn't turn down the road, one of our men walked down the alley in time to see her getting in a vehicle with someone and taking off. He got the identification number from the transport, but was unable to pick them up on the street. We have teams driving around trying to spot the vehicle now."

"It could be innocent. The woman could be going away with a man for a few days," Varick volunteered.

"I want her dead. It no longer matters what she knows. We can't take the risk of her coming back for blackmail," Hanoree raged.

"Yes, Lord Hanoree, it will be done." The man left the room, and Varick filled a glass with extra wine and drugs. He handed the drink to Hanoree.

"I hate to say you were right, but you were." Hanoree sipped the drink. His mood flickered from rage to cold determination to mellow reflection. "I shouldn't have been cautious. It was you who advised me that the empress was thinking of hiring a dumas and gave me the courage to take action."

"I am always at your service, my Emperor," Varick said. "You have no major appointments today. Why don't we cancel what is there, and you can spend the morning planning our next steps? I will let you know if the woman is spotted."

Trying to clear his mind, Hanoree shook his head. His demeanor was going from mellow to sluggish and would soon approach stupor. He frowned at the glass of wine, wondering what Lord Varick added this time. Hanoree was soon asleep in his quarters.

Twenty-Six

Houston flew the personal transport above the highway, weaving in and out of traffic. Before long, they were cruising along in the countryside with little traffic. He noticed a tail. "Wake up. I think we have trouble."

Beliani sat up and blinked at the wide farmlands, bare in the winter cold. She looked over her shoulder. "Are you sure?"

The large blue air cruiser switched lanes and sped up. There was a sharp sound as their vehicle took a glancing hit from a blaster. Someone in the other air car was trying to shoot them down.

"Hold on, we're going to lose them." He sped up the air car and jumped up to the next level. In an illegal turn, he whirled the vehicle and headed in the opposite direction. "Can you fire one of these?"

Beliani took the proffered weapon and fired a few rounds at the back of the other car as it tried to turn and follow them. One was a pretty good hit. The air cruiser spun and landed.

He activated the communicator. A communications officer answered and said the general had left orders to patch Houston through. He pointed toward the navigation screen. "See what large city is on this route. We're going to have to change plans."

Beliani climbed over the seat and began to enter commands into the console. "This is Route Nino7. It goes back toward the Imperial City before it curves toward the east. Nothing good is ahead."

General Evans came on the line. Houston explained where they were, and the general consulted a navigation officer.

"You need to stay on Route Nino7 for three miles or so. You'll come to a much smaller crossroad—it's ground travel. Turn right and follow the road for twenty miles until it crosses another major passway. Go north on the passway and follow the signs for the port city of Gilliam. It has several ships and a small airbus transport to the neighboring kingdoms. Get a room outside the city, and we'll take care of your vehicle."

Houston followed the directions, stopping once along the way to refuel, get food, and take a bathroom break. Beliani was stuffing a large bite of sweet cake into her mouth as he came out. He purchased a hot beverage and a meat and cheese sandwich. Stale tasting, but filling. When they came out, their vehicle was gone. In its place was a smaller air car in deep blue. Where the other had been a sporty vehicle, this one was more of a family vehicle.

"How did they find us?" she asked.

"It's a League thing. They always put a tracking device on the other car." He opened the door and climbed in. Checking the glove box, he found a small package containing new IDs and airbus tickets.

Beliani buckled herself in and promptly fell asleep again. Houston blinked. He tried to avoid using one of the stimulants he carried in his bag. He was leery of its effect on his artificial heart-lung capacitor.

By the time they reached the outskirts of the port city, he was exhausted. Thirty-two hours without sleep, and he was going to drop. He turned in at a hostel with a vacancy sign. A traveler's inn, it was the kind of place businessmen and families frequented.

After getting everything from the aircar, they entered the room, which looked clean and comfortable. She flipped on the entertainment console.

He showered and looked around the room. The sun was

setting, and the street lights had come on, but the moon wasn't up. He was hungry enough to eat the pillow instead of sleeping on it. There were two choices: they could go to a restaurant or see what delivery options were available.

"Are we going to eat?"

"Yes, I'm starved," he answered. He looked from the window at the nearby buildings. "There's a place to eat at the end of the parking lot that looks open. We can walk there."

She ran a brush through her wig to adjust it, then added color to her lips and smiled. "Let's go."

They walked across the parking lot. Houston noted a mixture of vehicles: some simple ground transport, some air cars, and even a fancy air cruiser. The cruiser looked out of place at the inn. He made a note of it before he followed Beliani into the small restaurant. The smell of the spicy food sent waves of hunger twirling in his stomach.

Smoke from an open-flame roaster mixed with the smell of ale and spices. A man in bright robes and sashes was carving slices off three or four sides of meat. "Welcome. Do you prefer inside or outside seating?"

"Inside, please," said Beliani. Her tongue teased her top lip. Her eyes were sparkling with anticipation.

The server explained that the restaurant served four meats plus a choice of roast fowl or a nice fish stew.

"I'll have the roast jerney, inside meat please," she said. "What comes with it?"

"All meals come with the family vegetable sides, dark bread, and spice cake." The server looked at Houston.

"I'll take the Emperor's feast." He ordered the plate that featured all four meats and as much as he could drink of the house blue ale. One thing he could say about this planet—they knew their wines and ales. Some of the best in the seeded worlds came from Bengar.

They ate in companionable silence. The worst of their hunger sated, Beliani reached over and touched his arm. "Do you have a woman somewhere?"

A picture of Tegani's face and her smile flashed in his mind. He tensed. He had no right to let his thoughts go there. "Um, no, not really."

"Ha, your mouth says no; your face says yes. She is a lucky woman, I think." Beliani nibbled on her spice cake.

His cheeks heated. Maybe almost dying and spending so much time in rehab made him soft and vulnerable. Maybe he should take Beliani up on her not too subtle offer. Why couldn't he stop remembering Tegani and their kiss?

The heavy meal accentuated his fatigue, so they returned to the room in silence. The vehicle and the outside looked the same. He did a quick check, unlocked the door, then entered the room with a blaster drawn, just in case. After double-locking the door, he fixed a chair under the handle—nothing was getting in without a warning. The window was secure, but it wasn't blaster-proof. He sighed and crawled under the covers of his bed with his blaster loaded and handy.

A deep sleep engulfed him. A familiar dream gripped him with pain and fear. He saw the ambush and felt the impact of heavy blaster fire. There was a sound in the room, and he bolted awake with his blaster drawn. Morning light was filtering through the window curtains.

Beliani was awake and watching a news broadcast. Her face was pale. "My picture is on the news. Supposedly, I robbed the bar and shot someone. This is a joke. I own the bar."

"We'll be out of the Empire today. Hanoree must be getting desperate."

"I don't understand how he knew I ran."

"You said you were being watched. You were right." He began gathering his things.

They packed their few supplies and took out the airbus tickets. Their flight left in three hours. He checked the distance to the terminal. They could leave now and get breakfast there. Beliani was surprised that the car was gone.

He was less concerned about the air car because he knew the best way to keep from being located was to change vehicles and locations often. It was standard League procedure in situations like this.

An air cab drove up, and there was a knock at the door. "You ordered a transport taxi?"

"Yes, thank you, we're ready to leave." Houston said nothing to indicate their final destination.

When they arrived at the terminal, he tipped the driver and shouldered their bags. The cab flew off. Beliani headed in the direction of food. Hot java, meat, and bread rolls were drawing a crowd to a small shop in the terminal. They bought meat rolls and settled in the waiting area.

Houston's gaze scanned every corner of the building and every person. Everything seemed fine. When the boarding call was given, they walked onto the airbus and took their seats. As they were departing, several security officers came into the loading area.

"Get down," Houston ordered.

One officer was looking up at the windows. His partner, holding what appeared to be a picture, talked to the ticket clerk. The clerk shook his head and pointed to a camera mounted on one wall.

Houston had made sure Beliani avoided a direct angle. The airbus engines began to whir. An officer motioned frantically; his superior waved him away. They were too low-level to know their real purpose or the importance of their quarry. The airbus lifted off, and Houston sighed in relief. Soon, they would leave the Empire behind.

The flight was uneventful. Beliani grew more excited the closer to their destination they traveled. It was a good feeling, and even Houston was able to relax and smile.

They were met at the terminal and whisked to a League safe house where the general was waiting for them. Houston smiled and shook hands with his friend and commander—former commander.

"Good job, Colonel." Evans nodded at Beliani. "It's good to meet you."

"Thank you, General, I am glad to be here."

"The League has done our part. I trust you have the proof with you."

She smiled and removed her necklace. There was a small key attached to the chain. It was the kind of key used to open a safe deposit box at a bank.

"What does the key open?" General Evans frowned.

"My man kept proof Hanoree hired him. He put it into the bank and gave me this key."

Houston felt a rush of anger and disbelief. His hands clenched into fists. "Why didn't you bring the evidence? Now someone will have to go back to the Imperial City."

"I couldn't get it. The bank wouldn't let me into the vault. He was going to have me added before they killed him."

"How do you know there is proof?"

Beliani shifted and looked at Houston. "I've seen it. He has pictures of his contact and the exchange of credits. He recorded a statement naming Hanoree, and he took one of the empress's earrings to prove he was in the palace." She withdrew a small box from her pocket. She opened it to reveal a diamond and sapphire earring. "This is the other one. They were gifts from the emperor."

"Why didn't you tell me this?" he demanded.

"Because you would have tried to get them, and I would

be dead."

"But we don't have the evidence," he continued.

"The general has the key, and the bank will have to open it for the League," Beliani said with confidence.

General Evans grimaced. "That isn't true. We would have to petition the Council of Nobles. Only they have the official authority to open the box."

"You can ask the Nobles to have it opened." Beliani pouted.

"In order to approach the Council of Nobles, we need to have evidence, something to warrant breaking bank laws. We will have to wait until the birth of the baby. If the paternity test is in our favor, we can produce the key, and that should put an end to Hanoree."

Houston shook his head. He had risked his life to get this woman out of the Empire, and the League wouldn't even take the key to the Council of Nobles. This was why he was a soldier, not a diplomat. Interplanetary politics be damned; murder was murder.

General Evans shrugged. "I know this isn't what we wanted. If we had proof in hand, the League could act directly."

Beliani panicked. "You are going to keep me safe, aren't you? Get me off Bengar until this is over."

"For the time being, you will stay here. Your testimony may be necessary to convict Lord Hanoree," General Evans replied.

"I'm not going back to the Empire. You can't make me testify before the Nobles. They'll have me executed."

"We're not going to let them hurt you. I said you may be needed to testify, not that you would. Now, if you don't have any more revelations, we're done."

General Evans turned to Houston. He handed him an envelope with his ID and a travel pass to the space hub. "Good job. You can go home to Earth and finish your rehabilitation there."

Houston frowned. "Sister Tegani and the girl are in danger. I'll go back and finish this mission."

"I thought you would say that." The general pulled another envelope from his pocket. "This will get you back to Sayeri's. Please don't destroy your communicator this time."

Twenty-Seven

With no communications, Tegani began to fear Houston was off planet, working on another mission for the League, or worse, captured or dead. She was sitting by an open window, enjoying a cool breeze, when he returned to Sayeri's estate.

Houston got off the delivery transport and walked up to the house. He was wearing a heavy robe, one he would never need in this climate.

"It's Houston!" Ninallia squealed and ran to meet him.

Sayeri came hurrying from her office.

Tegani's heartrate quickened. She straightened her robes and glanced in a mirror. Her hair was growing out and was braided in the traditional Sister style. It was surprising how such a small thing could be so important to her self-esteem. She couldn't help the way her breath caught when she saw Houston standing in the long corridor. She willed herself not to rush into his arms.

Ninallia's rush was something of a fast waddle. The young emperor was growing well.

"Look at you, little one, getting big." Houston laughed and swung Ninallia around. He stopped when he saw Tegani. Ninallia looked up and followed his gaze.

"She's missed you, too, more than me," she said. She stepped aside and let Houston get closer to Tegani. There was a shy, almost awkwardness to his approach.

Tegani could see his uncertainty and gave him a welcoming smile. She extended her arms toward him, and he took her into a crushing embrace.

He held the embrace longer than was proper. When he let her go, they were both breathing heavily.

"Well, let's let Houston come inside, ladies." Sayeri laughed.

She led them into the great room, where Ninallia settled in a large chair and put her feet up. Her ankles swelled at times. "Now tell us about your adventures in the Empire. Were you able to locate this woman who claims to be the assassin's wife?"

"Yes, she was in the bar. In fact, Beliani owns the place and acts as a bartender." He brought them up-to-date.

"That witch! She could have given you the key in the beginning." Ninallia growled. This was followed by laughter as she gasped and clutched her stomach. "The emperor agrees!"

Everyone laughed. Sayeri and Tegani filled Houston in on the news from the Temple City. Sayeri promised to let him see a pair of beautiful horses she purchased from the League Trade Commission. Several of her neighbors were successfully breeding the animals, though many Bengarians felt the animals were not worth the effort. Riding horseback was slow to catch on, and horse meat even less so. Horses were graceful and powerful as they galloped across the open grasslands. Tegani figured that was why beef cattle were more popular and practical. But she enjoyed watching the horses.

~ * ~

Houston's mouth watered as the smell of grilling steaks reached him. What a wonderful homecoming. He froze at the thought. Was this what a homecoming felt like? Why did he feel he was home? He looked at the three women who felt more like family than anyone had in a long time. How hard would it be when he left them to return to space?

The meal was one of the best. The Bengarian tubers were tasty, but he preferred Earth potatoes. Ninallia laughed, and Tegani looked happy. He ate more than usual, as evidenced by the tightness in his belt.

A piercing alarm sounded, and everyone jumped up from the table. The intruder alarm. Security sensors had been triggered by someone entering the estate without going through the checkpoint.

Houston bolted from his chair with a weapon in hand. Sayeri was on her communicator. The intruder had shown up like a blip on the sensors and then disappeared.

"You and Ninallia stay here," he told Tegani. "Lock this door, and don't open it for anyone."

Tegani took the small blaster he put in her hand. Ninallia was standing with her hands on her stomach, with tears streaming down her face.

Sayeri put her arm around the girl. "It's okay. It may not be anything."

The curtain shifted, and a figure stepped through the window. Houston whirled to fire. The trigger froze. He prepared to launch himself at the figure when Tegani called out. "Arturon, what are you doing here?"

The tableau froze.

Arturon bowed to Tegani. "Thank you, Sister, it's good to see you."

Puzzled, Houston lowered the blaster, thankful he hadn't fired. He knew of First Brother, Arturon. Houston bowed and extended his hand. "I'm glad to meet you, Brother."

Arturon bowed, then shook the proffered hand. "I regret my duplicity. It cannot be known I am here."

"Why are you here? My Lady is in danger. You should be there," Sayeri said.

"My Lady sent me because paternity must be verified as soon as the baby is born, and I am one of those authorized to handle royal paternity matters."

"You traveled all this way to verify the paternity before

Hanoree has time to dispute or destroy the evidence?"

Arturon looked at Sayeri and smiled. "Yes, My Lady has foreseen much trouble."

The door opened, and in ran young Peterno straight into his grandmother's arms. Everyone stopped as Sayeri comforted him.

Tegani's wide eyes looked from the child to Arturon. That caught Houston's attention. When he looked, he realized the resemblance was striking. Arturon glanced from the child to Sayeri. Utter confusion and amazement shone in his expression.

Tegani touched Houston's arm, nodding toward the door. Ninallia stood and followed him and Tegani, giving Sayeri and Arturon privacy.

~ * ~

Sayeri stroked her grandson's hair. She smiled at Arturon. "It's been a long time, Arturon. There are things I should have told you. Say hello to your grandson, Peterno."

Peterno looked up at Arturon with those uncannily similar eyes and smiled shyly. "Grandfather?"

"How?"

Sayeri motioned for Arturon to sit and explained, "I learned I was pregnant as soon as I got back to the Empire, and was in great disgrace when I refused to name you as the father. I couldn't because they would have ruined you. I knew I couldn't marry you and live in the Temple City, so I married Nabaro and came to live here. Our daughter, Hennina, was born, and Nabaro accepted her as his own."

She gave a shrug and sighed. "She inherited my wild nature and ran off to live with a trader, leaving me with Peterno."

The belated confession was spilled in such a matter of fact way that Arturon sat in silence. It was a shock to find the boy was his grandson, and he had a daughter he had never met. The revelation seemed to leave him dazed. Tears filled his eyes.

They'd been foolish youngsters in love long ago.

She walked to a portrait of a young girl standing next to a grape arbor. Their daughter. Hennina had Arturon's eyes, her mother's hair, and smile. The artist captured something of a wild nature in the portrait, as well as a love of life and kindness.

Arturon stared at the portrait. Sayeri put her arms around him from behind. Her body pressed against him, and her head leaned against his shoulder. "Please say you forgive me."

He turned Sayeri around and held her in his arms. He kissed her hair, then her lips. *Was it possible to find love again after so many years?*

Sayeri drew back. "We should let My Lady know you have arrived." She squeezed his hand and waited for him to contact My Lady.

My Lady responded quickly, her mental voice as clear and crisp as ever. *Arturon, we trust you had a safe journey. Is everyone well there?*

Yes, My Lady, it appears so. The girl is healthy, and the child appears to be growing inside her.

And Lady Sayeri? My Lady asked, a hint of irony in her voice.

Sayeri is well, My Lady. She sends her best wishes.

She is a brave woman, Arturon. Take care of them as best you can. What do you think of this League colonel?

He seems to be a good man. I sense honor and loyalty in him. He hesitated. *He loves Tegani or, so he believes.*

And what does our Sister feel?

She is in love, My Lady.

Oh dear, I did not foresee this.

Don't worry, I won't mention this to Tegani. Perhaps the colonel can be persuaded to become a permanent resident of Bengar.

"Arturon." Sayeri's voice called through the fog of his connection. "Tell My Lady goodbye and come to dinner."

Sayeri had never been respectful of rank or position.

~ * ~

Tegani sat on the wide veranda, moving the porch swing back and forth. Her thoughts echoed the pattern. It was understandable that the League and the Order would predicate their involvement on the birth of a true heir. There was no reason to automatically believe Ninallia. She could be a fraud, or Madama Ector could have been lying about which dumas carried the royal heir. Tegani didn't even want to imagine that scenario.

Seeing Arturon and Sayeri together brought other feelings. How sad they missed all those years together. What about her feelings for Houston? She was bound to Ninallia until this was resolved; then her loyalty was to the Order. Could she abandon her training and go with Houston?

"You look serious. Aren't you glad to see Arturon?" Ninallia joined her on the swing.

"Yes, I worry about My Lady," Tegani lied.

Too much was already apparent to Ninallia because of her abilities, and Tegani was not ready to share her personal feelings. She looked at the girl sitting next to her on the swing. Pregnancy made her face glow. She wondered if Ninallia realized how much her life would change if her son became emperor.

"Now you're worrying about me. I am too, but we must not let Hanoree get away with murder." Ninallia placed a hand on her stomach. "If I had known whose child I would carry, I don't know if I would have agreed to be a dumas." Her eyes narrowed. "Hanoree will get to my son over my dead body."

"You're looking and sounding fierce," laughed Tegani. There was something frightening about the sudden determination in Ninallia's eyes.

"I hate Hanoree. He killed my friends from the hostel. He is the reason Madama Ector is dead. My mother and aunt are…"

"They are quite safe," said Arturon, coming onto the

veranda and catching their conversation.

Ninallia squealed with joy and launched her rounded body at the senior Brother. He laughed and caught her in his arms. "We were able to get them to safety before Hanoree could act, if in fact he knows about them. They are under guard for the time being, and your mother is receiving medical attention and is doing well."

Tears of joy flowed down Ninallia's face. Tegani smiled and hugged her old mentor.

Clouds darkened the sky, so she suggested they go inside before the rain started.

Twenty-Eight

Hanoree was growing restless. The Council of Nobles refused to crown him emperor. The First Minister, a man Hanoree now considered an ally, spoke up for him. He counseled Hanoree to remain calm.

"You do not want to appear eager to take the throne. The Empire and the Council are in shock and in mourning. They are afraid to act. They do not wish to dishonor the late emperor, and neither should we."

Hanoree smiled. *Let the old fool think he will retain his position once I am crowned.*

Varick came into the room and stopped when he saw the First Minister, then bowed to both men.

"You will excuse us. My aide no doubt brings a list of household matters from my wife," Hanoree said.

The First Minister bowed and excused himself. Hanoree smiled and returned the bow. After the First Minister left, Hanoree turned to Varick. "The man's an old fool. I hate to depend on him to prod the Nobles into action."

"Yes, my Emperor," Varick commented in a dry tone. "I have been busy on your behalf. I believe I have news of the greatest importance. There has been communication between the Order and Lady Sayeri in the Kingdom of Madori. It seems she may be harboring our fugitive. This proves the Order was involved in her escape."

A white heat of anger engulfed Hanoree. He refused to let it take control. If he attacked a holding in Madori, its maniac ruler might unleash a terrible round of bombs. He stopped short of beginning the next Great War among the kingdoms. "I want someone inside the compound. I want the mother and child dead."

"It will be hard for Sayeri is not easily fooled. If you will leave it to me, I think I can find the right individual for the job."

"See that you do. I will take care of Sayeri later." The two men shared some wine. "Should I contact the old witch in the Temple City? I would love to see her face when I tell her I know where the fugitives are."

"Oh no, my Emperor, give my assassin a chance. Do not forewarn them," Varick said in an almost teasing manner.

Hanoree saw the wisdom and assented. "Have you heard anything said among the Nobles? Are there any rumors about me?"

"They worry you will be a stronger emperor than your uncle, and they are jealous of your power. The late emperor was too weak in his dealings with the Nobles." Varick refilled Hanoree's glass but added no drug.

Hanoree smiled and drained the glass. "What shall we provide our guests for entertainment tonight?"

"Something subdued. Remember, we are in mourning."

He chuckled, and Hanoree joined him until he and Varick were laughing like schoolboys sharing a dirty joke.

Twenty-Nine

Months passed, winter turned into the rainy season in the Southern Kingdom, marking the beginning of spring. Ninallia thought about the changes in her friends. Arturon and Sayeri had rekindled their romance. She could see the smiles and gentle touches they exchanged. Happiness gave a glow to Sayeri's face. Ninallia frowned. Houston and Tegani were still dancing around their feelings for each other.

Her due date was nearing, causing her to walk in slow, cumbersome steps. She was uncomfortable and eager to get the child born. To make matters worse, the nursery maid hired by Sayeri was unable to take the job. The replacement seemed like a nice girl, and she came with excellent references, but there was something solemn and almost sad about her. She was too quiet to suit Ninallia.

The rain slackened to a cool, damp mist. She decided to venture onto the veranda when a sharp pain nearly doubled her over. A flood of wetness ran between her legs. Sayeri had prepared her for this—her water had broken. She turned to go back in and slipped. She fell hard onto the stone floor of the veranda and cried out in pain.

Ninallia's call found someone, and her friends rushed to find her lying on the cold, wet stones of the veranda. They eased Ninallia to a sitting position, then the men gently lifted and carried her inside.

The healer arrived and examined her. "There are a few bruises, but nothing is broken. She's young, healthy, and is in the early stages of labor. The baby will be here soon." He smiled as he gave the good news.

"Praise the Spirits," Sayeri said.

Ninallia yelped in pain as contractions began. It was a long evening of waiting, pacing, pushing, and sweating with effort. Before dawn, the new emperor was born.

"He's beautiful," Tegani sighed.

"All babies are beautiful," Sayeri added.

Beaming, Ninallia held her son as Arturon drew the necessary material for a paternity test.

He assured them, "The late emperor's information is on file in both the Bengarian and League databases. I've uploaded the data from the sample, and now we wait for the results."

~ * ~

"What do they mean by a week?" Ninallia fumed. "It cannot take longer than a day or two."

"Of course not, if we want to alert Hanoree to the fact that the child has been born. The tests are being run secretly, and the results will be sent to us by an indirect route. Have patience, dear girl. We are almost at the end of this journey."

A week came and went with no word on the test results. Ninallia recovered, and Hiroto was eating, sleeping, and growing as babies were meant to do. The nursery maid shared the duties, giving Ninallia time to rest. She insisted on having the crib in her bedroom, so her son could sleep near.

It was the middle of the second week. The nursery maid brought a warm cup of tea and milk for Ninallia. "You drink this, and I'll get the baby ready for bed."

"Thank you, Dorna." Ninallia placed the squirming infant in the nurse's hands, and he was soon settled in his crib.

"Goodnight, Miss Ninallia," said Dorna as she closed the door.

Ninallia had finally started warming up to Dorna, and their relationship had turned companionable. Ninallia started to drink the tea, and a sudden fit of sneezing caused her to spill it. Dorna would insist on fixing her another cup, and the nurse needed her own rest. Hiroto seemed to thrive on keeping everyone busy.

Ninallia got up long enough to take off the wet covers and remake the bed, then tried to sleep.

It wasn't long before she heard a sound. She froze as Dorna slipped back into Ninallia's room. "Shush, baby, this won't hurt a bit," Dorna crooned.

"What are you doing?" Ninallia cried in alarm.

Dorna drew a knife from her pocket. "Don't make a sound. Stay there, or I'll use the knife, and it won't be painless."

"Dorna, why?" In horror, she watched as Dorna used a thumb to open the vial.

"There can only be one emperor; Hanoree is our emperor. Anyone else will lead to a civil war." She tilted the vial down to the infant's mouth.

"No!" Ninallia screamed as she lunged toward Dorna and fell.

A dark figure crashed through the window and wrestled the knife from her hand. Houston pushed her to the floor. She scrambled for the vial and swallowed the liquid. Within seconds, a strange look appeared on her face, and her hands flew to her throat. She died quickly.

The commotion woke the others, and soon they were crowded into Ninallia's room, staring in disbelief at Dorna's body.

"I can't believe this. I've known Lady Kittel for many years, and she recommended Dorna." Sayeri was beside herself with anger and grief. She stared at the infant. "At least he is unharmed, thank the Spirits."

"Apparently Hanoree's hands extend even here," Arturon said.

Ninallia was rocking Hiroto and crying. She could not

stop. After catching her breath, she asked. "How did you know?"

"You called me. I heard you say *Houston, I need you. The window. Hurry*. I got a picture of what was happening, and I came in through the window."

"Amazing, she can send to non-gifted people," Arturon observed.

"Thank the Spirits," said Sayeri. "I think we need to get some sleep and decide on a new plan of action in the morning."

Ninallia agreed but wasn't sure she'd sleep.

~ * ~

Tegani slept fitfully. It was evident Hanoree knew where Ninallia was hiding. He had known long enough to arrange for that stupid girl to kill the baby. Tegani shuddered, remembering how close the woman had come to succeeding. When the first light of morning began to peek through the window, she got up.

Sayeri and Arturon were in the kitchen at the small table, drinking a hot beverage. Houston was sleeping on the floor near Ninallia's bed and Hiroto's crib.

"Morning, Sister. Brother," Tegani said as she poured her own cup.

She and the others were somber. She couldn't stop remembering how narrowly they had escaped disaster and how lucky they were that the heir and Ninallia were both alive and well.

"Do you think Hanoree is the reason the paternity test is delayed?" Sayeri asked.

"We must assume so. I foresaw something like this and sent multiple samples under different names. We will receive the results we need in time." Arturon looked older this morning. The troubled night showed on his face and the way he held himself. His usual ramrod straight posture was slightly stooped.

"I think it is time to take the fight to Hanoree," said Tegani. She had given this much thought in the sleepless night. "What if we make our case publicly? We don't have to accuse Hanoree. We can present Ninallia's son as emperor. Make the announcement public."

"Why not make sure the whole planet is watching?" Houston came into the room. Behind him, a pale Ninallia carried Hiroto.

"Can you do that?" asked Tegani.

"I think Interplanetary Governor Bashari can make it happen," he answered.

"My Lady can persuade the nine kingdoms to broadcast the news. With the rest of Bengar watching, Hanoree can hardly suppress the broadcast." Arturon began to show signs of his usual strong nature.

"Has anyone stopped to think we don't have any paternity results, and we may not get them anytime soon?" Ninallia asked.

"Hanoree doesn't know that. We will proceed as if the results are in and we have them in hand. It's bluffing, but it's the best chance of getting our little emperor before the Council of Nobles alive."

"I agree," said Arturon. "If we declare ourselves, any friends we have on the council will have to step up or prove their cowardly natures."

"Do we have any friends on the council?" Ninallia asked.

"There are many who served Emperor Rhealgar, and they may choose to support his son instead of Hanoree. They must guess or suspect he was behind the murders." Sayeri put an arm around Ninallia.

"Let's get it arranged. I'll contact My Lady, and Houston can contact the League," Arturon said, standing and heading for the door.

"I think I should let Lord Ellino know what we're doing. He deserves a heads up." Sayeri hurried out.

"Courage, ladies. This is what we have been working for,"

said Houston.

The broadcast was shown planet-wide and relayed to every world in the League.

Thirty

The public announcement spread throughout the Empire and the many kingdoms. There was an immediate uproar. All discussion of crowning Hanoree was dropped by the Council of Nobles, and they argued over what this could mean for the Empire.

Hanoree's face loomed in Sayeri's communication screen. The conversation was also shown on another screen where Arturon, Houston, Tegani, and Ninallia watched unseen.

Hanoree began, "Of course, we will welcome the baby if he is proven to be the legitimate heir. I will be happy to serve him. I am astounded you have waited to inform us you have been hosting the baby and his mother."

"Lord Hanoree, given the deaths of the late empress and emperor, it cannot be surprising. Have you solved their murders?" Sayeri smiled into the screen.

Red rose to Hanoree's cheeks. "I can guarantee we are doing everything to apprehend those responsible, and as guardian and regent pro-tem, safety will be my first concern."

No trace of shock or dismay showed on Sayeri's face, though she was feeling both. How could those stupid Nobles have been reckless enough to let Hanoree protect the child? Having Hanoree serve as the guardian was as good as signing the child's death warrant. There would be nothing traceable.

An accident or illness would befall the child. "Congratulations, Hanoree. I had not heard of your appointment."

"You've long distanced yourself from court, Sayeri. You cannot be current of what is happening here."

Sayeri raised one elegant eyebrow. "What do you propose

as guardian?"

"I decree you should bring the heir to the Imperial Palace at once, where I can oversee his safety." Hanoree smiled benignly.

"I will see that your suggestion is taken into consideration," Sayeri answered, lowering her eyes demurely.

"Taken into consideration by whom?" demanded Hanoree.

She was astounded at his cluelessness. "To his mother's consideration, of course, Hanoree. She has custodial rights and control of the infant for the first eighteen months. I have been away from court, but I know the law."

"The girl is no Dowager Empress! The empress died with her husband." Hanoree virtually exploded.

She sighed and continued, her tone chiding, trying to explain to a reluctant school boy. "Hanoree, has your education been lacking? The Dowager Empress is defined as the mother of an emperor. The emperor's mother is here and well. I will consult her and present your position."

Hanoree sputtered and huffily ended the call.

Sayeri, who made her own recording of the communication, laughed and turned away. It was a small victory.

"Let's keep him wondering a bit longer. I'm sure he is researching the qualifications for a Dowager Empress. There has never been a surrogate mother in the royal line. Technically, Ninallia is the biological mother, as the empress did not have a viable egg for fertilization," Arturon said. "I can use that when I present her to the council as his regent."

They put Hanoree off for three days. Ignoring his fuming and demands that they turn over the infant emperor. They agreed for a conversation between Hanoree and Ninallia to take place. Sayeri altered one of her finest dresses to fit Ninallia for the transmission. Her hairdresser was brought in, and soon Ninallia was almost unrecognizable. She looked like an elegant vision in lace, diamonds, and pearls. She was every inch the empress in her splendor. The girl's court posture and manner, practiced for months, was on display, her bearing regal.

~ * ~

Hanoree was stunned when he was greeted by Ninallia. She looked nothing like a girl from the slums who sold her body as a surrogate. Still, he bowed. "We have been awaiting your decision. I must tell you, it is for the safety of the child I am concerned. "When can we expect you to turn him over?"

Ninallia brought one finely manicured hand to her breast. "I will not turn over my child to anyone. I will accompany him to the Imperial Palace."

"Of course, we await your arrival." Hanoree smiled.

"As you wish. When will my escort arrive?"

"Escort?" What was she up to?

"Is it customary for an emperor to travel without an Imperial escort?"

Hanoree recovered. "Of course, I shall arrange to travel to meet you."

"I prefer to choose my own escort. The First Minister and Lord Nebron will be sufficient. You need not exert yourself. I am sure you will be too busy conducting matters of the Empire."

At this nod to his authority, Hanoree smiled. The girl wasn't going to dispute his guardianship beyond insisting she get a chance to live in the Imperial Palace for a bit. Perhaps he could even marry her to his son after the baby met its inevitable accident. Perhaps he would make her his mistress.

"As you wish, I will arrange the escort as soon as the First Minister and Lord Nebron are available."

"Thank you, Lord Hanoree." Ninallia inclined her head in a small bow.

It was the bow one extended to an inferior at court. If he responded with an equally small bow, he would be seen as assuming too much. He hesitated, then gave a deeper bow.

~ * ~

When the communication ended, Tegani and Sayeri congratulated Ninallia on her performance.

"Now, if the paternity test will just come in." Tegani was worried. If Hanoree could use his private army to surround the Temple City, he could destroy a report. How long would it take?

She and the others gave a collective sigh of relief when a messenger arrived carrying the results the next day. He explained there was no safe way to send the results electronically, so he volunteered to deliver them by hand. The results were on a data chip, and the certification was both digital and hard copy.

Arturon did the honors of opening and reading the results. No one doubted the results would be positive, but seeing the official proof was exhilarating.

Ninallia's eyes filled with tears. Tegani was happy Madama had not lied to her. Her son, Hiroto, was the true emperor. A small part of Tegani wished it weren't so. Any chance of a normal childhood for them was gone. Their lives would belong to the Empire.

"Courage, child, life at court will not be all bad." Sayeri put her hand on Ninallia's shoulder. "There will be parties, and the palace is grand."

"I think we should do a family history on Ninallia. There are those at court who will be doing one as soon as her identity is revealed. The historians will do the research," said Arturon. "You can be sure others will seek anything on her ancestry they can use to challenge her authority as regent."

Ninallia laughed. "I grew up hearing my mother say we were almost Nobles. Her family came from the eastern province of the Empire, like the empress."

"It was the reason Madama Ector chose you. You have the same coloring as the empress." Arturon replied. He found the communication terminal and began to key in information.

Ninallia gave him her parents' names and her grandparents' names and even one great-grandmother she recalled meeting as a very small child. The biological wars that occurred twice in the last two hundred years made genetic and hereditary information vital, and genetic databases were extensive.

Soon Arturon whistled. "I never imagined we would find this."

He told them that in the last century, the Emperor Hapirion ruled the Empire during a time of great expansion. He was something of a womanizer, having several mistresses, including one Noble lady in the Eastern province. She was a young widow and never lived at court. She bore a child long after her husband died, and there were rumors that he was the emperor's bastard son. He received royal favors until the emperor died. When the emperor died, and his heir took the throne, the young man's fortunes took a turn for the worse, and he was soon almost penniless.

"What does that mean?" Ninallia asked.

"It means your mother carried the emperor's blood. And she was also related to the empress."

Tegani laughed. Sometimes life took twists and turns. The many times great-granddaughter of a royal bastard was now a Dowager Empress. "So, when do we release this?"

Hiroto began to cry in the next room. Without a nursemaid, Ninallia and Sayeri scampered to tend him.

Tegani smiled. Hiroto was a handsome child with Ninallia's eyes and his father's strong features.

Thirty-One

"My Emperor, it would not be hard to arrange an accident on the journey to the Imperial City." Varick stood uncomfortably in Hanoree's presence. His assassin failed, and now Sayeri and the Order declared the child as the true heir.

"How could we arrange this with Lord Nebron and the First Minister in attendance? Your grasp of the situation is slipping." Hanoree glared at him.

"There are undetectable poisons," Varick offered.

"Okay, we will try your plan. I will arrange for you to be in the entourage. You will take care of this personally. In the meantime, I will prepare plan B in case you fail."

"What is plan B?" He dared not balk at Hanoree's plan. He would have to do this job himself.

"We have the Temple City surrounded, and I have hired mercenaries to reinforce our position. We will take the city and kill My Lady of Wisdom and her First Brother."

This seemed like a futile mission to Varick, but he did not question Hanoree. He saw no benefit in starting a war with the Order. It would gain them nothing, but he would continue to follow Hanoree's commands and reap the benefits.

~ * ~

Ninallia straightened in her chair. The dress and ornaments Sayeri insisted were necessary for her first meeting with the Empire's escort draped on her, heavy and artificial. Anxiety and perspiration were hidden by layers of cosmetics, perfumes, and fabric. Her son lay in the bassinet beside her, sleeping peacefully. She struggled to smile as the guests were introduced.

Sayeri had warned Ninallia that Lord Varick was among the escorts, but the sight of him filled her with a mixture of fear and rage. She smiled at the stricken look on his face when Arturon stood beside her and read the results of the paternity test. In his League uniform, Houston hovered on her other side.

"This is outrageous," sputtered Varick, looking at the First Minister seemingly for support. "By what authority has this child been tested without Imperial edict? The Order is forbidden to insert itself in Imperial matters."

Sayeri stepped forward. Ninallia waved her hand to signal her to stop. "By my authority as Dowager Empress and great-great-granddaughter of Emperor Hapirion, I have authorized this and transmitted these results along with those of my own bloodline to the Noble houses in the Empire and the twelve kingdoms."

"As half-sister and the closest blood kin of the late empress, I approved the test," Sayeri added.

The First Minister shook his head. "As head of the Council of Nobles, I was informed and agreed to the test. Perhaps you have forgotten who holds that position."

All color drained from Varick's face. Confusion and anger registered. "You betrayed the Emperor."

"Hanoree is not the emperor. He expressed his desire that the paternity of this child be established, and I have done so. Do you doubt the veracity of the First Brother or the testing center?" The First Minister's icy tone did not appear to be lost on Varick or the others present.

Bowing in deference, Varick stepped back behind the other guests. Ninallia inclined her head. Hanoree would be outraged over these developments. More importantly, her son's paternity was established and could not be disputed.

The First Minister made a formal bow, then took Ninallia's hand and kissed it. She almost gasped in surprise as something was slipped into her palm. She lowered her arm to her side and slipped the data chip into a fold of her dress.

The First Minister turned to his entourage and said, "Sayeri has graciously provided us accommodations in her guest quarters. Let's take the opportunity to rest. We will leave for the Imperial City tomorrow."

Ninallia did not rise as the visitors departed. Her legs felt too weak, and she didn't want to draw attention to the small data chip. Her heart did not slow until the last member of her official escort had exited the room and the doors closed. Without a word, she handed the chip to Houston.

He put it into a small viewer and projected it onto the table before him. It was in code. He frowned and looked from Tegani to Arturon.

Arturon was smiling and nodding as he read the message. "This is good news indeed." He explained, "This is very old code taught only at the Temple City. The First Minister's wife was an acolyte. This is a list of the Nobles and their loyalty. He thinks we have a chance if we can prove Hanoree's involvement in the deaths of the emperor and empress."

Ninallia scooped up her son from the bassinet and swung him in her arms.

"This is not all good news. It means Hanoree will be more determined to prevent the royal heir from reaching the city," Sayeri cautioned. "He is not stupid."

Ninallia held her son. This started as a means to save her family financially, now she loved Hiroto beyond measure. She would do anything to protect him.

Sayeri slipped an arm around Ninallia and placed a kiss on Hiroto's small head. "We won't let anything happen to either of you."

~ * ~

Hanoree dismissed his servants, except for the guards outside his chamber. Varick would be reporting soon. The news that the child had been tested and confirmed as the heir of the late emperor hit the Council of Nobles like a bomb. It had been strategically timed and widely distributed, which meant there was no way to contain it. This report would confirm who was behind the support for this child.

A soft pinging alerted him that Varick was reporting in. Hanoree turned on his monitor. Varick twitched with nervous energy. The man knew his life was forfeit if he failed.

"The First Minister is a traitor. He is behind this attempt or at least aiding the Order." The words sounded as if Varick were pleading for his life.

Hanoree clenched his fist. He had not given the old man enough credit. "He will not live long. Who else was present?"

Varick relaxed. "I managed to have the whole meeting taped. You will see for yourself that the Order is behind this. The First Brother himself confirmed the paternity. There was also a member of the League."

Hanoree blinked, and he took in a deep breath. This was unexpected. His communications with the League were ongoing and seemed positive. The ambassador must have been lying. He pushed down his anger and signaled for Varick to play the footage from the meeting. The tape was made by one of the minors in the escort party. The angle was not good, but it was adequate for Hanoree to recognize Arturon and Sayeri.

His jaw twitched. He would pay back both with a vengeance. The view shifted to the young woman sitting beside a bassinet.

An idea began to bloom in Hanoree's fertile imagination. If he married this girl, it would solidify his right as the regent. It was an absurd plan. His children were her age. There was also the matter of his wife. Lady Hanoree was his senior by a few years and had brought quite a large dowry and social clout to him when they married. Without her family connections, he would never have amassed his fortune. She was, however, showing her age. She could perhaps suffer a deadly illness or an unfortunate accident. A young wife and more children could be a good thing.

He shook his head. He was being foolish. There would be nothing wrong with appearing to welcome both the baby and his mother.

Hanoree strode to the long mirror in one corner of the room, which was also a secret viewing panel. It allowed him to watch anyone waiting for an audience and listen to their conversations. He studied his reflection. A man of average height, with a head full of hair and good teeth that could pass for a younger man. There was much a young, impressionable girl might admire in him. Taking a small amount of his calming drug, he rang for the Minister of Protocol.

When the small, elegantly clad man entered, he bowed fractionally. Hanoree did not miss the insult but schooled his features into a gracious smile. He began almost apologetically, "I am afraid I must ask your favor and rely on you for guidance."

The minister preened and relaxed. "I am at your service, Lord Hanoree."

Hanoree smiled and continued, "The infant has been confirmed as the son of my late uncle, Emperor Rhealgar. An escort will be bringing the heir and his mother to the Imperial City soon. I feel some sort of celebration is in order, but we are in mourning. I need your wisdom. We must honor the heir without offending."

The minister's head bobbed. "Lord Hanoree, set your mind at ease. Even the strictest of society will not find fault with a celebration in such a circumstance; the people will demand it."

"You will oversee this for me? Invite the Nobles. Make sure they know this will not be an official recognition of the heir. The Council of Nobles will, of course, decide if he will be declared emperor."

"I will be honored, my lord." The minister's face was alight with anticipation.

"Good, check with the Minister of the Treasury for funding. Do not spare any expense. I will rely on you also to prepare the royal nursery and a suitable bedchamber for his mother."

The minister bowed. He was eager to be off, and Hanoree dismissed him with a motion of his hand. He smiled as the door to the chamber closed. Soon, the palace and the city would be aware of his gracious preparation for the new heir. Now for the unpleasant task of informing his wife that she would not be attending the festivities.

Thirty-Two

Tegani sat beside Ninallia in a private compartment on the air transport. Her hair had grown, although not to its previous length. She wore nothing to identify her as a Sister of the Order. She still felt the shame of losing her standing, though she knew it was necessary and temporary. A Sister of the Order would hardly be allowed to serve as lady-in-waiting to the Dowager Empress.

She had promised to stay with Ninallia and continue her training. The girl's skill and ability gave hope that she would be a formidable regent should she be allowed to rule for her son until his coming of age.

Sayeri sat opposite them, next to Hiroto. She had been reluctant to leave her home but considered it important to help Ninallia. Her grandson lay sleeping with his head on her lap. Tegani nodded to the young boy, and a smile passed between them. He was the spitting image of Arturon. One day, he might even possess some of his grandfather's abilities.

There had been a disagreement about the transport. Houston had not been pleased that he was assigned to a different transport. He ended up in a different compartment along with the First Minister and Varick. Arturon was making his own way to the Imperial City.

Tegani was nervous to be without the presence of Houston or Arturon, though Houston was in an adjoining compartment. There was something she did not trust. A strange feeling of danger tensed her body, and she could not rest. She watched the others close their eyes, and the gentle motion of the transport finally lulled her.

Sister Tegani, can you hear me?

Stiff with fear, Tegani sat up. She recognized at once the mental voice of Arturon.

Tegani, you must get the emperor and Ninallia out of your compartment now. There is great danger.

She was on her feet. Ninallia was alert and picking up her son. The girl's ability to hear even those messages directed to others was uncanny. Sayeri gathered her grandson.

Tegani said, "We need to get into another compartment."

Sayeri reached the door and found it locked. Shifting Peterno, she banged on the door calling for the guards. She pulled the emergency switch. The pilot ignored the sound. This time, she kicked the door. Tegani tried the back door, but it was also locked. She caught the scent of gas. Oh Spirits.

They must hurry. Tegani did not know what kind of lock or what kind of gas they were facing. Concentrating, she focused on the ventilation system. If she could vent the gas into the exhaust, it would become harmless outside the transport. This would mean they would be cold, though.

She began to work, seeing the system in her mind even as she said, "Get the blankets and heavy robes. We will need them."

The gas smell lessened. Tegani marveled that the gas was so easily detectable. Why not an odorless gas? She realized it was meant to be detected, and perhaps Hanoree meant for it to be traced back to the Order. How, she was not certain, but she understood why. He was going to blame their deaths on the Order and launch a full-scale war. She shivered. The temperature was falling inside the compartment. Now that the gas had dissipated, she located the path to the locking system and released the back door. It hissed open, letting in warmer, fresh air.

The startled expression on the faces of the guards transmitted their guilt. The men started to draw their weapons. The mind-scream Ninallia emitted momentarily stunned them as it would anyone who could not normally receive.

Tegani slammed her fist into the face of one guard and kicked the other hard in the groin. Weapons went flying, and Sayeri picked one up and aimed it at the men. She looked from Ninallia to Tegani. Tegani nodded in Ninallia's direction, and a look of understanding passed between them.

"Who put you up to this?" Sayeri demanded.

The men were silent. If they knew who hired them, they were not going to reveal the information.

The air transport train began its descent. After Tegani tied the men up, she joined Ninallia and Lady Sayeri in the main compartment. She adjusted the system back to normal, and the heating system warmed them fast.

If the pilot and co-pilot were surprised to discover their passengers were alive, they hid it well. Guards were summoned to take the assassins into custody. The delay heightened the frenzy of the crowds gathered to welcome the baby emperor.

Ninallia clutched her son to her body and walked behind Houston. With thousands of people here, there was no way to prevent another attempt on their lives. Imperial security formed a barrier around the party. Tegani relaxed a fraction, but Hiroto whimpered—he was likely hungry. Through the crowd, she heard a voice calling. Someone was trying to part the crowd to reach them.

~ * ~

As a man approached, Ninallia recognized Hanoree from the news. He looked very excited to see them. It was hard to imagine him killing the emperor and empress. Smiling affectionately, he hurried to her and swept her a bow so low his hat brushed the ground.

"Greetings, cousin." He cooed at the baby in her arms. His hand brushed her arm and rested there a little too long. "You must be tired." He waved his hand to summon a young woman dressed in a servant's clothes. "Baski can take the baby. The palace nursery has been set up."

"Thank you, Hanoree. My nurse is here with us." She handed the baby to Tegani and laid her hand on Hanoree's arm to lessen the insult.

Together they walked toward the palace. She could feel Tegani behind her, but Ninallia didn't dare to use any mind communication. Hanoree must not suspect Tegani was a Sister of the Order or that she was a secret acolyte. He continued to chatter as they walked along. Did he think Ninallia was stupid? He had tried to have her son killed twice. She would never trust him or give him an opportunity to harm them again.

She remained on guard. The luxury and beauty of the palace should have made her stare in wonder, but she barely noticed. She followed Hanoree down hall after hall until he stopped with a flourish and opened the door to the royal nursery. It was indeed lovely, with everything a child could want or need.

"Where are my rooms?" She walked around examining the crib and small bed for the nurse.

"I thought you would like a room in the empress's wing. Not the royal apartment, of course, until after the coronation." He smiled. "Something with a lovely view of the gardens, perhaps?"

She walked over and opened the door to an adjacent room. It was furnished comfortably but was not in the grand manner as the rest of the palace. A large bookcase contained a collection of schoolbooks. The royal tutor's room. Unused for many years, it was spacious and comfortable-looking. "I think this will suit me well. If you will send for someone to set this in order, I will be most grateful."

"This room is not adequate for someone of your status," Hanoree sputtered. After a few minutes of her silent refusal to change her mind, he ordered the rooms be made ready.

"I think I would like my old rooms, if they are available,"

said Sayeri. "They're not far from these rooms. It's a quiet part of the palace."

His face twisted as if he were swallowing something unpleasant. "Of course, Sayeri."

~ * ~

Hiroto was sleeping in Tegani's arms as Ninallia followed Hanoree to inspect the other room. Tegani shifted the baby. He didn't wake as they waited for his mother. She wished Houston were here to judge the accommodations and guard them. There must be something she could do to get him permission to join them.

There was a hot flush of anger on Ninallia's face as they entered the room.

"If you will excuse me, I will see to the arrangements and check on dinner." Hanoree bowed and left.

Sayeri turned as Hanoree left the room. "He acts as if this is his palace and we are guests. The late emperor didn't trust Hanoree, and the empress despised him. How he struts around here as if he owns the whole palace is sickening."

Tegani blinked in astonishment at Sayeri's vehemence. The late empress's half-sister had seemed indifferent to what was happening in the royal palace and very content with her life away from court.

"He told me Houston may not join us." Ninallia took Hiroto and paced.

"We must stay on guard," Tegani commented. She wished she could talk to My Lady. Ninallia and her son were both in danger, and she felt inadequate to protect them. She thanked the Spirits for Sayeri and Houston.

"I think I know someone who may help," Sayeri said in a hesitant tone. Her voice was soft, as if she doubted her own idea. She did not volunteer anything else.

A slow smile came to Ninallia's face. "After I demanded to

question the Council of Nobles as to why a royal guest and possible Dowager Empress would be denied a personal bodyguard, he backed down. He offered one of his own guards. I refused."

Sayeri clapped her hands. "Very good, child, stand up to him. It is better to let him know right away that he cannot run over you. You are the Dowager Empress, and if I have anything to say about it, you will act as regent for your son."

"In this place, the walls have ears," cautioned Tegani.

This brought a nod of agreement from Lady Sayeri. The women were united in their quest to put Ninallia's son on the emperor's throne.

A small chime sounded, and Sayeri turned toward the door. A young maid stood in the entrance. She bowed toward Ninallia. "A meal is being prepared, and Lord Hanoree has sent me to care for your son while you and the others join him in the royal dining room."

Sayeri stepped forward. "There is no need. I am much too tired from travel to endure a formal meal. I will stay with Hiroto. Ninallia and Tegani can enjoy Hanoree's company." There was a definite mocking tone to her voice.

The girl looked down in embarrassment. Ninallia touched her arm. "Please tell Lord Hanoree I will be pleased to join him."

Once the girl left, Ninallia glanced from Tegani to Sayeri. She looked as tired as Tegani felt. "Must I dress formally for this dinner?" Ninallia asked.

"I'm afraid so," Sayeri answered.

There wasn't much time to dress, and many of their things were not unpacked.

"Both of you get yourselves bathed," she continued. "I will find something suitable for you to wear."

Ninallia eased herself into the bath and washed her hair. Tegani sat beside Hiroto's cradle, singing as she rocked him back and forth. As Ninallia stepped out, there was a commotion as

Sayeri returned with a group of women and several servants carrying bags. Wrapped in a towel, Ninallia froze. The two women walked around her, touching her wet hair and appraising her.

"Lovely skin," commented one woman holding up a purple ribbon next to Ninallia's face.

"Too thin," fretted another.

Sayeri laughed and introduced the woman who oversaw the late empress's wardrobe.

The older woman bowed. "I have two gowns that might serve. You are lucky they are ready ahead of time, and Lady Vasto has not picked them up."

Ninallia was soon dressed in a blue gown. The seamstress made a few tucks at the waist. "Be careful, this is a temporary alteration."

Tegani was clothed in a beautiful, if less ornate, silver gown, and her hair curled around her face artfully.

Sayeri clapped her hands in delight. "You are two beautiful women."

Tegani and Ninallia were escorted to the dining room. Tegani noticed Hanoree glowering as she and Ninallia entered the dining room in regal splendor. Ninallia was every inch the picture of a young empress. During the dinner, her manners were impeccable.

Hanoree must be furious if his sources had assured him the girl was raised in poverty in a low-class neighborhood. She appeared so calm and self-assured, and her coloring and bearing were like the late empress. Tegani didn't think even the strongest detractors would find little fault with her appearance or behavior.

Thirty-Three

In the dining room, Tegani and the others were finishing when alarms cut through the air. Startled, she looked across at Hanoree. His face showed shock and confusion. Either he was an accomplished actor, or he was as surprised as she was. Ninallia was demanding to be taken back to her room.

"Calm down, it can't be anything to do with the baby," Tegani said.

"Sayeri is sending screams of distress," Ninallia answered.

At a run, Tegani followed Ninallia back to their rooms. Hanoree and his personal guard were behind them.

A nervous Imperial lieutenant stood in the hallway. He bowed to Ninallia and spoke to Hanoree. "The child is missing. Sayeri's guards said no one came in or out. We will have to review the surveillance tapes and see if there are any secret entrances to the suite."

Tegani tried to comfort Ninallia. She paced back and forth, gulping in breaths of air and wiping away tears. Sayeri, whose face was drained of color, stood in shock. After a few minutes, Tegani picked up on the message. By the slack look on Sayeri's face, she heard too. Ninallia was broadcasting at an unbelievable level. Anyone with the least bit of talent and training from the Order would hear, and not just here in the Imperial City. Her ability might extend planet-wide.

Arturon's connection broke through to Tegani and Sayeri. It was followed soon by My Lady herself. "Sisters, you must be calm. I do not think the child has been harmed. Hanoree does not want anything to happen to Hiroto under his care. If he has

Hiroto, he has some plan to use the child as a bargaining tool."

Guards announced the arrival of Houston, who gaped at Ninallia. He moved next to Sister Tegani and whispered, "I heard her in my head, much stronger this time. I think the League picked up the signals. They and the Order have issued a planet-wide alert."

"The Order is behind this." Hanoree glowered. "I will convene the Council of Nobles, and we will demand the child be returned."

Sayeri started to speak when Ninallia held up her hand. The softness and insecurity of her youth were stripped away. A young mother, barely more than a child herself, she stood, a woman of steel, and turned to face Hanoree. "I don't think this is the time for groundless accusations."

He took a step back and bowed deferentially. She motioned to Houston. "This is my head of security, Colonel Houston. I assure you he is impartial and independent. He has my total trust and will be in control of the search for my son. I want him to have access to those recordings and anything else he needs to do his job. I also want him to vet a security team to take over my personal safety."

"Only Imperial security is allowed to operate inside the Palace," Hanoree answered.

"That was not a request. It is my right and decree as Dowager Empress, acting as regent for my son."

Sayeri glanced at Tegani. Ninallia was not trained in Imperial law, but My Lady was. She must be guiding the girl through their mental link. Until such a time as the Council of Nobles met and decreed otherwise, Ninallia was, by Imperial law, his regent. Tegani bit back a smile.

Ninallia wasn't done with Hanoree. She fixed him with a look stern enough to have done an ancient dowager justice. "Since my son and I were placed in your protection, cousin, I hold you responsible for his safe return. I expect your complete cooperation with Colonel Houston. Is that clear?"

A small group of Nobles made their way into the room. From the looks on the faces of several, they were enjoying seeing Lord Hanoree being taken down a peg. One elderly Noble went to one knee. "My Lady, as a representative of the Council of Nobles, I offer you my support."

It was an oath of fealty from the Empire's largest and most powerful province. Hanoree sputtered as he failed to find words to express the disbelief in his eyes.

Tegani listened as Ninallia followed My Lady's focused instructions. Inside, the girl must be a mass of raw nerves. The support of My Lady and countless other followers of the Order gave them both inner strength.

~ * ~

Ninallia buried her head in Houston's shoulder while Tegani paced the room, and Sayeri, still in shock, stared into space.

"If it helps, I think Hanoree is speaking the truth. He does not have the baby," he said.

"But where is he?" Ninallia's voice cracked, and she looked even younger than her sixteen years. She started to say more, but stopped. She shook her head. "He is okay. I don't know where he is, but he is safe for now."

Houston, Sayeri, and Tegani talked all at once, their voices excited. "How do you know? Can you tell anything about where he is?"

Questions bounced around the room. Ninallia shook her head. She was overcome with relief that her son was well; nothing else mattered.

"We must find him before Hanoree does," said Tegani.

"I do not think Hanoree will harm him now. The council would suspect he was behind it, and he needs their support if he wants to become emperor." Sayeri took in a deep breath.

"I hope you are right," said Ninallia, and her eyes filled with tears. She had never been separated from her son, and her emotions were like a tidal wave crashing against the shore.

Houston contacted the general and updated him on the disappearance of the young emperor. There was true sympathy on the general's face as he assured Ninallia the League would do everything possible to help find her son.

She waved off an offered sedative to help her sleep, laying in her bed trying to get back the brief connection with her son. How was he dealing with being separated from her? She tossed and turned. *When I find who has done this, I will rip them apart with my own hands.* Such a thought, far from rational, calmed her. *Silly girl, you are a young woman and not very big or strong. What can you do?* A sense of her place settled over her. *I am the Dowager Empress, mother of the royal heir. I may not be strong like Colonel Houston or powerful like Sister Tegani, but I will rule as regent until my son comes of age. I will make his enemies my enemies. I will destroy anyone who tries to harm him.* Picturing herself as a mother lioness protecting her cubs, Ninallia fell asleep.

Something woke her. A movement against her body, a small warm shape, penetrated the primeval dream. She sat up and almost pushed her son off the bed. The young emperor began to cry, and she scooped him up in her arms and held him. She rocked back and forth as tears of joy and relief coursed down her cheeks.

Sayeri hurried into the room. She stopped in amazement. "How?"

Ninallia shook her head and kissed her son. "I don't know."

Houston burst through the door with his weapon drawn, but quickly lowered it.

"What's going on? I can't seem to focus." Tegani came into the room looking disoriented and unsteady on her feet.

"Someone has returned Hiroto," Sayeri said. She fixed Tegani a cup of strong tea.

After sipping the tea, Tegani reached for Hiroto. "Let me see the child."

Ninallia held her child fiercely.

"I want to check him to make sure he is okay," Tegani said.

Ninallia lowered her head. She was so happy to see her son that she had not done a thorough examination. She handed Hiroto to Sister Tegani. He shifted and made sounds of distress.

It took several minutes to find the tiny tattoo and even smaller place where a small blood sample had been extracted. Someone had taken a sample to compare the results with those of the sample submitted and verified by the Order.

"Who would do this?" asked Ninallia.

"A better question is who could have gotten past the Imperial guards, a trained League colonel, and a Sister of the Order. They didn't even wake Ninallia when they brought him back." Houston's voice was deep and grave. "How can I protect Hiroto if someone has the power to take him at any time?"

The baby wiggled and cooed as Sayeri leaned over him and studied the small tattoo. Houston handed her a small magnifying glass. She squinted, then nodded. "I am not positive, but this looks like the ancient symbol for the House of Hambbie, one used before the empire was formed two hundred years ago."

"Who would use that symbol and why?" Houston asked.

After a few minutes of silence, Sayeri broke into laughter, shaking her head as if she couldn't believe the answer herself. "The Dowager Empress."

"I'm the Dowager Empress," said Ninallia. She lifted her chin.

"There is another Dowager Empress. The late emperor's mother, Miette, is alive. She must be in her eighties now. I met her once as a small child. The council banished her from court for being too political, and even her son approved her banishment. She has lived in seclusion for over twenty years."

Ninallia shook her head. This woman was her son's grandmother. She must wield a great deal of influence and power. Still, Ninallia would have a few choice words for the old woman if they ever crossed paths. She smiled. Her son was back, and he was fine. That was the most important thing.

"I will ask My Lady why Dowager Empress Miette would involve herself. Only someone trained by the Order could have slipped in here unnoticed," Tegani said.

It wasn't long before My Lady responded. *I was a young sister when Miette came to the Imperial throne. She studied with the Order for a year, as was the custom for Royals in her day. She has remarkable power and ambition, too much ambition. Javian was the Father of Wisdom then, and he refused her further training, fearing the Nobles. They would not allow a full Sister to become empress, and he agreed. The Order has always tried to stay neutral.*

So, what do you think Miette is planning? Why is she involving herself in royal politics after this long a time? Tegani forwarded Houston's question.

I believe she wants to be sure Hiroto carries her bloodline. What she will do now that it has been confirmed, I do not know. Don't get involved with her scheming. In fact, do not let her know you suspect her involvement. She will make her plans known in her own time, and at least we are warned.

My Lady's answer caused silence to settle over Ninallia and the others. They agreed not to mention the tattoo or Miette to Hanoree.

It wasn't long before Ninallia was summoned to Hanoree, who seemed relieved to see the baby reunited with her. He could not explain what happened or why, but said the Council of Nobles would be pleased.

Later, Houston reported he'd spent the rest of the day with the head of Imperial security, trying to locate any weaknesses. Every room was searched for secret passages and listening devices. Meals, even snacks, would be tested before eaten, though Tegani assured him that Miette wouldn't poison them.

"She drugged Ninallia, you, and Sayeri. She got past me, or someone did, and I intend to find who and why," he snapped.

"Do you think she would be in league with Hanoree?" Ninallia asked.

"No," Tegani and Sayeri answered at the same time, their responses quite emphatic.

Thirty-Four

The next day, Ninallia groaned when reminded that she was expected to attend a banquet for the Council of Nobles. She did not want to leave her son again, yet how could she explain her son's disappearance without revealing too much?

Sayeri tapped her lips, then said, "Tegani can attend and keep Hiroto with her at a lesser table. Perhaps we can even arrange Houston's presence."

"I think we should play down his disappearance. If the news reached the council, having him at the banquet will set their minds at ease. My Lady is trying to find out what Miette is up to," Tegani said.

Thankfully, Ninallia could rely on Sayeri's skill and experience in court etiquette.

~ * ~

Hanoree began to reevaluate his plans. If this child were indeed the emperor's son, as the eldest male member of the line, he should be appointed as regent. The very idea that they appoint this teenage girl would be preposterous. What could such a child, one not raised in the palace, know of how to govern?

She needed a strong hand to guide her, his hand. She was young and perhaps susceptible to flattery. For now, she was wary of him and surrounded by people who were aligned with the Order. He must convince the council that this was a bad thing.

Summoning Varick, Hanoree sent an urgent message to his wife and son. He demanded they present themselves at the palace as soon as possible. His wife would make a good companion for the girl, and no one would question her presence. His son would play an even more important role. He would woo the girl into an alliance. If not, perhaps she would disgrace herself, and the council would exile her and let Hanoree stay as regent. After several years of his good leadership, the council would crown him emperor after the young boy tragically died. A good plan.

~ * ~

Lord Pater Hanoree was not pleased to be summoned to his father's office at the Imperial Palace. At eighteen, he preferred to spend his time with friends drinking, taking drugs, and getting into trouble. His father's position protected him from the law, and his inheritance provided him with ample funds to indulge in his vices.

Hanoree looked up, a scowl forming on his face. "Is that what you think is appropriate to wear in the Palace?"

Pater bristled. "I assure you, it is very fashionable."

"Not here in the palace. You are my son and represent one of the highest Noble families. You are related to the emperor."

Pater sighed. It would do no good to argue. His father had a point. "I will dress more appropriately in the future."

Hanoree smiled. "You have heard of my late uncle's child?"

Pater turned his head to hide his smile. He would have loved to have seen his father's reaction to the news. "A very unfortunate birth to be sure."

"The council has not confirmed the heir. They seem satisfied to accept the word of the Order's First Brother," Hanoree snapped.

Pater shrugged. "What can you do?"

"What can we do is a better question. The heir's mother is a child herself. A sixteen-year-old dumas who finds herself a pawn of the Order. If we can discredit her by scandal, the council will not make her regent."

Pater made a face. "She is a bit young for my taste, but I

suppose I can introduce her to a few vices."

Hanoree smiled and waved for Pater to leave.

He bristled. "I am not a servant, you know. You haven't asked how mother is doing or if I need anything. I know she would like to visit the Imperial City."

He thought this would anger his father. It didn't. He just waved him off. Failing to get a rise out of his father, Pater left.

That night at the banquet, he made an entrance dressed in elegant clothes. He spotted the so-called Dowager Empress standing by a serious-looking man. He must be the human his father had warned him about. The man looked like a soldier—dangerous.

After a short time, Pater caught Ninallia's attention. He smiled in a friendly manner and then looked away.

Shortly after, he walked up near her in the buffet line and whispered, "Could Lord Hanoree be any more boring?"

She smiled at Pater. "That will get you in trouble."

He laughed. "He's my father. If I can't say it, no one can. He puts me to sleep with his speeches."

"You bore easily," she teased.

"If you want some fun, I know the best places in the Imperial City."

"I have a young son. I am afraid I cannot explore the city."

"Oh, come on. Don't let them keep you locked up here. Sayeri and your nurse can watch your son for one night. Unless you are afraid of the city or are too young." He lifted a brow.

When she smiled, he knew he had her.

~ * ~

Ninallia tensed when she recognized the area. She even recognized the name of the club. It had a notorious reputation. Pater must not realize she was aware of the dangerous side of the Imperial City. This club was popular with those seeking drugs. It catered to wealthy, desolate young Nobles.

Her palms moistened. She regretted her rash decision to go with Pater even as she followed him into the club and they were seated at a table. He ordered drinks. She didn't drink but listened to him talk. Not long after they'd sat, she thought, *this is a mistake.* If the Council of Nobles found her here, she was finished, and her son's reputation could be at risk. *Sayeri will never forgive my stupidity, and Tegani and Houston will be furious if they find out. If I hurry and make it back to the palace, no one will be any the wiser.*

Pater should have known her reputation was in danger. She watched him sniff something and down a drink. She pretended to sip her drink. What should she do? "I need to visit the ladies' room." Clutching her bag, Ninallia got up.

Pater's eyes were red and glassy. His head swayed in time to the loud music. He pointed in the direction of the bathrooms. It was easy for her to exit the back and find herself in an alley behind the club. She decided to go to a better area of the city before she hailed a transport. No one in the palace needed to know where she had been.

Her fine clothes were attracting attention from people on the street. She ducked into a small shop that was open late and purchased a simple shift dress, then hurried into a public toilet and changed. At least the young woman who hailed a transport would never be recognized as the mother of the Imperial heir.

Ninallia got out of the transport blocks from the palace. She managed to slip in through a back gate. Some skills learned on the streets of the Imperial City were useful.

As she entered her room, she was met by the Tegani. "Where have you been? Don't you know people are looking for you?"

Ninallia sighed, and her hopes of her absence being unnoticed died. Tegani sent a message to Sayeri, and Ninallia heard the response. She was embarrassed and sorry to have frightened her friends. Hiroto began to cry, and she rocked him back and forth. She was relieved that her friend was so happy to see her to stay angry for long.

Soon after, Sayeri came into Ninallia's room. Sitting down next to Ninallia, she asked, "What were you thinking, child?"

Tears filled Ninallia's eyes. "I think I just wanted a friend my own age. I miss my school friends and wanted to have fun and not worry about things."

Sayeri took Ninallia into her arms and held her. Hiroto snuggled between them. After a time, she spoke. "There will always be people who will mean you harm while pretending to be friends. Seek your training to see the truth."

"Pater said the Order wants to use me to rule our world," Ninallia stammered. Tears flowed down her cheeks. Hiroto squeaked in protest. Ninallia laughed and placed him in his crib.

"The Order has its agenda. They want to find who killed the royal couple and set things right. After that, who knows?" Sayeri said. "I love you as my own, and I know Colonel Houston would die to protect you and your son. Tegani is the same. She would defend you from the Order if she thought you were in danger from it. They are your friends."

Ninallia smiled. "I am sorry for being stupid. I wish I could beat Pater over the head."

Sayeri laughed. "Houston took care of him, and I spoke with the Dowager Empress Miette. She is old but wields much power in the royal family. She has agreed to take charge of Pater temporarily. Lord Hanoree cannot protest because Pater tested positive for drugs. He also told the Dowager Empress Miette his father put him up to discrediting you."

Ninallia smiled. "Can we have the council arrest Hanoree?"

Sayeri shook her head. "Miette does not want to act against Hanoree now. He is the half-nephew of the late emperor and second in line."

"But he is evil and would bring harm to the people,"

Ninallia said.

"There have been evil and incompetent emperors before. What matters to her is that the bloodline of the emperors remains the same."

Ninallia did not share this view. But when she thought of her son and her determination to make sure he inherited the emperor's throne, was she any different than the Dowager Empress Miette? Soon, her eyelids began to feel heavy, and she slept.

~ * ~

It didn't take long for news of Pater's failure to reach his father. Lady Hanoree sent word that she was joining him at the Imperial Palace. It interfered with his plans, and she was always spoiling their son. She also kept close tabs on him and insisted he escort her to court functions. He could not visit his mistress at will.

Hanoree paced the room in frustration. Varick brought him a message from his grandmother. She wanted to meet with both parents about Pater's future. Hanoree's wife was wealthy, but the Dowager Empress Miette wielded power as well as wealth. He would have to placate the old woman.

Hanoree sent Varick to check on Pater, and he reported that Pater was in his rooms guarded by men loyal to Empress Miette. Her personal physician was checking him.

He could imagine her reprimanding Pater and warning him that he needed to get his life together if he expected to inherit from her. She would promise to help if he obeyed the rules and got involved in no plots. She might also offer a hefty financial inducement.

Thirty-Five

Hanoree checked to ensure the bank vault of the assassin remained unopened. He could not access it himself, so he didn't know what evidence it contained. With the Order's interest, he assumed the worst. He trusted imperial banking laws. None of the Council of Nobles would vote for access, fearing their own accounts might be opened to scrutiny.

He admitted to himself, if not to Varick, he and the Order were at a stalemate. Hanoree was under pressure to remove Imperial troops from surrounding the Order's capital. He had the royal heir, but he wanted to provoke an attack by the Order or discredit him, so he called in an expert.

Lady Orand was not an expert on genetics, but she was an expert on royal inheritance law and a stickler for the rules. A lesser known, but important, fact was that she did not like the Dowager Empress Miette.

He smiled ingratiatingly at Lady Orand and held out his hand to the older woman. "Thank you for taking the time to meet with me. I know I can turn to you, dear lady, in this delicate time."

Lady Orand puffed up at the compliment. Her head tilted. "How may I be of assistance, Lord Hanoree? I am an old woman and retired from court and politics."

He gave her a pleading look. "Your expertise and influence are legendary. I hope I can count on your discretion also. This matter is most private."

She straightened in her chair. "Of course, my lord."

"You are aware of the infant pretender who claims to be the son of the late emperor? I fear these people have duped my royal grandmother. She is old and has lost much of her good judgement."

Her lips twisted into a slight smile. "I have heard the blood tests have confirmed his paternity."

"Is there no legal way to protect the Empire from such dishonorable people?" Hanoree asked.

"I can think of a few instances where the Nobles ruled against a blood heir."

He sighed. "So, there are instances?"

Lady Orand patted a flat stomach. "Perhaps we could continue this conversation over lunch?"

He responded by ordering tea and a lunch he promised would be outstanding.

Over tea and appetizers, she continued, "If the emperor was an unwitting party to the dumas contract, it would be void." She popped another stuffed olive into her mouth and chewed. She swallowed. "That would be almost impossible to prove now, but another factor would be the moral character of the dumas. This, too, would be hard to prove since she is young."

Hanoree tried to control his irritation. "Is there no other circumstance?"

Waiters came in serving lunch, and her answer was delayed until after the servants retired, and they were eating. "A lesser-known objection would be if the family line of the dumas were proven to be heretical or dishonorable."

Hanoree clenched his hands to suppress his anger. The girl came from the slums. Any connection to the royal line was over one hundred years in the past. He stopped. It would be easy enough to trace her line, even though it was obscure. Because it was bound to be, he could make sure it was dishonorable.

Lowering his lids, he peered at Lady Orand. "Can you recommend someone to investigate discreetly? I would hate for word of my doubts to reach the Dowager Empress. She is very sensitive."

Lady Orand smiled. "I would not trust anyone other than myself with such a delicate mission. You can depend upon my confidentiality."

Having obtained his goal, Hanoree was anxious to be rid of Lady Orand. When she finally departed, he made a note to send chocolates. If gluttony was her weakness, he would certainly feed it.

He was now free to focus on his second mission—he must get into the bank vault and retrieve whatever was in it. Also, he needed to find the missing wife of the assassin, but did not have any clues where she might have gone. He sent men to interview the employees and patrons of the bar she ran. Satisfied the right wheels were in motion at last, he poured another glass of wine and retired to bed.

Much too early the next morning, his houseman tapped at his chamber. Hanoree fought to free himself from the blankets and from the dream of sporting with his mistress. How dare he be roused at such an unpleasant time? He glared at the houseman.

"Forgive me, my lord. Your wife has arrived, and she wishes to breakfast with you. I thought it best to come to you. She is in the kitchen ordering the cook's day."

Hanoree jumped from his bed and started dressing. His cook was a prize possession; he was also temperamental. Spirits knew his wife could try the patience of the most patient of souls. "Tell Lady Hanoree I will receive her in my private salon. Please escort her there. I will join her after I finish dressing. Give the cook a suitable bonus with my apologies."

The houseman bowed low before hurrying to obey his master's wishes.

~ * ~

He saw Lady Hanoree standing near the fireplace. She seemed to be studying the flames and fighting to contain her agitation.

She turned as Hanoree entered and did not wait for the servant to leave.

"What are you doing to my son? Is it not bad enough that you ruin your life and my reputation with your debauchery? Our son and heir has been introduced to drug dens."

Hanoree raised his hand. "Please, wife, I am as shocked as you over Pater's behavior. I admit to having been distracted by other matters. I am glad you have come to take charge of Pater."

Lady Hanoree huffed as she glared at her husband. "What matters have you been concerned with that are more important than our son?"

"I am concerned with his future. You have hidden yourself in the country, but you must be aware of this pretender." That was a bold statement since his wife stayed away from court to avoid the public embarrassment of his many affairs.

She bristled.

He extended his hand in a placating gesture. "Come now, my dear wife, I need someone who can keep an eye on Sayeri and this pretender of a girl. She is not worthy of a crown. You are the one who should be sworn in as empress. Is it not our time?"

Hanoree watched her expression change to reflect her growing ambition. For the first time in years, they enjoyed a pleasant breakfast. He could trust her to spy on the pretender and throw a barb or two in the way of that upstart and her child. Few knew the ways of court better than Lady Hanoree.

After they ate, she left, happy and determined to see their son and make sure he was on the mend.

Hanoree drank his drug-laced wine to calm his nerves. When both were taking effect, he returned to bed. He slept soundly, dreaming of wearing the Imperial crown.

Thirty-Six

My Lady waited for spring to reach the Temple City. Hanoree controlled an army, and they were surrounding her city. Her allies were working with the rest of the Council of Nobles to rein in his power. Hanoree's soldiers blocked the roads, but air drops of supplies were coming in, thanks to the League. There were also ways to get around the blockade if one knew the area. She and her people were used to this weather. They were nice and warm, while Hanoree's army was cold and miserable all winter.

My Lady sipped tea. Inaction was difficult when one was being provoked. She missed having Arturon with her. They shared an excellent connection, but it was not the same as having him here. His absence was for the best. If the Temple City fell, the Order could not afford to lose both leaders at one time. She was troubled by her latest report from the general. The assassin's wife had run away from the safe house. Until they found her, there was no hope of getting into the assassin's bank vault.

Her morning reports brought further bad news. Inquiries were being made into the history and loyalties of Ninallia's family. My Lady feared a challenge to the legitimacy of the heir. There were many Sisters and Brothers throughout the kingdoms, but most in the Empire were hiding, and their lives were in danger. She did not want to risk their safety.

A formal request came from the Empire for the return of the assassin's wife and for information about the location of Ninallia's mother and aunt, who were last seen in the Imperial City not long before the deaths of the emperor and empress. After protests, they issued a clarification that her mother and aunt were not connected to the assassinations.

My Lady felt a sharp jab of pain in her chest. Not now, she thought, it cannot be my time to go. She willed her body to calm. The pain passed, and she shook her head. How much longer could she stay the resolve of the body? She could not tell Arturon, for he would hurry back to the Temple City and be trapped here. She trusted the Spirits would allow her to remain until this crisis was handled.

"My Lady, you are not well?" a voice behind her spoke. Her personal healer stood by the chamber door.

How long had she been there? She turned and smiled. "It is nothing." My Lady tried to sound confident.

"It is your heart," snapped the healer. She laid her hands on the older woman. She looked troubled. "I will mix medicine that will help for a time. You need surgery."

"Not now, my friend. Not now."

~ * ~

Arturon was heartened by the reports he received from the Temple City. The League general kept his promise during the winter months, and the city was never without food and supplies. However, Hanoree's army did not withdraw as promised by the Council of Nobles.

Until the troops withdrew, Arturon could not return, and he sensed My Lady's health was failing. She pretended otherwise, but he could feel it; the stress was taking its toll. Warned about Hanoree, Arturon worked to combat his efforts. He couldn't understand how the League allowed Beliani, the assassin's wife, to escape and disappear into one of the largest cities on Bengar. Pray the Spirits, they were doing a better job protecting Ninallia's mother and aunt.

He knew Tegani and Houston would protect Ninallia and Hiroto. Arturon would only bring suspicion on the Order if he stayed at the Imperial Palace. Since he could not return to the Temple City of Uban, his best plan was to locate Beliani and convince her to testify against Hanoree. There was no reason for the woman to be loyal to the Order, and he did not blame her for being afraid. Hanoree would be happy to see her dead. She was wise to avoid capture.

Dressed in simple robes, Arturon was disguised as an ordinary Brother taking a sabbatical. He entered the bar once owned by Beliani. Looking around the room, he stopped in surprise. There were three Imperial soldiers at the bar talking animatedly to the barkeep.

"I am new here," the man protested. "I never even met the previous owner."

"Who would know her the best?" the soldiers demanded.

He indicated two of the barmaids, motioning for one of them to come over. She looked annoyed at the presence of officials and took her time joining them.

Arturon shifted in his seat, ordering a mug of ale and listening to what was being said without being caught. Turning away from the bar, he pretended interest in what was happening outside the window. He focused his hearing and caught most of the conversation.

"Always full of herself, Beliani was. She acted like she was better than me, but I can tell you we grew up in the same neighborhood. She thought that husband of hers made her special. It doesn't surprise me that he was a crook."

"How do you know he was a crook?" they asked.

"Why else would Imperial security be interested in his death and her whereabouts?"

"You knew her growing up? Where was that?"

"Rison City. It's on the coast. As soon as I save enough credits, I am going back there. Say what you will, the Imperial City is a dirty and hard place for poor people."

After a few more questions, the soldiers seemed satisfied.

He averted his head and appeared to be interested in his ale. They walked right past Arturon. There was no use in questioning anyone here. Lord Hanoree's men would have frightened the workers. Arturon paid for his drink and was leaving when someone grabbed his arm. Startled, he almost swung a fist at the person.

A gap-toothed old woman smiled up at him. "Brother, will you join an old woman for a little ale? I seek penance."

"The Spirits grant forgiveness." He bowed and sat at her table.

Sharp eyes stared at Arturon from a weathered face. Something about this old woman told him she was not what she seemed. She dipped a piece of bread into her soup and put it in her mouth. After a swallow of ale, she spoke. "Imperial guards are hunting my Beliani, guards loyal to Lord Hanoree."

Arturon blinked. How could this simple old woman be aware of such a thing? He considered her face and could detect no guile. "An unusual observation, grandmother."

The old woman laughed and fished a piece of meat from the soup and chewed it with her bad teeth. She sucked the juices and then spit what was left into a napkin. "You are a true Brother of the Order?"

He bowed slightly. "I have that honor."

"Can you get a message to someone higher up in the Order?"

He smiled. The old woman might be seeking alms, but he did not think so. "My words reach My Lady of Wisdom, as do all of her people."

"Tell her she has to forgive and help my daughter. Lord Hanoree will kill Beliani because of what her awful husband did."

Waving over the barmaid, he ordered another ale and some sweet bread pudding. He wanted to appear to be a lesser Brother helping a poor woman by taking care of her meal. He placed a few credits on the table. "Do you know where your daughter is?"

The old woman's face lit up. She cleared her throat and answered, "Not where she is. My Beliani is too kind to place me in danger. I know where she was."

Arturon frowned and waited until she finished most of the pudding. "Will this help us?"

"There is a place in a Southern Kingdom that is known for assisting those who wish to change their identity and start over, or to hide. Beliani told me her husband planned to go there after his last mission. He promised to start over with her."

He had heard of this place. There were, in fact, several such places. "You think she's gone there?"

She reached into her pocket. Feigning a coughing fit, she dropped her napkin. He bent and picked it up, slipping a small folded note into his robe. They grew quiet as she finished her pudding. Arturon blessed her and put an alms bag with a few credits into her hand. He nodded to a couple of customers who seemed to be watching. He stopped and blessed a woman and baby near the door.

The old woman seemed very concerned with helping her daughter. Arturon waited until he was back in his room that evening to open the message, though it seemed to burn in his robes. It was simple: *I think of you often. You would not recognize your own daughter now. One day, I hope you can visit the Adamari coast. La Cabbra is beautiful. Ibella.*

Slowly, he reread the note. There was something not right in the message. At first glance, it was simple and direct. He folded it and was almost finished with his small supper before it hit him. There was no coastal city of La Cabbra in Adimar. There was a small, rather poor city called La Cabbra, but it was far from the coast. However, there was a large port city, popular with travelers, called La Cabbra, some three hundred miles south on the coast of Risar. It would be easy for Beliani to hide and start over there.

The next morning, Arturon booked passage to the city. As a Brother of the Order, his entrance was free into all kingdoms, but would be noted. He was posing as a lesser Brother, but assumed Imperial forces and Hanoree either knew or could uncover his identity. They would be watching him, so he must be careful not to lead them to Beliani.

Thirty-Seven

Ninallia eyed Lady Hanoree skeptically. It was customary for ladies to be presented when they arrived at court. It implied Lady Hanoree was acknowledging Ninallia's position as mother of the heir. Given who and what her husband was, Ninallia doubted her intentions.

After greeting Sayeri, Lady Hanoree tilted her head at Ninallia for a moment. "Well, you have a look of the late empress. I suppose my husband is being a royal pain."

She smiled and inclined her head.

Lady Hanoree glanced toward the crib where the young emperor was sleeping. "May I see him?"

"Of course," Ninallia answered, and Lady Hanoree walked over to the crib. Hiroto woke and looked up at her with wide lavender eyes. She gasped and stepped back. Startled, Ninallia reached for her son.

Sayeri took Lady Hanoree's arm. "Silence, Sister, remember your oath."

"But he is born."

"Yes, I know, but this is not for us to say."

Lady Hanoree's face was flushed. "Does My Lady know?"

Sayeri shook her head. "I have not dared tell her."

"But the First Brother has seen?"

"Few are gifted to see this. He is not. You are bound by your oath."

"I never joined the Order." Lady Hanoree rubbed her hands on her skirts.

"You were trained. You have the sight."

Lady Hanoree kept shaking her head. "I have not joined the Order."

"You took the novice oath and are bound," Sayeri repeated.

Ninallia watched the two women and lifted Hiroto into her arms. What was going on?

Lady Hanoree tugged at her skirts. She appeared to be in a position she found unbearable.

Sayeri placed her hands on the woman's shoulders. "Keep your silence, Sister. Let the Spirits rule in this matter."

Lady Hanoree left the room. When Sayeri would have followed, Ninallia stood in her way with her arms crossed. She gave Sayeri a look that dared her to try deceiving her. "What was that about?" she demanded.

"It is a gift few have. I did not realize she shared the gift, or I would have prepared her or prevented the audience."

"What did she see when she looked at my son?"

"I do not know. Lady Hanoree would need to answer that."

"Perhaps I should recall her. I mean to have an answer to this now."

Sayeri walked to the crib. She smiled down at Hiroto. "Many are born with ability; the Order trains the best of these. It does not matter what station the person is born to."

Ninallia understood this. Royal protocol and duty would prevent her from going to the Temple City herself for training. As she looked at her friend and advisor, she realized it was more than that.

Sayeri continued, "Once in a thousand years, sometimes longer, a child is born who is special. The gifts manifest without training. We say that such a child is born to the Order. Their lives are controlled by the Spirits, and they are guided by the Order."

"An emperor cannot be trained by the Order," Ninallia said. She was confused. If this were true, why not leave and allow

Hanoree to rule?

"He will not be trained by the Order. That does not mean he has not been chosen by the Spirits. The wisdom of the Order will be manifest in him."

"Is this prophecy, lady?" Ninallia asked.

"If My Lady knew of this, she could tell me what to do."

"Can't you speak to her?"

"I dare not. Too many Sisters and Brothers might hear, and word would get out."

Ninallia agreed. "Lady Hanoree knew at once; she recognized the prophecy. We must find a way for My Lady to see my son. If what you say is true, won't she see it too?"

"Sending her images of the child will rouse suspicion." She pursed her lips for a moment, then sent for Sister Tegani.

Once Tegani arrived, Sayeri discussed an idea Ninallia supported. The Council might approve a short video of the young mother and baby. It would appear harmless if they did not present him as the emperor. The whole planet was eager to see Hiroto.

"Why are we doing this?" Tegani asked, tilting her head.

"It is not your gift, Sister. My Lady must see the face of the child," said Sayeri.

Her eyes narrowed.

Ninallia gave her a hug. "My Lady will decide if we are correct."

"I see," said Sister Tegani. "If this was something of great importance to the Order, why do I, with many more years of training than Sayeri, not know?" When her question was answered with silence, she added, "How can I help?" She helped arrange for a video of Ninallia and her young son.

"Make sure you get a good close-up of the child's face," instructed Sayeri.

The council, prompted by Hanoree, expressed concerns

about the video. After reviewing it, there was nothing specific they could object to. The people of the Imperial City were clamoring to see the child, as was most of Bengar. The video met the council's demand for controlled exposure.

~ * ~

My Lady of Wisdom was resting in her room. One of the Sisters came in to check on her and asked if she would like to have the entertainment vid tuned to the news from the Empire. She said yes and was surprised to hear there was to be a video of the child. Why hadn't Sister Tegani informed her of this? Of course, she would watch.

The camera first showed Ninallia's face. My Lady smiled. After panning the royal nursery, the camera zoomed in on the young child. He seemed to realize the attention was on him and looked into the view screen with a smile. He waved a tiny fist.

My Lady cried out. Servants rushed in as she was weeping. When they brought her water, she started laughing and crying at the same time. What joyous news!

~ * ~

Tegani felt My Lady's reaction, and Tegani's eyes grew wide as the reason was revealed to her. She looked from the cradle to Sayeri, astonished.

"I needed My Lady to confirm it before I spoke," said Sayeri.

Tegani picked up little Hiroto. She laughed. If she heard My Lady, Arturon had also heard. She wished she could have seen his face. She kissed the boy. What would this mean for the empire?

Sayeri knew the prophecy best. She told it to Ninallia as she rocked her son. "In a time of great danger, there will come one born to the Order who will rule the empire. He will defend Bengar and rule his people well, but his life will not be easy."

Ninallia shook her head. "I do not care if my son fulfills

prophesies. I want him to be happy and healthy. All this was doing was putting a target on his sweet head. Houston must be informed that there was greater danger."

Since he was not a native of Bengar, they debated how much to tell him.

Ninallia said, "Houston has risked his life for my son and for me. It is not fair to keep him in the dark."

Sister Tegani gave her a grateful smile. Because Ninallia knew Tegani's feelings for Houston, it would have been hard for the girl to exclude him.

Thirty-Eight

With shock, Arturon looked around the bustling city. The revelation from My Lady came as a complete surprise. He had been with Ninallia and the baby many times, and he had never seen the prophecy. "It is a gift given to a few, revealed in time," the gentle voice of My Lady had told him.

He wished he knew more about Beliani. With surgery, she could look like anyone. There were places where they did face alteration and even skin color changes. It seemed like a hopeless quest. At least the weather here was fine, and the food excellent. He chided himself. Such thoughts were not worthy of a Brother of the Order.

Arturon discreetly inquired if a newcomer with the name Ibella lived in the area. In a city this size, he was trying to find a needle in a haystack. He sat over lunch in a shorefront café to think. People changed their faces and names; they could not change who they were. In the Imperial City, Beliani ran a tavern that served a low-end clientele. Perhaps she would take a job in such a tavern here. She could fool the Imperial forces, but not him. He felt sure he would recognize her if he were in the same room with her since he was trained to recognize auras.

His waitress gave him an unusual look. "You're a Brother of the Order?"

He bowed. He was not in disguise. "I am on a sabbatical and errand for the Temple."

"Would you be able to tell if a very young child was gifted? If I should take her to the Temple?"

Arturon answered simply, "The Temple welcomes

everyone to be tested."

The waitress smiled. "I know, I was not raised here. My people are very devout and loyal to the Order."

This was a very secular kingdom. There were Brothers and Sisters here, but the Order wielded little influence on the rulers.

"I know she is young, but would you be willing to touch her? If she is gifted, I want to raise the funds to take her to the Temple. Could you tell me if she is worthy?"

He started to protest a busy schedule. The woman waved her hands, and an older woman came in holding a young girl with unruly red hair. The child appeared to be about three and was obviously of mixed race. With the number of foreign trade in the area, he was not surprised. What did surprise him was the strength of the child's ability. He touched her head and peered into her eyes.

"You have done well to bring her to me." He gazed at the grandmother. "You will help her raise this child?"

The old woman pledged her assistance. Arturon whispered a blessing and placed a small bag of credits in her hand. "Save this until the child is six, then bring her to the Temple City." He inquired if she knew the name of a tavern that would make a good hiding place for a newcomer to the city.

The woman shook her head. "This is a port city, lots of tourists, also many sailors and dockworkers."

"A place where someone who doesn't speak the language well could find work?" he pressed.

The two women glanced at each other. "Where would this stranger be from?"

He hesitated a second. "I believe she would be from the Empire, the Imperial City."

The old woman made a face. The younger woman answered, "Those places are further down toward the end of the ports. There are four bars frequented by sailors from the Empire."

Arturon made note of the tavern names and their direction. This narrowed his search and saved him days of work. He was much more hopeful when he bade the women goodbye. They had blessed him in return for his advice.

The grandmother whispered a warning before she left. "Brother, guard your purse in those places; they are not safe. Thieves will attack anyone who goes there unarmed."

Arturon smiled. Any thieves or ruffians who attacked a Brother of the Order would soon regret their mistake. He was skilled in fighting.

The sea air was beginning to cool the area, and the taverns he was seeking were at least a mile from where he left the two women. It was rundown and smelled strongly. Few of the ships docked here belonged to the Imperial fleet. Smaller companies used the port, and he suspected many of these traded in contraband.

There was distrust, almost hostility, when he entered the first place and ordered a meat pie and ale. The pie tasted at least a day old, and the ale was bitter. The other customers watched him nervously.

"Have you heard of a woman named Ibella? She arrived in the area from Adimar. She speaks Imperial."

The bartender shook his head. "We value the privacy of our customers."

As Arturon was leaving, a man slipped off the barstool and bumped into him. It was a common pickpocket routine. The man whispered, "Try the Two Dragons Inn."

Arturon allowed the man to take five credits from his pocket. Would seem a great joke, and the information was worth its price.

The wind picked up, and he pulled his robes closer. He knew the inn would be open for many hours, but he decided to wait until the next day. No respectable Brother of the Order would be in this neighborhood late, unless it was an emergency, and he did not want to draw attention to himself.

The room where he was staying was simple, clean, and warm. He ordered tea. There would be hot rolls and coffee for breakfast. He took a moment to contact Sayeri and Tegani. They reported things in the Imperial City were much the same. *Has Lady Hanoree kept our secret from her husband?*

Yes, but it will not be long before Hanoree notices her reticence to discredit the heir. She visited her son yesterday and talked with Miette about his future. Miette could go a long way to help him, if he gives up a few of his vices and takes his future seriously, Sayeri replied.

Arturon wished his friends well and broke their connection. He wanted to be in the Imperial City, but it was critical for him to find Beliani and gain access to the bank vault for the proof of Hanoree's perfidy they needed.

He was preparing to turn off the light in the room when there was a soft knock. Surprised, he peeked out and saw a figure wrapped in dark, flowing robes. Strange green colored eyes looked at the door. He opened the door and recognized Beliani. The once fair-skinned beauty was now dark and exotic.

She glowered at Arturon. "How did you find me?" she demanded. "You will have Hanoree's men on me."

"Your mother told me where to look."

Beliani, now known as Ibella, looked at him with concern. "She is okay?"

"She is well. How did you know I was looking for you?"

"I have friends who heard you mention my name."

"You left the protection of the League."

"I value my life. They were going to keep me in custody until this crisis is over. They wanted me to testify against Lord Hanoree," Ibella explained.

"We need you to access the evidence. We are not sure there is a bank box."

She looked uneasy. Arturon knew she was going to tell a lie. He frowned, giving her a look that frightened most novices into a confession of their trespass.

"Okay, it's too late to convince Hanoree I won't testify against him," she admitted.

"Doesn't someone else having the information make you safer? It gives Hanoree another target."

She gave Arturon the name of the bank and the code to the deposit box. "You won't find credits or jewels in the box. Those were kept in a separate box, under my name. The evidence against Rico and against Lord Hanoree are the only things in his box." Tears came to her eyes. "He wasn't a bad man. He was a good husband."

He could have reminded her that her husband made his living killing and stealing. His murder of the emperor and empress spread fear and unrest throughout the Empire.

Arturon shook his head. "If you get in trouble, try to make it to the League. They will protect you. If you can't get to them, you should seek refuge in the Temple City."

"And freeze my tail off, no thank you. I want to get off planet, not under League safe house arrest this time."

"You know the League cannot involve themselves."

She laughed. "They are involved up to their asses."

He inclined his head in agreement, hoping she understood her best bet for surviving this was to have as many other people as possible be privy to the information.

"He knew the identity of his client. The contact worked for Lord Hanoree."

"And you can prove this?" Arturon asked.

"No, he's dead. I saw it on the news feed. I knew they would come for me, so I ran."

"Why didn't you tell the general?"

"Because it would be my word against Lord Hanoree, if I

lived to testify."

Arturon frowned. "Can you name the man?"

"No, I knew his face. He was found in an alley with his guts cut out."

A flash of memory hit Arturon. There had been something on the news feed, a grisly murder. Hanoree murdered or had people murdered at will. He must be stopped.

Thirty-Nine

Ninallia was enjoying a late breakfast when she was interrupted by an older woman pushing her way into her room.

"Excuse me, my dear, I have a few questions if I may."

"I don't believe we have met before," Ninallia said.

The woman puffed up. "I am Lady Orand. I am sure you would not be familiar with my name, given your background."

Ninallia tensed. How should she handle this? She wished Sayeri were here. As if in answer to her silent summons, Sayeri came back into the room. She took one look at Lady Orand and stepped beside Ninallia.

"How may we help you, Lady Orand?" Sayeri asked.

Lady Orand smiled. "I was hoping to have a private chat with this girl."

Sayeri crossed her arms. "My Lady, Ninallia is the mother of the heir."

"He hasn't been confirmed yet. I am working on verifying a few facts."

Ninallia decided it was her turn to speak. "Arturon has already verified his paternity."

"I have read his statement, but the council has many guidelines to the succession."

Sayeri shook her head. "You have been hired by the council as an expert?"

Lady Orand hesitated. "I have been consulted by a private individual on behalf of the Council of Nobles."

"I see, I don't suppose you are at liberty to disclose Lord Hanoree's name?" Sayeri asked.

There was an intake of breath, and Lady Orand sputtered, "My clients are confidential."

"Then I see no reason to allow you to interview Lady Ninallia."

"She is no lady born," Lady Orand said.

"She is the mother of the Imperial heir. Her credentials have been made public to the council. Perhaps you are out of touch. Didn't you realize this?"

By the shocked look on Lady Orand's face, the jab hit the target. She made some vague remarks about the loyalty of one's ancestors to the Empire, then left.

"What an unpleasant woman," Ninallia said. She was relieved Sayeri had come to her aid and was not intimidated by Lady Orand.

Sayeri put her hand on Ninallia. "If there are any skeletons in your family closet, Lady Orand will find them. I see no reason to help her do so."

A chill swept through Ninallia. How would she know if her ancestors were involved in anything illegal? Her son was the son and heir of the emperor, and she was his mother. What else should matter?

~ * ~

Arturon slept fitfully. His subconscious tried to devise a plan. He memorized the information and destroyed the paper. He was sipping his morning tea when there was a loud banging at his door.

"Coming." He wrapped his robe tightly around himself and opened the door.

Two local police officers stood there. They seemed taken aback to be facing a Brother of the Order.

One of the officers bowed. "Brother, forgive this intrusion. We were told a certain barmaid, named Ibella, visited this room last night.

Arturon smiled, thinking they might be investigating prostitution. "Yes, Ibella came here."

The officers shifted, scratching at their necks. "Can you tell us the nature of her visit?"

"Is there a problem?"

"I hate to inform you, Brother. Ibella has been found murdered."

Arturon wobbled. He reached and put a hand on the table to steady himself. She was in his room last night; now she was dead. "I am sorry to hear this. I came here on behalf of her mother. The woman is old and frail. She asked me to seek a reconciliation with her daughter."

Tension slipped from the officers. Now they were happy to accept his explanation and avoid conflict with the Order, but he knew they would check and confirm his story. He had not left his room after Beliani's visit.

"I am sorry to burden you with sad news for the mother, Brother. How long will you be in the city? Our supervisor will want to speak with you, and you could be called to testify."

As he answered, Arturon was very cordial to the officers and walked them to the door. He didn't know what to do. He would be watched if he tried to leave the city. It was possible the authorities would discover his identity, and the First Brother of the Order should not be found in the area. His presence would raise too many questions.

Arturon was sure it would take months for the investigation to be completed. He was also sure the security forces here would be unable to find this killer. If this was, as he suspected, a murder by Lord Hanoree's forces, the murderer was out of the kingdom already.

One thing was certain: if Arturon was to be in this port city long-term, he needed a different place to stay. He preferred simple meals and much more privacy. His first mission after breakfast was to find living quarters. There were nice tourist areas and seedy port areas. Something private and nice without being extravagant or showy would fit his needs. He sent a message to Sayeri and explained his situation. She told him about the problems Lady Orand was causing.

I do not think there is anything to worry about, he said. Short of treason, there is nothing serious enough to negate the inheritance.

Sayeri agreed. She wanted Arturon's presence in the Imperial City but understood the importance of his mission. She wished him safety and luck in uncovering Beliani's murder.

He broke the connection. He would have to be very careful with any inquiries about Ibella. The police would not share information with him, and he could not appear too eager to help them. After going downstairs, he passed the young woman at the desk as he headed outside. He stopped when she yawned and rubbed her eyes.

"Bless you, my child, you look tired."

"Thank you, Brother, my relief will be here soon. I have worked all night."

Arturon nodded and started to walk on, but halted when the woman hesitated as if she wanted to say something. He tilted his head and smiled.

"Forgive me, Brother, I was the one who told them the woman they were looking for visited your room. I told them she was not there long enough for illicit purpose, and that you did not go out."

"No problem, daughter. Both statements are true, and the Order would never want anyone to lie." He exhaled slowly. "Did you see the woman leave? Did you notice if she was alone or see anyone following her?"

The woman blinked. She looked up as if to remember the night. By her reaction, Arturon felt sure the two officers had not asked her this question. "Yes, I see everyone who goes in and out. I told the officers she left alone. I did see an odd-looking man standing across the way, watching our building. When she was gone, he was not there anymore. He could have followed her."

"Can you describe him? Why was he strange or odd looking?"

The woman described the man, who appeared to be dressed in an expensive foreign costume. His manner as he stood across the way watching the hotel had seemed nervous. It wasn't much to go on, but Arturon thanked her. "That could be important. Be sure to tell the investigators when they return."

He did not tell her about Ibella's murder. If the local police didn't mention the murder, he would not. At least this was a small lead on the killer. Strolling into the café near the corner, he scanned the crowd.

"Morning, Brother. You are a long way from the Temple City," a young waiter said. He was fresh-faced and pleasant.

Arturon could tell he was at the beginning of his shift. "Yes, I am on sabbatical. Can I have some hot chai and maybe a sweet roll?"

"Yes, of course, Brother," the waiter answered.

Arturon nodded at the customers. "You do good business. How late are you open?"

"We're open all night. We serve breakfast for the night workers when they get off."

Perhaps some of these workers would remember the mysterious man. Waiting until he received his chai, he listened and decided to strike up a conversation with two men in a booth near him. Again, his presence in the city was remarked upon.

"Brothers enjoy travel the same as anyone," he said. "Unfortunately, my rest was disturbed by the police. I am afraid they are searching for a man dressed in foreign clothes who followed a woman from the hotel."

One man shrugged. The other man spoke up. "I saw a man like that standing around looking shifty. He was too well-dressed to be a vagrant or night worker. No posh restaurants here."

He blushed when the waiter carrying his order obviously overheard the comment because he frowned. "I meant no offense. The food is great here, but it's not fancy, and the price is affordable."

"Have you seen the man before?"

Both men agreed that the stranger was new to the area. They could add little to his description.

Arturon watched the people going up and down the street; one of them would be a police person assigned to follow him. He sent a message to the Brothers and Sisters hiding in the area. Three agreed to go to the transport center and watch, but feared the description was too sketchy for them to spot the killer.

Inquiring about hostels or houses that could be leased for short periods of time, he found few available. He agreed at last to accept the hospitality of a friend of the Order who lived in the area. She had left the Order to care for an elderly parent.

Angena bowed low. "It is an honor to serve the First Brother."

Arturon returned the bow, raising a hand. "I am here on official business, and my mission requires that I be anonymous. I count on your discretion to remain so. I am a simple Brother on sabbatical. There was an incident involving a murder, and I may be interviewed further, though I am not under suspicion."

Forty

Lady Hanoree was acting very strangely. Hanoree watched her with concern. He expected her to be more aggressive in trying to discredit the girl. Instead, she seemed to be almost deferential. "Why are you acting friendly? You are almost acting as if you approve of the heir."

"You fool," she snapped. "How do you expect me to get any information if I antagonize the girl and Sayeri? I want to gain their trust. I am pretending to be grateful they did not expose your son's recent behavior."

He had the grace to act chagrined. He expected to find a complaint before the council. Whether it was the Dowager Empress Miette's influence or some strategy of Sayeri, he was happy.

"What have you learned?" he said, trying to sound reasonable.

"The girl is from the Imperial City, but her family is originally from the Southern Province. The Imperial line began there a century or two ago."

"I can find that on any news feed. What do you know that is not common knowledge?"

"Her mother and aunt are missing, but she doesn't seem overly concerned. I think either the Order or the League is hiding them."

This was something he did not know, and he found the news interesting. If he could locate and control Ninallia's family, he might be able to control her. "Do you think she knows where they are?"

Lady Honoree paused a moment before she said, "No, I don't, but she seems unconcerned for a girl who sold herself as a dumas to get money for her mother's medical needs."

Hanoree smiled. "That's it. I can use this information. I didn't know the girl's mother is ill. She may be hiding in a clinic. What was the illness?"

"She didn't say. I could ask, but since she doesn't speak of the mother or aunt, it would seem odd for me to bring it up."

Hanoree stroked her hand. "You are wise, my love."

Lady Hanoree changed the subject when she said, "Is there any news of Pater?"

Hanoree reported that Pater was currently in a clinic recommended by Dowager Empress Miette. Their son was not happy. Only the promise of an increased allowance when he completed the treatment kept him in there.

Lady Hanoree laughed. "Don't let him fool you. The Dowager Empress Miette is promising to fund him if he behaves. He is playing both of you. Make sure his tests are clean before you transfer any credits into his account."

They agreed that perhaps this was the best thing to happen to their son. He needed the old dowager's iron hand on his neck for a while. That or a stint in the Imperial guard or army was Pater's best hope for rehabilitation.

Hanoree spent a harmonious evening with his wife. When she left to prepare for a court appearance the next day, he took a relaxant and was preparing for bed when his guard knocked.

He closed his eyes and took in a breath. Fifteen minutes later, and he would have been calm enough to face anything. Calm, he reminded himself, but perhaps not sharp enough. "Come in."

A messenger entered. The man was too nervous-looking to be delivering a good report. Hanoree's stomach tightened.

"My Lord, I have news. The wife of the assassin has been

killed."

"She was not to be killed until I was certain of her information." A dangerous fury filled Hanoree. "How do we know her information was true and not a lie?"

The messenger looked down. The carpet pattern seemed to fascinate him. "Someone killed her before we were able to question her."

The volume of Hanoree's response brought servants rushing in. He waved them away.

"Where is this professional who cannot follow simple orders?" Hanoree had lowered the volume, not the menace in his voice.

The messenger shrugged. "I am not privy to my master's plans."

"Take this message to your master. This is what happens to those who fail me." Hanoree pulled a weapon.

The messenger's face showed puzzlement before Hanoree shot him. His body would deliver a strong message. Hanoree rang for his servants to dispose of the body and clean the evidence from his conference room.

His associate would either produce the person or face the consequences. His stomach churned, and he sent for his healer for something to settle his nerves. Could he not trust anyone to handle the simplest tasks? The man should have brought the woman back, and Hanoree would have gotten the information from her. Then he could have become a hero by having her executed. He didn't know what evidence the assassin might have shared with the woman or others.

He dressed and decided to join the other Nobles for lunch. Perhaps something new would turn up. If not, at least the woman was dead. She could not testify to anything her husband told her, and any reports would be third-hand at best. He wanted to get back the credits he paid Rico for the job. There were also several items missing from the royal apartment. As the future emperor, they belonged to him. That doxy wouldn't have known their value.

~ * ~

Sister Tegani listened gravely as Arturon spoke in her mind. Beliani was dead, and the local authorities were looking for her murderer, but they had few clues. Perhaps someone wanted more than her life. Someone wanted the information and evidence she possessed at the time. He planned to return to the Imperial City as soon as the authorities permitted.

Hanoree was Tegani's prime suspect. It would be nothing for him to hire killers. She watched him. He seemed to be agitated. His eyes were bright, and his movements jittery. It was early, and there had not been much drinking in the palace yet. His wife was much calmer. Tegani noted that she remained loyal to at least part of her Temple training and that Dowager Empress Miette's presence at court seemed to be permanent. The council Nobles seemed overly festive and nervous—eating, talking animatedly, and laughing with each other.

"My spies tell me there was a body removed from Hanoree's chambers this morning," Lady Sayeri whispered.

Tegani gasped. This was something she was not used to. The Order did not operate in such a manner. She longed for the tranquility of the Temple City. Lord Hanoree threatened both.

"No one knows what will happen. The council members are afraid, and the young Nobles are excited. Everyone is scheming to gain power."

"They cannot deny the First Brother's evidence!"

Sayeri pointed to where Lady Orand stood in animated conversation with one of the council members. The lord looked anything but happy to be listening to whatever she was saying. "Lady Orand is digging for anything treasonous in Ninallia's family history. She will fabricate something, no doubt, but My

Lady will be able to contradict her. No one keeps better records than the Order; no one can falsify those."

Supper was served, and Sayeri took the arm of a young Noble, following the group into the dining hall. Ninallia was seated at a table next to Lady Hanoree. It was an unusual seating arrangement. Tegani was seated at another table, and Hanoree sat across from her.

She met his eyes and smiled. If he thought to intimidate her, he would be disappointed.

Everyone stood as Dowager Empress Miette entered. She was dressed in deep mourning. Long absent from court, her presence caught everyone's attention and turned the meal into a formal occasion. The servants rushed around in confusion. A council member rose from the head table to offer her his seat. She shook her head and walked over to the table where Ninallia was seated. At her sharp look, two young lords jumped up, and servants placed one of the finest chairs across from Ninallia.

The first course was served. In the kitchen, the Imperial chef scurried to prepare a dessert worthy of the Dowager Empress.

It took a few minutes for the lords and ladies to relax and enjoy the meal. Lady Orand's efforts to gain the attention of the Dowager Empress and perhaps move closer were met with a chilly stare. She retreated behind her soup. That made Tegani smile.

"Now, child, tell me how my delightful grandson is doing," Miette said.

"He is well, your majesty," Ninallia answered in a modest tone.

"There are many people here tonight who do not wish him or you well."

There was a gasp, and the table grew quiet. The Dowager Empress Miette looked pointedly to where Hanoree sat watching them. "I am not among them. Always remember you can depend on me."

"Thank you, Your Majesty." Ninallia smiled.

Tegani was sure that the statement would be spread throughout the palace before the dishes were removed and washed.

Miette looked pointedly around the table, and they began talking of other things. Lady Hanoree was very quiet. Surely, she hadn't missed Dowager Empress Miette's warning. It was meant for her and Lord Hanoree. Empress Miette would help Pater, but not support Hanoree as emperor. He would not be pleased. But that pleased Tegani.

The servants brought in a flaming pudding. From what Sayeri told Tegani, this had been a favorite of Miette's and her husband's when they ruled. She clapped her hands in delight.

~ * ~

Back in her quarters, Ninallia picked up her son and gave him a kiss. What was she getting him into? Backstabbing and even murder seemed common at court. It was as if these people thought they were above the law. When her son ruled, it would not be so. She would teach him to be a good and just ruler. He seemed to agree with her thoughts. A tiny hand reached up and touched her chin. He babbled happily. A shadow of sorrow fell across her when she thought of how many people were dead because of his birth.

Sayeri came over to Ninallia and smiled at them.

"You miss your grandson," Ninallia said. "I'm sorry that I am keeping you from him."

"Yes, I do, but my people will take good care of him and have him completely spoiled when I return." Sayeri laughed. She gave Ninallia a hug and whispered, "This will not go on much longer. The council must decide soon, and Arturon will return."

"He loves you," Ninallia said, returning the hug. Arturon and Sayeri had missed so much in the past. They deserved happiness.

"He is the First Brother; his place is in the Temple City. He will succeed My Lady."

"That doesn't mean you can't travel back and forth. He should spend time with his grandson, and he would love spending time with you."

"You are a romantic child," Sayeri scolded, but there were tears in her eyes.

The baby cooed, and she and Sayeri watched him laugh and play. Hiroto was growing strong and was a happy and well-behaved infant. How the prophecy would manifest itself and how it would affect them was part of the mysterious future.

Ninallia let him play on the floor and crawl around. When he tired, she tucked him into his crib, and he fell asleep. Sayeri helped Ninallia undress and climb into a small bed next to the cradle.

~ * ~

Sayeri kissed Ninallia's forehead and lowered the light. Outside the room, she noticed Houston on guard in the hallway and stopped to discuss the day's events.

"The League knows Beliani has been murdered and was not surprised," he said. "She chose to leave their protection. With no contact for weeks, her death was predictable. The general assured me the League will continue to monitor the situation at the Temple City and stand ready to lend air support and even drop ground troops if needed."

Sayeri shook her head. "The League cannot intervene unless My Lady of Wisdom asks for help or her life is in danger. We need to tread warily; the people will not support an emperor put on the throne by the Order or by the League."

"That old woman will never ask for help," Houston said.

"Never be too sure. She means for Hiroto to take the throne. She sees it as destiny. He is a child of prophecy."

"The enemy of my enemy is my friend," Houston quoted.

"No, the League is an ally in this. They just don't realize how critical it is to our future," Sayeri replied.

Forty-One

The palace was waking up. Houston watched the servants carrying breakfast trays and housecleaning supplies. He was guarding the royal nursery where Ninallia and her son slept. A maid carrying clean linens for the crib came near and caught his attention. She was tall with a voluptuous body. He didn't recognize her, and something was not right. He was well-trained and knew most of the servants. Also, there was nothing of the servant in her face. It was hard and arrogant.

He stepped between her and the door. "You are new?"

"Yes, my lord," the woman replied.

That sent off alarms. No palace-trained servant would call him that. Servants talked, and they would know he was an outsider. "I will take those." He indicated the linens.

"I have to change the crib. It is my job, my lord."

"I will take those. The child may still be sleeping."

The woman looked down and turned as if to go. Taking a few steps, she whirled and threw the linens at him. He started to lunge for her when he felt a sting. Glancing down, he saw hundreds of tiny spiders crawling all over the linens and on him.

The door of the room opened, and Tegani ran out. She stomped on the spiders and called for help. Other servants came running, and when they saw the spiders, they shouted. Soon, servants brought toxic spray and killed the spiders. After a moment, Tegani managed to get Houston into her room.

"Ninallia and Hiroto are safe," she said. "Sayeri got them out through the other door. You need to lay down and let me see your skin. I have called for a healer."

Weakness made his legs tremble. His heart pounded, and his skin was damp and cold. By the time the healer arrived, he was laying on the bed.

The healer's face was grave. "This is a very toxic spider; the venom attacks the heart. How many times was he bitten?"

Tegani blushed. "I found three bites, but I have not removed his clothing."

"I do not know anything about human physiology. For a Bengarian, the bites are often fatal and would be if the person had heart problems."

"I have an artificial heart-lung capacitor," Houston said.

The healer prescribed something to slow the blood flow to the heart and bed rest. "The spider venom acts quickly. No anti-venom can be given." He patted Houston's shoulder. "Venom cannot stop a machine."

Tegani thanked the healer as he left, then gave a hovering Sayeri the good news. "I think he will be okay, but he will need rest. What have you heard?"

Sayeri replied, "No one has been able to find the maid, and the whole palace is in chaos. Many of the Nobles want to leave, but they are afraid to go because they might carry a spider to their homes in their luggage. The council is meeting to decide how best to rid the palace of the spiders. They fear spreading them to the rest of the Imperial City."

If one or two of the spiders escaped, they would infest the city. The Dowager Empress Miette sent a servant to check on Ninallia and her personal healer to look at Houston. A servant handed him a personal note from her. It read: *We cannot thank you enough. Such a bite would be fatal for an infant.*

What she did not say was implied. She would use her resources to get to the bottom of this attempt on her grandson's life.

Houston lay back in the bed. The medicine slowed his

heart rate, and the capacitor seemed to be working, but his legs and arms trembled. The healer said he would be fine after rest. If the poison was going to be fatal, it would have been soon after the bite.

Houston smiled at Tegani when she brought him lunch. He was hungry. "Thank you, Sister."

She stayed for a few minutes. They didn't speak. He found comfort in her presence.

~ * ~

Hanoree was terrified of spiders. He wanted to return to his own palace, and Lady Hanoree was demanding that she be allowed to do so. She was not convinced this was not his doing, though she should know he would not sanction such a plan. The city would learn of the spiders and be in a panic.

He mulled over the facts. Who would want the heir killed so much that he or she would risk the lives of everyone in the palace? An insane scheme that would cause chaos in the empire and throw suspicion on everyone. Perhaps it was a political enemy from one of the other kingdoms.

He mentally reviewed the ambassadors and Nobles from outside the Empire who might be involved. Perhaps surveillance vids would help identify the culprit. The idea of tiny poisonous spiders sent chills up his spine. He motioned for Varick to bring him another glass of wine and tried to make some sense of the situation.

Hanoree's musings were interrupted by a signal from his comm station. There were some early vids he needed to review. The Nobles were being asked if they recognized the suspect caught on tape flinging the spider filled linens at Houston.

Hanoree squinted at the screen. The woman wasn't familiar, and her looks were unique. Her features appeared foreign; he would remember that face. Perhaps he could spread rumors that somehow the Order staged the attack. He hesitated.

Since the First Brother authenticated the child's paternity, he would hardly be a suspect. Perhaps he should pursue the true culprits.

Imperial guards knocked on the door to inform Hanoree that they needed to fumigate his quarters. If he wanted to have luncheon in the dining hall, they would let him know when they were finished.

"Of course." He gathered his robe and headed out.

His security cameras would ensure the guards did not do any snooping. Bowing to the guards to enter, he joined his wife for lunch. Her nerves were even more rattled than his.

In the dining hall, the Nobles chatted as they ate. He noted several suspicious and even hostile looks cast his way. "What do they think I have to do with this?"

"As you say, they are fools," Lady Hanoree answered. She looked toward a table where Miette was trying to ignore Lady Orand, who appeared to be pressing some point. "Perhaps you need to call your dog off?"

He laughed. "I wouldn't wager against Miette in that fight. In fact, if she doesn't send Lady Orand packing, I will be mistaken in her ability."

As soon as he voiced the words, Lady Orand stood up in a huff, left the table, and the dining hall. He tried to stifle his laughter and saw his wife doing the same. Even as they did, other diners looked at them with even more suspicion.

~ * ~

Ninallia caused a stir when she entered the dining hall carrying Hiroto. She looked around at the faces and could not fathom what she had done wrong.

"Ninallia, child," called Miette.

She motioned toward Lady Orand's vacated seat. She spoke to a servant and sent him scurrying to find a baby chair.

Every eye was on Ninallia as she took the seat next to

Miette, who remarked a bit loudly, "How lovely that the baby can join us. I know you could not be persuaded to abandon him after such an ordeal."

To their credit, many Nobles agreed. They soon resumed eating. Most of the conversation concerned spiders and their venom. Ninallia heard whispers about possible enemies lurking in the palace. Others lamented that not even the Imperial Palace was safe in these troubled times.

Because the fumigation would take a few hours, entertainers were brought in to sing and play instruments for the guests. Wine eased their nerves, and the guests began to feel merry. The music and laughter filled the room and carried throughout the palace. Ninallia found herself relaxing.

~ * ~

Tegani heard the music. Houston was sleeping, and she refused to leave him with a guard to go to the dining hall. A tray had been brought in. Much heartier food than she had fed Houston. She smiled, thinking how he would grumble at this. She decided to save him the cake for when he woke.

Arturon contacted her. *The others are in an area with too much noise and interference.* His mind touch was filled with concern.

Everyone is safe, and Houston is recovering from the bites.

I will return as soon as I can. Arturon would have heard of these spiders and would know they were not native to the Empire.

Don't do anything to put yourself in danger.

I won't. I believe the authorities have eliminated me for now. I can plead business and give the Order's pledge. I will return to testify if needed. The Order has never gone back on a pledge. My word should be sufficient.

Tegani sighed. She would welcome Arturon's presence. She represented the Order, even though she was masquerading as Ninallia's companion. Her hair was long again, but no beads were woven into it, and she did not wear a Sister's robes. She was very discreet when she used any of her abilities, and communication with the Temple City was out of the question. She relied on Sayeri, but Arturon was more than her senior in the Order; he was a mentor and friend.

She missed the Temple City. Would she ever be able to go there again? She felt a strong bond with Ninallia and her child, and what she experienced with Houston was both exciting and scary. A relationship with an off-worlder would never be sanctioned. Life in the Temple City would be too restrictive for him. Perhaps she would find a position here in the Imperial City.

Houston stirred. He opened his eyes. "How long have I been sleeping?"

"A few hours. The medicine helps you sleep, and your body fights the poison. You are doing well. It is a good thing you have an artificial heart. Not many people would survive four bites."

He asked, "Did anyone else get bitten?"

"I don't know. The entire palace and grounds are being treated to kill the spiders. Arturon is on his way to the Empire. He should be here soon."

Houston smiled. He started to say more, then drifted back to sleep. The strong sedatives slowed the spread of the poison in his system, and he remained asleep most of the day. She would ask the healer when it would be safe for him to stop taking them.

It was not long before security reported the spider situation was under control. Two servants had also been bitten. Because the healers took quick action, they were treated, and their recovery was hopeful. The smell of the insecticide was strong but reassuring. The crews had started to treat the palace grounds.

~ * ~

Hanoree knew he was a suspect and wanted to be the one to solve the mystery of the spiders to prove his innocence before the rest of the council. He researched the spider and looked again and again at the images of the woman.

The spiders were native to one kingdom, and it was many miles away in the southern part of Bengar. He blinked when he saw the people. They were tall with distinctive dark hair and eyes. The woman in the photo looked very similar.

He was even more puzzled. Why would someone from an unimportant southern kingdom try to kill the heir? He corrected his thinking. Must make sure he never thought of the child as the heir to the throne, because it would be necessary to kill him later.

~ * ~

Arturon cleared his departure with local officials, and he traveled light, carrying everything in one bag. He boarded the transport and relaxed. This time, he splurged on a private compartment. He wanted to spend the time doing research, and he needed privacy.

He did a search for the kind of clothes the witnesses described and the scant physical description they provided. Not much to work with. When images arrived of the woman who attempted to kill the heir, he reviewed those. She was also identifiable by her foreign look.

Arturon noticed that the two shared several similar features. In fact, both could be from the same kingdom. Something kept nagging at him. His thoughts were interrupted by a porter serving refreshments.

Arturon ate some fruit, cheese, and bread. He was offered wine but abstained. He drank the house tea, though it was not up to the standards he preferred. He returned to work, connecting to the Orders database. It was risky, but Spirits willing, the benefits would be worth it.

When he considered the images of the woman with the spiders and read where the spiders were native to, he made an unusual discovery. The spiders were native to Hattar, one of the southern kingdoms. It was a small, unimportant kingdom. He ran a query, searching for known assassins from Hattar. After a moment, there was a hit.

It was almost too easy; there she was, the woman who had posed as a maid. He reviewed the information the Order had on her and was surprised such a voluptuous woman had also used a male alias and persona. He sent the information to the Order and to the Imperial officials. Once Beliani was dead, why had the woman tried to kill the heir? Arturon was thankful Houston had been there to protect Hiroto and relieved that he was alive.

Arturon would soon be back where he could help protect them. My Lady was quiet, and he feared her health might not be well. A gentle touch found her mind sharp and reassuring.

With her identity and images now public, even Imperial security will be able to find her, My Lady said.

Arturon smiled.

My Lady did not mince words when it came to her views on Imperial security and government. *When the boy rules, he will make things better.*

Arturon wished he shared her confidence that Hiroto would reach the throne.

~ * ~

Hanoree received similar information from his spies, and he shared the report with Varick.

"It won't take long, now that they know her identity, to have her in custody," Varick assured him.

A ping told Hanoree there was an incoming message. The face of Beliani's assassin filled his screen. He almost fainted at her audacity.

A husky female voice spoke with a pronounced accent. "You look for me; I have found you. If I am captured, I will tell of your plot. If I am killed, many sources are set to identify you as the one who arranged the murder of your emperor. I will tell the council that you hired me to kill the baby. You need for me to go away, Lord Hanoree. Credits, lots of credits, will make that possible."

She had the nerve to blackmail him. Was there no end to her madness? Hanoree couldn't be sure if Beliani had talked or if this woman was bluffing, but he did not want to take a chance. She would find out how foolish it was to challenge him. Once he had the witch, he would show her what torture was like.

~ * ~

Arturon was relieved to learn that Houston was recovering from the effects of the spider venom. He was better, but still weak. Tegani had relayed information to him about Houston's recovery.

The League was working with the Order secretly. They did not have many operatives on Bengar but would provide surveillance equipment and assistance.

Once in the Imperial City, Arturon made his way to the palace and found Tegani's room. When he tapped on the door, a male voice bade him come in. A weak Houston lay on the bed, dark stubble highlighting his pale face.

Houston held out his hand in the Earth custom of a handshake. Arturon took his hand and returned a half-bow. He was too reserved to inquire why Houston was in Tegani's bed, but sensed the two had feelings for each other. How would Tegani feel when Houston's mission was complete and he returned to his people? He hoped Houston would find a reason to stay on Bengar.

"The healer is very pleased with your progress. If you are up and about tomorrow, I was wondering if I might call on your assistance and expertise."

"I can go right now." Houston started to get up.

Laughing, Arturon assured him the matter could wait. Tegani and Sayeri protested the next morning when Houston prepared to go with Arturon. "He needs more rest."

"I am fine. I could use some exercise," Houston responded.

"I am going with you," Tegani said.

"Sister, your duty is here protecting the heir. I am sorry you do not trust me to protect your friend," Arturon said.

She lowered her head. "Forgive me, Brother. I will strive to follow your teaching."

"We are going to retrieve the evidence against Hanoree," Arturon explained.

"You have the bank and code?" asked Houston.

"I will need your assistance to retrieve it. And a disguise, and as you would call it, cover," Arturon answered.

After a couple of hours of shopping and preparation, a tall, older man dressed warmly and walking with a cane approached the bank. Once inside, Arturon approached the clerk and handed her the box information. She slid the sign-in sheet to him. He had practiced the name and wrote it with confidence. The clerk nodded in the direction of the large vault room.

Houston had instructed Arturon to hold his head to one side and use the scarf to prevent security from being able to identify him. Outside, the pedestrian traffic seemed normal. He could see Houston nearby, listening on a headphone. He would warn Arturon if any Imperial forces approached, and he would be able to hear if there were any problems inside or any signs of trouble.

Arturon uttered a soft explicative.

"Are you okay?" Houston responded. "I'm on my way in."

"It's empty. Stay there. I am coming out."

Arturon fidgeted when he joined Houston. They bought sandwiches and walked to a park table. It was far enough from traffic and other tables to be private. If they made an unusual looking couple, it was not one that would cause undue notice.

"Hanoree cannot have the evidence," Houston said

"No, he would have made a move against Ninallia by

now," agreed Arturon.

"Who would have known there was a vault?"

Houston chewed on the delicious sandwiches. Their flaky crust oozed with velvety cheese and spicy meat. "This is heaven to my taste buds after the mush they fed me during my recovery from the spider bites." He paused, tilted his head. "Something occurs to me. It is something so impossible and outlandish, I almost cast the idea aside. Someone has the evidence, and they are blackmailing Hanoree."

~ * ~

Arturon laughed. "That makes a twisted kind of sense."

Houston definitely had come up with a probable cause. For a while, he and Houston sat in companionable silence as they finished eating lunch. After Arturon agreed with Houston to meet back at the palace later. They went their separate directions.

Leaving the food place, Arturon reported their conclusion to My Lady.

She responded, *who would be bold, or crazy, enough to blackmail Hanoree? That would be a death wish. Beliani is dead because she thought she could hide from him on her own. This killer is a madman or a fool. Protect the others if you can.*

Yes, My Lady, I will do my best, Arturon answered and then broke the connection.

He returned to the palace to talk with Sister Tegani and Sayeri. They were in Sayeri's room, enjoying their own lunch. He poured himself a cup of tea and gave them a summary of the day.

"If the stakes were not so high, I could wish the blackmailer success," said Sayeri.

"That means Beliani's murderer and the woman who attempted to kill Hiroto with spiders are one and the same," said Tegani.

Arturon shot her a sharp look. "As you say, there is a connection. We are dealing with a cunning or, perhaps, foolish person. If she or he has contacted Hanoree, they are dead. If he finds the blackmailer, he is in control of the evidence against him, and we are in danger."

~ * ~

The Dowager Empress Miette shook her head. As a young woman, she had been trained for two years at the Temple, but as a royal, she was not a member of the Order. Many times, My Lady was on the opposite side of a political situation. Miette respected My Lady but did not let that interfere with ambition.

One of her loyal ladies was a member of the Order, though not active for years. My Lady had reached out to Miette through her. It confirmed her suspicions that Lord Hanoree might be connected to the death of the emperor.

Miette bowed her head. She had continued to support Hanoree after the emperor's death, determined that the bloodline would continue. Now with this news and the heir, she was reconsidering him. She sent her own spies to locate the murderer and proof of Hanoree's complicity in treason and murder.

Forty-Two

Hanoree was enjoying tea with Varick when another message from the killer came in.

"You don't want me to be caught or killed, Lord Hanoree. Perhaps you need to understand what I have." There was silence, then the killer laughed. "I visited a certain bank vault. It wasn't hard. I wasn't the first. Beliani's box was empty. She took the credits and certain jewelry when she fled. She spent quite a bit on cosmetic surgery trying to hide. I found the important stuff in her husband's box. What was his name? Rico? You know, you hired him, didn't you? He named you, gave details, and left proof of your guilt."

"You have nothing."

"Oh, I have your head. Your hands are all over the assassination. You must help me to protect yourself. I need credits and a way to leave the Empire undetected. It is too dangerous here. I didn't count on this many people trying to take you down."

He decided to play along. "What do you need?"

"Credits, a new identity, passage out of the Empire, or off Bengar should do it. Not much, considering I am giving you the Empire."

"How are you giving me the Empire?" he shouted. "The infant is the heir."

"Please, Hanoree, can't you even take care of one little baby? He cannot be that hard to kill."

Hanoree wanted to scream with rage. This woman tried to kill the heir with her crazy spider attack. He failed when he tried to get rid of the girl and that pretender to his throne. Something always got in his way. He could take care of two birds with one stone. "Would you consider finishing the job for me?"

The woman gave a bitter laugh. "Perhaps you help me, and I don't turn this information over to the Order or the council. I think any one of them would pay me handsomely. If you don't want to work with me, I am sure one of them will. You have made yourself many enemies."

Hanoree wanted to throw something across the room or smash something. Taking several slow breaths. "I can get you new identity papers and travel documents. Where can I reach you?"

She laughed again. "Get the papers ready, and I will contact you in two days for a drop-off place. Until then, try to at least call off your people."

After he signed off, Hanoree signaled Varick and ordered that the investigation should slow, and they should, if possible, hinder others who were trying to find the killer. Because his heart was racing, and his head was banging, Hanoree took two sedatives and swallowed them with wine. He commanded that no one was to disturb him and locked himself within his chambers.

~ * ~

The League's new ambassador on Bengar was interrupted at his dinner by an urgent message. He almost refused the request. What he saw when he turned on his view screen was an attractive woman in dark robes with dark red lips.

"Good evening, Ambassador. I believe you have been looking for me. I have information you want, and I will share it with you for safe passage off Bengar and funds for a new start. I am not picky, almost any League world will do."

"We do not interfere in the politics of other worlds."

The woman laughed. "Save the lies. You can help me get off Bengar and get what you want, or you can refuse, and I will either be killed or I will destroy the evidence. Either way, the truth will not come out."

"How do I know you have the proof? I need more information."

"Just call your people off and get me passage from Bengar. I promise you won't be disappointed."

The ambassador huffed again and said he would have to consult with his superiors.

"Just don't try to double-cross me or the evidence disappears and so do I."

The ambassador swore and hit the desk with his fist. "The League will not be blackmailed."

She chuckled and broke the connection. The woman had nerve. The problem was that the information was important enough to make his superiors in the League order him to cooperate with her.

~ * ~

Tegani listened to Arturon's report, and then she received a message from the Nobles. She could not believe their plan; it was crazy. They wanted Hiroto and Ninallia to go on a tour throughout the Empire to introduce them to the people. This was, of course, before any official declaration or ordination of the child.

"How can they want Ninallia to do this? It will be exposing her child to danger, and they refuse to crown him emperor."

Houston agreed with her. There should be some official recognition of the child before such a step was taken.

Sayeri touched Ninallia's hand. "I don't blame you if you refuse. The council is receiving letters of protest because they have not acknowledged the heir. This is just a way of pacifying the people and delaying until they see what people like Lady Orand dig up."

At Lady Orand's name, Tegani sighed. Was there a more objectionable woman at court? If there was, she did not want to meet her. She pried into everything and made snide comments, starting rumors where she could. Even Dowager Empress Miette was not exempt from criticism.

The latest rumor she spread was that the Dowager Empress was feeble and senile. In reality, Miette was in remarkable health for her age, and her mind was sharp. It would not be long until she had enough and squashed Lady Orand's pretentions.

Tegani couldn't wait to see Lady Orand's defeat, and Sayeri must be happier than ever, her grandson would not grow up in the toxic environment that was court life in the Imperial City.

"I think we should do it. My son will rule these people, and they should see him," said Ninallia.

"Both of you will be in danger. The palace is secure. There are surveillance devices everywhere," Houston reminded her.

Ninallia shook her head. "We cannot hide here. The emperor and empress were not assassinated on tour. They were killed in their beds, here in the palace, amid all the security the Empire has to offer."

Sayeri agreed, "Yes, my lady. I will talk with the council and arrange something."

"Tell the council we will agree if my chief of security oversees protecting the heir," Ninallia added.

"Chief of Security?"

She raised her cup to Houston and said, "Remember, I appointed you Chief of Security for His Royal Highness Hiroto, the heir apparent and future emperor."

Everyone laughed, then Arturon spoke. "Ninallia is correct. If we want the people to accept her son as emperor, we must present him as such."

They agreed. Sayeri began offering suggestions at once. "A full tour of the Empire will last at least a month, so we will spend many days on the road. There will be lots of dinners and ceremonies. You will need several court dresses. The baby will need robes and a traveling nursery. Almost every stop will have accommodations, but he will sleep better and feel more secure with familiar things around him. I don't see how we can be ready in less than three weeks."

This was short notice for such an endeavor. Everyone agreed it was possible, and Sayeri was dispatched to meet with the council. Houston and Arturon sat talking over security issues.

Tegani and Ninallia got Hiroto up and dressed. He was full of energy this morning and ready for breakfast. Now that he was crawling and pulling up on things, it took a lot to keep him entertained and out of trouble. He wanted to hold the spoon, but managed to get more food on himself than inside his stomach. After breakfast, it was time for a bath.

Tegani and Sayeri made the need for these workers almost nonexistent. Tegani doted on Hiroto and Sayeri almost as much. Arturon laughed and warned them that Hiroto would be a very spoiled emperor indeed with these women in his life.

"There will be time enough for rules and proper court etiquette when he is older. Now I want my son to feel loved and safe," Ninallia said.

They received a message from the Dowager Empress Miette. She had learned of the tour and was pleased and wanted to lend her approval to the plans. Also, she would send some of the late emperor's baby clothes. They would be brought out of storage, cleaned, and serve her grandson.

Tegani thought that was most appropriate.

When the servants arrived with the clothes from the Dowager Empress, Ninallia was almost brought to tears. Miette herself arrived, and the afternoon took on the festive air of a party. Tegani, along with the others, sorted the clothes and tried a few on a wiggling Hiroto.

"I remember sitting with my ladies and hand stitching some of these. Not the fancy ones; I never was much of a seamstress.

Hanoree's mother was the daughter of my first marriage, a very unhappy time. My son was different. I loved his father so. They will be suitable for appearances."

Hiroto soon became fussy, and Ninallia rocked him until he quieted, and then Tegani put him down for a nap.

Miette said, "I want to give you a formal send-off with my approval. It can be shown on the news nets. I will join you at a few stops, but I am afraid the entire trip would be too much for me."

Ninallia murmured words of sympathy and agreement.

Miette was not finished. "Sayeri is perfect to act as a chaperone and to take charge of the day-to-day affairs. You will need ladies-in-waiting as traveling companions." Her head tilted slightly as she studied Tegani. "Since this one is to be included in your group, she will need adequate clothing for her status, as will Ninallia."

Tegani protested. She had sufficient garments and didn't need anything fancier. Miette would hear none of that.

When Ninallia also protested, Miette looked at Ninallia. "You are the mother of the royal heir. You need to dress and act for that role. It is what people expect."

Seeing Miette was not to be persuaded, Tegani and Ninallia conceded. She and Ninallia would go and meet with her personal seamstress.

~ * ~

Hanoree heard the plans and insisted that Lady Hanoree offer to join the heir's court. He was affronted that Sayeri was selected to act as chaperone and leader of the ladies-in-waiting. It was common for the most senior or highly connected lady be chosen, and his wife should have the honor.

When he learned that Miette had presented the imposter with his uncle's baby clothes, he was furious. He was the rightful heir; his own mother was Miette's firstborn.

Lady Hanoree calmed her husband. She assured him Lady Orand was finding suspicious ancestors in Ninallia's background. She reluctantly agreed to spend a month traveling around the Empire, but assured him she would prefer her own estate.

Hanoree thought for some excuse to join the tour. He decided his presence would only lend support for the child's claim to his throne. He did not want to appear supportive or too opposed to Hiroto's claim. When the child was discredited or eliminated some other way, he would step up and accept the throne. Hanoree was the most qualified to be emperor, and he had already produced and raised an heir. He was capable of producing another heir should something happen to his wife.

A pleasant thought occurred to him. While Lady Hanoree was on tour with the imposter, he could see his mistress. That prospect cheered him. If he were discreet, his wife need never know.

He voiced no objections when his wife announced that she needed to purchase at least three new gowns for the tour. He almost put the killer out of his mind. *What information can the blackmailer have anyway? I am always careful and have never met the assassin in person. There isn't anything that can be traced back to me.*

He decided not to cooperate and act as an innocent blackmail victim. The composite sketch and descriptions of this woman could be published. It would be easy to create a link to the assassination of his uncle, and it would be her word against his. He sent the info to the news links and laughed. He could prove she was blackmailing him. Even that worry-wort, Varick, could not find any fault in his plan.

Forty-Three

Houston stared in disbelief at the group of Nobles. He extended his hands in entreaty. "I have to have something to work with. Our entire party will be a sitting duck if our itinerary is made public. The transport can be attacked at any stop on the tour. You are putting the lives of the heir and his mother in danger along with several of your own."

Arturon gave Houston an encouraging smile, but no amount of reasoning changed the minds of the Nobles.

Arturon placed a hand on Houston's shoulder and whispered in his ear, "I can have the eyes and ears of the Order watching and reporting anything suspicious."

Houston turned on the images of the transport that the royal tour would be using. His mind was churning with ideas. Guards would need to be stationed at each door. Snipers, perhaps provided by the League, could ride on top of the transport.

The others could not wear body armor all the time, but the heir should be kept in a protected enclosure for the majority. He had been around Tegani and Arturon long enough to believe in their ability and those of the Order. Their help in keeping Ninallia and the baby safe would be very valuable, but the logistics would be a nightmare.

The transport was loaded, and the royal procession began. Despite Houston's objections, it was a very public departure. Crowds lined the sides of the tracks and sidewalks. Guards were stationed at every window in the transport and on top of the transport. They were on rooftops along the route. The latest in surveillance equipment was hidden throughout the area, recording everything.

Sure that the killer was out there, he peered out over the crowd. Perhaps as an ordinary-looking worker or just one of those gathered to see the heir. His neck itched with concern.

~ * ~

Hanoree received the photo of his wife. It was from the tour, and there was a red X between her eyes. The message was clear. It was another threat to force him to pay. If this killer thought he was some weak fool to be blackmailed, she was wrong. He would warn security of the threat against his wife. That would make him seem a victim instead of one of the guilty parties. There must be some way to stop this person without exposing the evidence against himself. Perhaps he could make it appear the killer was framing him for the murder and blackmailing him.

He spun scenarios in his mind. None of them quite worked. It depended on what proof the assassin had hidden in the bank box and what this killer knew.

He contacted the tour and was pleased to be put through to Houston. Hanoree reported the photo and sent a copy to him.

"Can you think of any reason someone would want to blackmail you? Has there been any request for payment?" Houston asked.

Hanoree hesitated. He couldn't admit he was being blackmailed about his involvement in the assassination of his uncle. "Not yet, Colonel. I believe they are trying to frighten me before making demands."

"You think there is more than one person working together?"

Hanoree coughed. "I am sorry. I don't know if this is a lone person or a group. A man in my position sometimes acquires enemies. My wife, on the other hand—I can think of no one who would want to harm her."

~ * ~

Houston looked at the image Hanoree provided on his view screen. Hanoree's words sounded reasonable, and he had done the right thing by contacting him. Houston was also sure of a few things: Hanoree was lying, he knew something, and he was afraid. His eyes were bright, and there was a shakiness to his manner only an expert would detect.

Houston thanked him and signed off. Houston studied the photo of Lady Hanoree, which was obviously taken at the transport station in the Imperial City. He decided to see what the computer experts here could do with the image. He would also interview Lady Hanoree and assign her extra guards for the rest of the tour.

Tegani entered the car carrying a tray of food. She set the tray down near the large desk set up as a security command center. "You missed breakfast."

He smiled. The food smelled delicious, and he was hungry. He often forgot to eat when he was in the middle of a mission. After taking the lid off the tray, he picked up a meat pastry. As he bit into it, he glanced at her. She was beautiful. The gown became her much more than the robes she usually wore. The dressers had done something special to her hair. The lush brown curls fell around her shoulders instead of braids or being pulled back. He wished he could take her in his arms and kiss her. Perhaps when this was over, they could be together.

No, when this was over, she would return to the Order. What did he have to offer her? Why would she want a washed-up colonel who didn't know where his home was? She deserved a palace.

"Houston?" By her tone, Tegani had repeated his name.

He blushed, so caught up in his thoughts, he hadn't realized he was staring at her. *Get hold of yourself, man.* He smiled and told her what was happening, then asked, "How well have you gotten to know Lady Hanoree? Has she said anything that might indicate she is being blackmailed?"

"No, I would have told you." Sister Tegani gasped when she saw the photo.

"We will use the computer to analyze this and project the angle and possible location from which the picture was taken. We can search the images from the transport station and see if we can identify the person who took the photo. It is a long shot, but maybe it will work."

After a few minutes of silence, they said goodbye, and he went to the passenger car to tell the others about the threat. He did not want to frighten Lady Hanoree. Who could blame her if she decided to return home?

"No blackmailer will dictate to me," Lady Hanoree answered. "I am impressed with the security you have set up, and I think I will be safer here than traveling home with an escort."

~*~

Sayeri was of a more pragmatic nature. She knew there was no future with Arturon. She loved him, but she could not ask him to give up his life with the Order. That did not mean that she could not steal happiness while she could. She waited until everyone had gone to their compartments for the night. She slipped a silk robe over her nightgown and knocked on his door.

Arturon answered the door. He had taken off his official robes and stood there in loose night garments. Sayeri gave him a mischievous grin, and he took her in his arms, drawing her inside. The door slid shut. They laughed like teenagers when they overslept, and Sayeri hid in his closet when a servant arrived to bring his breakfast tray.

When she slipped back into her room, she dressed quickly and joined Ninallia and Tegani. They greeted her, and she fixed a small plate of breakfast rolls. She noticed Ninallia was watching her with a small smile. She blushed. If either of her friends were aware of her late-night absence, they were too polite to mention it.

~ * ~

Imperial footage was uploaded to League computers, which possessed the ability to locate and track the assassin. The break came on the second day of the trip. The picture of Lady Hanoree led to video footage of the killer taking a photo. Surveillance cameras followed the progress of the killer while Houston reported the results.

"Hours after the photo, she boarded a direct transport heading toward the second stop on our tour. There was a quick response, and security was sent to meet that transport. I have issued orders that no one is to be allowed off the transport until she is apprehended."

He wanted to be in on the take down, but he could not leave his post guarding Ninallia and Hiroto, even for this. Brothers and Sisters of the Order were with the security soldiers. It was one of the Sisters who identified the woman who was disguised as an old woman. She spotted security at once and ran back through the transport, waving a blaster.

The weapon was shot from her hand. Two security agents grabbed her arms. She fought like a lioness before finally being subdued by four men. As she was being handcuffed, she screamed out, "I am an innocent woman! Lord Hanoree paid to have the emperor killed. The proof will be released today!"

Later, as she promised, proof against Hanoree was released. Security was dispatched to take him into custody. Imperial guards reported the arrest to Houston. In deference to Lady Hanoree and his son, and by order of the Dowager Empress Miette, Houston agreed that there should be minimal news coverage of Hanoree's involvement in the assassination, and he was taken from the Empire. Varick was arrested and would stand trial for his complicity in the matter.

The tour was cut short, and the party returned to the

Imperial City. The Council of Nobles met and approved the coronation of the Emperor Hiroto. Houston was relieved that Ninallia was appointed as her son's regent.

A couple of days later, Houston met with Ninallia for the first time since her coronation. She gave him a huge smile. "I owe you so much, Colonel. If I am not too presumptuous, what are your plans now? Another adventurous case for the League?"

"I have no plans, Your Highness."

His formality made a smile cross Ninallia's face. "I was hoping you were free. I find myself in need of a trusted Minister of Security."

"I don't think the council would approve an off-worlder."

"The council will accommodate my wishes. You have earned their respect."

He bowed. "I will accept the position, Your Highness."

Ninallia tilted her head and grinned. "It will also be among your duties to escort Tegani to official functions whenever possible."

He looked down and stifled his laugh with a cough. "I think I can manage that duty, Your Highness."

Epilogue

Ninallia sat in her quarters, watching Hiroto. She was lonely without her friends. Arturon was in the Temple City to provide support as My Lady underwent much-needed heart surgery. Lady Sayeri had returned to her estate and her grandson, anticipating Arturon's promised visits. Life in the palace fell into a routine for Ninallia.

One morning, a messenger arrived with a note from the Dowager Empress Miette. It read: *I am not up to lunch in the palace dining hall today. Would be pleased if you and my darling grandson would join me in my quarters. Cook will prepare something special.* It was an unusual request, but Ninallia readily accepted.

The Dowager Empress's chambers were in another wing of the palace. One that Ninallia had never been in, and she had to follow one of the palace servants to find it. She wondered if one day, after Hiroto was grown and married, this would be where she lived. *No, I want to live in a small house on Sayeri's estate.*

Her guide stopped and knocked on an elaborately carved door.

"Come in." Miette's voice sounded strong and cheerful.

Ninallia took Hiroto from his nurse and entered, expecting to find an elaborately decorated apartment. Instead, everything was elegant, yet simple, with personal items scattered around the room.

"Thank you for joining me," Miette said, taking Hiroto in her arms. This private Miette seemed far different than the Dowager Empress Miette, who bullied and manipulated the court. "I hope you don't mind that I have invited a few other guests. They are most eager to see you."

A smaller door on the other side of the room opened, and three people Ninallia knew and loved came in: her mother, Vicori, Aunt Rese, and her old friend, Mento the baker. Her mother was thin and a little frail, but much better than before. Rese appeared ten years younger. She stood straight, and the lines of stress and worry were gone. Mento looked like he had been enjoying sunshine and fresh air. He had even slimmed down.

Ninallia rushed into her mother's arms, and they embraced for a long time.

"Oh, my baby, I have missed you." She finally released Ninallia and reached for her grandson.

Ninallia hugged Vicori and then Mento.

Mento explained, "When you left, and Vicori and Rese disappeared, I was devastated. One day, a Sister came in and gave me a note from Rese. I sold everything, packed up, and then joined them. The clinic is in a large resort town with lots of sunshine and clean, dry air, great for the lungs. I got a great exchange on my Imperial credits, so I had enough to buy a small house and a new bakery. Those people really like my fruitcake. I was such a success that I had to hire Rese to help. Pretty soon, I convinced her to marry me."

"Now you can all come here to live with me!" Ninallia said.

The room got quiet, and then Rese spoke. "No, your mother's lungs can't take the air here long, and the stress of living in the palace would be too much for any of us. Mento and I are so happy, and I don't think any of us are suited for palace life."

Ninallia tried to blink back tears of disappointment. "But I miss you so much. I will come and visit you and bring Hiroto."

Aunt Rese looked alarmed. "Would we be safe if people knew our connection to the palace? Could we have the kind of peaceful life Vicori needs?"

Miette put an arm around her. "They will come for visits, and when they do, we will have a party here in my quarters, away from the prying eyes of people like Lady Orand."

Ninallia nodded. This was another price she would have to pay to see her son on the throne. She wondered how many more sacrifices would be needed.

About the Author

Teresa Howard is a retired teacher, author, and time traveler. She is a science fiction author with a passion for genealogy, or a genealogist with a passion for writing science fiction. You decide.

These seemingly opposing passions bring her characters from the ancient past to the distant future. Many of her stories feature both.

In her novel, The Reluctant Empress, she blends heredity and bloodlines into a futuristic coming-of-age tale where DNA and paternity are keys to resolving the conflict.

She lives in Hoover, Al, but her home is wherever her characters are.

Readers can find more about Teresa at:

Website/Blog: http://teresahoward.webnode.com/
Facebook: https://www.facebook.com/TeresaHowardauthor/
Twitter: https://twitter.com/aldebar123

www.ingramcontent.com/pod-product-compliance
Lightning Source LLC
LaVergne TN
LVHW090557110826
845146LV00001B/164

* 9 7 9 8 8 9 1 2 6 5 3 8 7 *